DRIVEN TO PROTECT

GAMBLE RACING
BOOK 4

RENÉE DAHLIA

DRIVEN TO PROTECT

RENÉE DAHLIA

Paid to protect him ... But at what cost?

Paulo's father's money bought him a seat in a Series One car, and now he needs to prove himself. Unfortunately, after a spectacular crash he finds it hard not to believe all the bad press about him. He escapes hospital to go to a dodgy bar, thinking a secret hook-up might get this all out of his system. Then he meets Cohen.

Working as a security guard in a run-down gay bar as a trans man has meant Cohen has seen a lot of things. But none as thrilling as when rich and famous Paulo offers him a new job. He can take the money and protect his boss without getting emotionally involved. Can't he?

As the racing season progresses, they have everything to prove. Paulo needs to be the driver he knows he can be, and Cohen needs to show that he can protect the man he's falling in love with.

FOREWORD

Welcome to DRIVEN TO PROTECT, the fourth book in the Gamble Racing series.

If you love gay sports romance with a protection/security guard theme, workplace tension, and a little mystery thrown in, Driven by Passion is the book for you. This series contains a few mystery plots that continue between each book; however, I have tried to make each book a stand-alone read.

Please note this story contains transphobia (mostly off page and implied), asshole parents, homophobia, travel to nations where being queer is illegal, bigoted Christianity, and a police chase (in USA but written from my Australian perspective – please don't laugh too much!).

This book is written in Australian English and some spelling and phrases may be unfamiliar to American readers.

If you are keen to keep up to date on new releases and, more importantly, sales, I recommend you sign up to my newsletter at reneedahlia.com or follow me on social media.

I hope you enjoy reading this book!

Renée

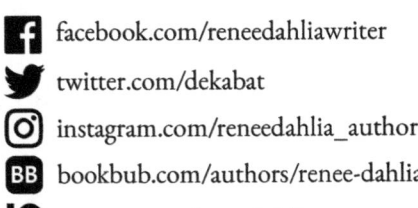

facebook.com/reneedahliawriter

twitter.com/dekabat

instagram.com/reneedahlia_author

bookbub.com/authors/renee-dahlia

patreon.com/reneedahlia

ABOUT THE AUTHOR

An avid reader, Renée Dahlia writes contemporary and historical queer romance. Renée is a bisexual cis woman who is fascinated by people and loves to explore human relationships, with a side of humour, through her writing. Renée has a degree in physics and mathematics, using this to write data-based magazine articles for the horse racing industry. Her love of horses often shines through in her fiction, and she loves a good intrigue and to escape the real world in the pages of a book. When she isn't reading or writing, Renée spends her time with her four children, usually watching them play cricket.

CHAPTER 1

OCTOBER. AUSTIN, TEXAS

Cohen was bored. He leaned against the entry door for Horny's, half-inside and half-out, watching the patrons and the few stragglers wandering along Sixth Street. Sunday evenings were always quiet at Horny's, the bar supposedly named after Texas' famous longhorn cattle. Cohen didn't expect to have to do much at all tonight. Given that his measly pay cheque didn't come with health benefits, he couldn't afford to get injured breaking up a fight, so he should embrace the boredom. His phone vibrated in his pocket.

> Lilly-Anne: How's life at Horny's?

His sister added a gif of a rodeo player being gored by a bull's horn. Gross. He preferred the NSFW ones she usually sent.

> Cohen: Same old

Lilly-Anne: Filled with horny guys?

Cohen: Ha ha

Lilly-Anne: Hey, how do you manage Mom's bullshit?

Cohen: Why?

Lilly-Anne: Felix asked me to marry him and I know she'll want to have a big wedding in Texas

Cohen: *flails wildly*
CONGRATULATIONS

Cohen: Yeah, she totally will.

Cohen: No is a whole sentence.

Cohen knew it wasn't that simple. Their mother was a typical Southern Belle; white and entitled. The type of person who said 'I'm not a racist, but' before saying something awful. The type of person who continued to dead-name Cohen and who Cohen avoided as much as possible.

Lilly-Anne: Ha. Yeah.

Cohen: What do you want?

Lilly-Anne: To stay here. But…

Cohen rolled his eyes. Lilly-Anne was a lawyer who took on some of the most complicated international taxation cases for the firm she worked for in France, and yet, outside of her work, her uncertainty stemmed from their mother's bullshit expectations. Being the older sister meant Lilly-Anne had spent her life being responsible; aside from the time she'd defied expectations to move to Paris with her now ex-girlfriend. Cohen glanced up from his phone and cast his gaze around the place. Nothing had changed. After a while, his phone buzzed again and he read the longwinded message from his sister about not wanting to disappoint people, and expectations, and being worried about their mother and what Mom was going to say about her marrying Felix—who was a Black Frenchman—and a whole dump of other insecure crap. Their mother had a lot to answer for in the way she'd undermined all Lilly-Anne's achievements; just because Lilly-Anne was a lawyer like their father.

For him, being a disappointment to both his parents had some benefits. He could just be himself; away from their crap. It wasn't all roses. He had a shitty low paying job and lived in a share-house miles from the city with a never-ending parade of people who couldn't quite afford the meagre rent.

Cohen was about to text back with something reassuring when a car pulled up at the curb and a man stepped out of the back seat. The young man—white, not quite six foot tall, slender, and probably in his early twenties—shoved his hands into his coat, a big heavy overcoat that looked like he'd borrowed it from his great-grandfather. It was fucking hot and sticky for a coat like that tonight.

"You sure you want to come in here?" Cohen asked. A few inches taller than himself, the man wore cheap jeans and had a ball cap pulled low over his face. His shoes... well, they were expensive and told a very different story.

"Yeah, I just need a night away from everything." He had a smooth British accent with a hint of South America. Not enough of a hint for Cohen to pinpoint exactly where he was from except that he was definitely not from around here.

"To disappear?" Cohen guessed. It was his job to profile people, and this man sounded like one of those rich kids who were educated internationally. Keeping him safe from all the grabby hands of the regulars was going to be a whole task tonight, even on a quiet night like this one. Cohen couldn't decide if it was a good thing; goodbye boredom, or a bad thing; no health coverage...

"Yeah." The man brushed past Cohen, nothing rude, just determined to get inside Horny's, and moved towards the bar, walking with a slight stiffness like he had a sore back or something. Dean poured him a whiskey and the man used a very expensive phone to pay for it. Cohen could see the palpable interest from all three patrons in Horny's. It was so unwise to flash anything of value around here. The man was just asking to be robbed. By the time Cohen had moved from the door to stand beside him, Stanley was already hovering beside him.

"Hey, leave him alone. Let him wallow in peace."

"And what are you going to do about it?" Stanley, one of the regulars, was a huge bear of a man; a gentle giant who used his size to his advantage. A man like the newbie was the perfect mark for Stanley, who would fuck him then rob him, and leave him thinking he'd had a great night. Plenty of men came here searching for exactly what Stanley offered. Normally, Cohen wouldn't bother interrupting. He wasn't paid enough for it to be any of his business. The other two patrons returned their focus to their game of pool.

"Stanley. I swear I could tip you on your ass before you've even bent down to steal his shoes."

The man shot Cohen a wide-eyed glance. "My shoes?" He had the most amazing eyes; deep brown with flecks of gold and black in them. Cohen flung his hand out and covered the man's phone with his own hand before Stanley could grab it.

"Perhaps you should leave." Cohen shouldn't care this much about a stranger; nice eyes and a handsome face weren't enough of a reason to get involved in the likely upcoming mess. The sudden urge to get the man out of here and away from the vultures hanging around waiting for a piece of him became a cold lump in Cohen's stomach.

"You'll protect me."

Cohen sighed. "Don't be naïve. Stanley and I could be working as a team."

"But you work here."

"And I get paid shit. I have all the motivation to rob clients, especially ones who aren't ever coming back here." Cohen didn't hate this job. It wasn't exactly his dream job, but it paid his bills and people tended to leave him alone. Mostly he just wanted to get through the night without some naïve rich fucker getting himself stabbed or shot. The man nodded and used his other hand to lift his whiskey to his mouth and sip. Cohen breathed in sharply. The last thing he ought to be doing was getting distracted by a pretty man and his full lips, or the warmth of his hand under his own hand. Cohen removed his hand.

"Just watch your back, and your phone. I have a job to do and it's not babysitting some rich pretty-boy who wants to be fucked by someone."

The flash in the man's eyes told Cohen that he'd guessed right. Well, he'd offer to do it, but Stanley was probably more the man's style. Big, burly, and a clumsy charm about him that hinted at the type of roughness men looked for when they dropped into Horny's. Nice looking wealthy young men didn't come to grubby gay bars on the Dirty Sixth unless they wanted something Cohen couldn't give them.

"You watch sports, boy?" Stanley slung his arm around the man who didn't move.

"Some."

"You see that car race today. Some fucking shit that."

The man pulled his hat lower and seemed to shrink further into his ridiculous coat. "Yeah?"

"I hope Sanchez is okay. Was a hell of a hit he took."

If Cohen hadn't been watching closely, he wouldn't have seen the muscles in the man's jaw tighten temporarily. Interesting.

"Gamble is my favourite team, you know. When I was a baby gay, it would've been unheard of to have an openly gay driver..."

"D'Grieg." The man whispered. Cohen tried to keep his attention on his surroundings—his job—but the newcomer was the most interesting thing to happen here in weeks.

"Yes. He's so out of my league, and his boyfriend is so

hot... It's just super cool to see that rep in sport, you know."
Stanley's chatter washed over Cohen. He knew nothing
about car racing. It always seemed so macho, yet here was
Stanley happily talking about some gay driver. Who knew?

"Yeah."

"You don't talk much, do you?"

"Didn't come here for talking." The man rubbed his
lower back, then drank another tiny sip of his whiskey.

"Well, you ain't going to get much drunk drinking that
slowly." Stanley hooted with laughter at his own joke.
Cohen leaned on the bar, watching the rest of the room,
but there was nothing to watch. Cohen pulled out his
phone to google this gay driver and saw Lilly-Anne's
message. Shit. Luckily it was quiet tonight, even for their
own usual standards, so he quickly replied.

> Cohen: Sorry. Work stuff. Give Felix a big
> kiss and we'll talk how to manage Mom
> later.

As if he was the expert in that; his strategy was to leave
home, then block her so he could decide when or if to talk
to her.

Stanley was still talking about the gay driver—D'Grieg,
who'd apparently won a race or something—and generally
being a pest to the newbie, while Johnno and Adam played
pool. The owner and barman, Dean, had disappeared out
behind the bar, probably smoking weed near the trash in
the laneway. Stanley elbowed the man, who closed his eyes
in time with Stanley's touch as if the nudge had really hurt.

"Yeah, see what I mean. That fucker Rainier just
clipped my man Sanchez." Stanley pointed at the television

above the bar where a couple of race cars smashed into each other. One car carried on racing, while the other spun around and slammed into the barrier. The man's mouth moved as if he were talking to himself. Something about it didn't make sense as the man didn't even look up at the television.

"Can you believe that?"

The man shook his head slightly, still not looking at the television. "Rainier didn't need to send it up the inside. Stole the racing line."

"Yes. You get it." Stanley gripped the man's shoulders tighter. "I fucking love that racing team. Seeing D'Grieg win today was amazing, you know."

The man flinched.

"Stanley." Cohen removed Stanley's hand from the man's shoulder. "Let the stranger drink in peace. I'm sure he didn't come here to chat about..." Cohen waved at the television. "Car racing."

"Not just any car racing. Series One. Cohen, don't tell me you don't watch the best racing in the world? Those guys who drive those cars are heroes. Fuck me. Can you imagine how fucking freaky it would be to sit in one of those cars at that speed?"

The man's fingers tightened around his glass of whiskey, but he didn't move.

"Come on, my dude. You obviously know about it if you knew Sanchez had the racing line. Two fucking DNFs in two years at this track. It's bullshit."

"Last year was engine failure."

Stanley threw his arms out and roared. "Fuck. You do know." In his energetic motion, he accidentally knocked the man's hat off. The taut muscles in the man's jaw stood out and he glanced up at the television for the first time. Cohen tensed, waiting for this to go wrong. Experience had taught him that accidents like this were often the trigger point for a fight. But the man didn't move. His stillness gave Cohen the chance to analyse him. He was incredibly handsome, in a baby-faced kind of way, like the singer in a boy band. His eyes were his most striking feature.

"Fuck me." Stanley's normally loud voice dropped to a whisper. "Sanchez? Holy fucking shit. Sanchez? At Horny's? What the fuck are you doing in the dirty six?"

"Just needed some time out." The man—Sanchez—still hadn't moved.

"Stanley. Maybe pick up the man's hat." Cohen needed to intervene before this went south. He didn't expect Stanley to obey him, yet he threw himself on the sticky floor of the pub, grabbed the hat, and brushed it off.

"Keep it." The man shrugged one shoulder.

"Seriously?" Stanley's reaction made no sense. The hat looked like one of those cheap tourist ones you could get at any cheap corner shop; nothing special.

"Yeah. Want me to sign it?" Sanchez radiated a lack of enthusiasm, like he didn't want to do that.

"Stanley, leave him alone."

"Fuck off Cohen." Stanley grinned. "This is Paulo Sanchez. He's, like, my second favourite driver."

The man barked out a surprised laugh; the loudest noise he'd made tonight. "Thank you."

Cohen gulped as the grin made Sanchez completely stunning. When his brown eyes glowed with good humour and his smile showed off a gorgeous dimple in his left cheek, he was staggering. Fucking hell.

"I'm guessing my teammate, D'Grieg, is your favourite?" The man's smile disappeared and he went back to staring into his whiskey.

"Fuck yeah. Oh my God, I can't believe it's really you. Sanchez?"

"That's me."

"This is the greatest day of my life." Stanley's smile was a delight. "I'm sorry I tried to steal your phone. God, so fucking embarrassing. I thought you were just some rich mark who wanted a good fucking."

CHAPTER 2

Paulo swallowed. Yes. He was a rich guy who'd come here seeking a good fucking. If he couldn't escape being famous here—in a rundown gay bar in a dodgy part of Austin—he never would. What were the odds he'd meet an S1 fan here? As soon as the big Black man with an impressive array of tattoos had slung his arm over Paulo's shoulders, he'd let himself hope that he'd found someone to fill the grubby need he had to get topped.

Three races in a row with no points only added to the frustration pulsing in his veins. Just his bloody luck that his best chance in months to get relief would be a fan of Gamble Racing and his teammate. Ondrej D'Grieg. Everyone's favourite queer pinup boy with his gorgeous historian boyfriend Hudson. He wasn't jealous of them or their love. He was envious that they were both the type of gay men that the media liked. Handsome in a wholesome, attractive way, as well as being generally nice people who were successful and rich. Nothing like his own messy pansexual adoration of people who confidently lived as themselves and fuck what the world thought. There was nothing Instagrammable about Paulo's desires, and photo shoots with supermodels like Delynda didn't even get close to the way he would rather be fucked than... He breathed out slowly. It was no one's business but his own, and literally only a problem because he was famous and because of who his father was.

"I didn't know you were into car racing, Stanley." The short-ish white security guard, who'd warned him about the exact thing Stanley had just admitted, said. He wasn't super short, just short for a security guard, a bit shorter than Paulo's five eleven. He had light brown hair, clipped in a military style, and a neatly trimmed goatee beard that made his face look longer and his jawline sharper. He moved with the effortless confidence of someone who knew exactly who he was. Paulo pushed the thought away immediately because that was exactly his type.

"You know my step-dad was a mechanic, and we used to watch the S1 together. Those were the days; remember when Socrates Drayton was World Champ?"

Paulo nodded. He hadn't been born when the owner of his team had won the World Championship, but he knew the history.

"Mechanic? Around here?" the security guard asked.

Stanley roared with laughter. "More of a chop shop than a legit mechanic. My step-sister runs the place now. I was always useless with tools. A danger to myself and everyone around me, Dad used to say."

Paulo let the conversation wash over him, grateful that the security guard drew Stanley's attention away from him.

He'd come here with the vague aim of finding someone like Stanley to fuck him, but now it seemed like a terrible idea. He wanted to hit something. Well, no, he wanted someone to hit him, then fuck him, and preferably now before he arrived in Brazil where his father had already outlined his plans to make sure there was no repeat of last year. His phone rang.

"You going to get that?" Stanley asked. He shrugged, staring at Monica's name on his screen. If he spoke to his race engineer, she'd likely scold him, but at least she'd keep his location a secret. He let it ring out to voice mail, then sent Monica a text.

> Paulo: I'm okay

> Monica: Where are you? People are worried

> Paulo: Just need some time out. I'm cool

> Monica: Ok. Just don't watch the news.

Fuck. If he was on the news... He quickly sent Monica a thumbs up, then slid his phone into the chest pocket of his coat. Nothing good could come from him being on the news, even if it was just the S1 channel. He slowed his breathing; just like Heather, his trainer, taught him. Keep his heart rate low. Make rational decisions.

"Do you have a pen?" He'd better sign that hat for Stanley before he bolted back to his real life; at least Stanley would get something out of tonight.

"There's probably one behind the bar." The security

guard walked away and Paulo tried to ignore the odd sense that floated by, like a cool rag swiped over his face after taking off his fire-proof suit. The most handsome man in the room was the security guard, not Stanley. Stanley looked like a big strong top who'd hold him down while he fucked him—a temporary distraction from his life--while the guard promised much more. He wore loose jeans, paired with a tight black sleeveless t-shirt. The shirt left nothing to the imagination; clinging to lean muscles, and he had a cocky swagger that Paulo adored. Confidence was his catnip because it was the one thing he didn't have most of the time. The only place he ever felt free and confident was behind the wheel of his car, and even then, he didn't live up to expectations.

"I'm still kicking out about this. What the fuck is a real life S1 driver doing here?"

Paulo admitted a half-truth. "Just needed some time away."

"Makes sense. I don't know how you guys do it. All that travel, and always having cameras in your face."

Paulo nodded. He'd grown up in the spotlight, a consequence of his family name, but everything had intensified once his father had bought him an S1 seat.

"I bet they've already made a ton of memes about your crash today. Shit. That was only today. Are you okay?" Stanley's sudden concern was hilariously too late, given the way he'd squeezed the bruises on his shoulder from his seatbelt earlier.

"I'm fine. They checked me over after." It was standard protocol after a crash like that and the hospital had been very thorough. He was a bit bruised, his lower back was a little stiff, and his neck would be sore tomorrow; nothing that Gamble's team of physios and trainers couldn't fix. A pen appeared beside his glass of whiskey. "Thank you." He glanced up at the security guard who nodded. He signed the hat with a personalised note for Stanley.

"I'd better go."

"Cohen. You go with him. Make sure no one else recognises him," Stanley said. Cohen. The name suited the security guard.

"It's fine. I'll just order a car."

Stanley laughed, a big booming laugh. "Not around here, you ain't. Cohen will get you where you need."

"I can't. I need this job. You go, Stanley."

"Why don't you both come with me?" Two men—very different types and both attractive—flanking him might be a fantasy come true; one he really shouldn't let himself think about. It was that kind of thinking that got him in trouble in Brazil last year.

Suddenly, Cohen vaulted over the bar and there was a cracking sound. Paulo spun on his chair. Cohen's foot connected with the face of a mean looking bald white man. Paulo leaped to his feet. A split second later, Stanley crash tackled him to the ground. All his breath rushed out of his lungs as his back hit the floor. He managed to turn his head to the side to see Cohen fighting two much bigger men. Cohen's speed—and impressive technique—more than made up for his lack of size. A gun skidded across the floor, spinning past Paulo's face.

"Get the fuck out of here."

"Stanley owes me."

"Not his life." Cohen punched one of the men in the

sternum and he bent over. "Now get out." Cohen twirled a knife in his hand—where had that come from?

"I'll have your money tomorrow." Sweat from Stanley's temples dripped onto Paulo's forehead. He'd bet anything that Stanley didn't have the money.

"You'd better." The two men walked backwards out of Horny's with Cohen stalking after them. Silence filled the bar and slowly Paulo realised that he was still lying on the floor with a heavy man on top of him. The pain from his bruised ribs shouldn't be this delicious. His desires were fucked up. What kind of person welcomed pain?

"I came here to get crushed, but I didn't expect it to be quite so public." Yeah, he probably shouldn't have said that out loud, judging by the surprised way Stanley's eyes flashed.

"Sanchez. I'm so sorry." Stanley scrambled to his feet. It was inelegant and clumsy, but then Stanley was a mountain of a man.

"I'm okay."

"You drivers always say that, even after the worst crashes." Stanley's big grin was adorable, and the perfect reminder to Paulo that S1 was the life he'd always wanted. Being one of the world's twenty best drivers was the life he'd chosen, and yes, the press liked to talk about his father's money which made him doubt whether he deserved to be there, but it was still his dream regardless of how he'd gotten there. He was a race winner this season. To be here— running away from fame with the excuse that he wanted to hook up with a stranger—was childish. Cohen stuck out his hand and Paulo grabbed it, even though he was perfectly capable of bouncing to his feet without the help. A bolt of electricity shot up his arm and he knew exactly what he needed.

Focus. He wasn't going to fuck up again because he would drive like he deserved his seat, like the race winner that he was. Tomorrow he would fly to Mexico, then after the race—and the podium he would earn—he had a fortnight until the circus that would be his home race in Brazil, and he wasn't going to let his father control the narrative around it again. He wasn't going to succumb to the pressure and fuck up like last year. What he needed—understanding washed over like a brilliant lightness—was his own security guard, his own protection that would prevent it happening again. If Cohen was much too short to look like a bodyguard, that was irrelevant. He'd just taken on two much bigger men and won.

Paulo needed him. Cohen—who didn't look threatening—yet was surprisingly fast and fierce for his size. Desire swirled awkwardly in Paulo's torso, and he pushed the sensation away because it was just the adrenalin in the aftermath of the fight. Yes, Cohen was confident, cocky, and most of all competent. The fact that he didn't fit the typical mould of a bodyguard, and that Paulo had a thing for people who were surprising, only added weight to his decision.

"Work for me." Paulo focused his stare on Cohen, so it would be obvious who he was talking to.

"What?"

"I need a bodyguard and you've just shown that you'd be great."

Stanley bounced on his feet. "Oh my God. Do it, Cohen."

Cohen glanced around the room, not in a nervous way, more like he was still doing this job, still focused on Horny's, and not Paulo's offer.

"I'll pay you more than you get here."

Cohen's mouth twitched at the corners. "Wouldn't be hard."

"Do you have a passport?" Paulo spent most of the year travelling. His bodyguard would need all the proper paperwork and it would be better if Cohen could fly to Mexico with him tomorrow.

"Yes. I visited my sister in France last year."

"Can you start now?"

"I'll need more than that."

"Like?" Paulo loved that Cohen's instinct was to negotiate, even when it was obvious this was the best job offer he'd likely ever get. Working for Paulo was a huge step up from here, and yet, Cohen still knew his value. It was fucking sexy. No, not sexy. The man was about to work for him. The confidence was exactly what Cohen would need to succeed as Paulo's bodyguard. Yeah, his offer was one hundred percent about Cohen's skill as a protector. Paulo blew out a short breath.

"How much will you pay me? What about a contract? Medical benefits? A job description?"

"If you come with me now, I'll give you a twenty-k signing bonus and we can work out the rest tomorrow."

Stanley gasped. "Just fucking do it."

"Okay. But I want all the medical benefits."

"Agreed." Paulo stuck out his hand and Cohen shook it, tingles flying up Paulo's arm again. For an athlete who had complete control over his body, it was unnerving to have an unregulated response to a simple touch. But he needed to get back to his hotel. Tonight had been a good lesson; it was time to grow up and take control because he'd chosen S1 and that choice meant dealing with everything that came with being a driver. Fame. The press. Having to ignore his grubby unconventional desires. Being pansexual wasn't the issue—not for him, although it would be for his father—it was the shame in wanting to be powerless during sex. His desires weren't what everyone expected of him.

"I hope you like travelling, Cohen. You're going to see the whole world." Stanley clapped Cohen on the back. "Remember us when you are being all glamourous."

A frown flashed over Cohen's face, something that looked a bit like regret. "Yeah, alright."

"Hey, Stanley. How much money do you owe?" Paulo asked.

"Four hundred."

"Shit." Four hundred thousand dollars was a lot of money, enough to justify at least two angry men sent to hurt Stanley.

"Yeah, I mean you probably earn that in like half a second, but it's a lot to me."

Oh. Stanley meant four hundred dollars, not nearly half a million. "Let me pay your debt."

"I can't let you do that."

"You just saved my life, Stanley. It's the least I can do." It wasn't technically true. He would've been fine without Stanley tackling him to the floor and lying on top of him, although the experience had been a hint of what Paulo had come here to find, so ... same thing.

Stanley's face glowed with a blush. "Ahh, thanks."

"There's an ATM on the next block, near where I parked my car. Give me a moment, and we can go together." Cohen disappeared behind the bar, and out through a door.

"He's probably going to get Dean for what that's worth. Hey, it's closing time." Stanley called out, and one of the men playing pool nodded. The only other two men in the bar left. Paulo hadn't even noticed them until now. "Thank you so much for offering to do this. Cohen deserves to be somewhere better than this shit hole."

"It's fine." Paulo wanted to say something inspiring to Stanley, but he had no clue where to begin.

"Let's go. Dean will lock up." Cohen reappeared, followed by a flimsy looking old man with a blank expression. "Dean owns the place. If it turns to shit, it's his fault." Then Cohen squared his shoulders and marched out of Horny's, leaving Paulo and Stanley no option but to follow, completely justifying Paulo's decision to employ him.

CHAPTER 3

A twenty thousand signing bonus. Fuck. It had better not be a fucking scam because Cohen had just quit his job on the promise of a signing bonus that almost equalled what he'd earn in a year at Horny's. And it wasn't just about money; this job was his chance to get away from Texas and the constant threat to his existence. Jesus—breathe, Cohen. Stanley wouldn't be this excited about meeting Paulo Sanchez if he wasn't the real deal. Plus, Sanchez had known about the car race and the accident without watching the television. Cohen walked towards the ATM with Stanley and his new boss following him; he wasn't employed to protect Sanchez yet, so he strode away without watching him. He watched everyone else though. Habit. The main street was unusually quiet, even for a Sunday night. The unsettling worry that he'd made a life changing choice on a whim wouldn't go away, like he was either about to get scammed or he was going to be thrust into something massive with no warning. Either way, it wasn't great. He liked to plan and understand the threats around him so he could mitigate against them. The temptation to pull out his phone and do an internet search on this whole situation clanged in his head like a loud bell. He stopped at the ATM, standing with his back to the wall, so he could watch the world while Paulo extracted money from the banged-up machine for Stanley. Paulo covered his hand as he typed in his pin, and then handed over the money to Stanley.

"Give me your number. We'll keep in touch about Horny's."

"Best day of my life, Sanchez. Say hi to D'Grieg for me."

Paulo stretched up on his toes and kissed Stanley on his cheek. "Later and thanks."

Stanley, who'd tucked the money away quickly, held his fingers to his cheek where Paulo had kissed it.

"My car is this way." Cohen ignored the buzz of jealousy in his gut. If Paulo was telling the truth, he was about to become Cohen's boss. He couldn't let himself care who Paulo kissed. A peck on the cheek. Honestly, what did that even matter? It wasn't until they were in his car, with Paulo sitting in the passenger seat, that Cohen spoke.

"What did you mean you'll keep in touch about Horny's?"

"I'm going to buy it and Stanley will run it."

"Seriously?" Cohen knew the bar was struggling. Dean could barely afford to pay him every week, drinking most of the meagre income. But he still couldn't comprehend a stranger walking in and buying a whole bar. Imagine having enough money to piss a bunch away on a crappy bar in the Dirty Six. Or on a signing bonus for a bodyguard ... except Cohen knew he was worth every cent; he just needed to find someone who recognised that. Paulo saw him. What a buzz. He couldn't let himself believe it just yet. Soon.

"Yes."

"What now?"

Paulo didn't answer for a long time, so Cohen just drove in circles around the block, trying not to think too hard about how much gas this was costing him.

"The job is simple. You'll be my personal security guard and will travel everywhere with me."

"Everywhere?"

"Yes."

"What exactly does that mean?" Cohen didn't want to sound ignorant, but he knew nothing about car racing.

"Series One consists of between twenty-one and twenty-five races each year, and each one is in a different country. There are only three races left this year; Mexico, Brazil, and Abu Dhabi. Then there's the winter break and pre-season testing before the new season starts in March. You can take personal leave during the winter break and the summer break, but you need to be with me for every race and every public appearance."

"Okay."

"Didn't you say you'd visited your sister in France?"

"Yes." Lilly-Anne lived in Paris, but he withheld the information for a moment.

"You'll be closer to her. I live in Monaco, so you'll need to move there. I'll subside your rent as part of your pay. Will that be fine?"

Cohen let himself smile a little. If this was real, his sister was going to be so thrilled. Stanley hadn't been joking when he'd said Cohen would see the world. "Yes." His voice cracked slightly and he covered it up with a cough.

"Good. First to your place and pack, then we'll get started."

"Wait. Do you want an ice first?" Cohen usually grabbed an ice from Jim-Jim's Water Ice after work to help keep him awake for the long drive home to the suburbs.

"A what?"

"An ice. It's bloody hot and I usually grab one on the way home from work."

"Okay. We need to go to your place, so you can pack."

A little while later, they stood outside the iconic Jim-Jim's Water Ice. The tiny little shop window was hidden in the side of the lottery building, with only a weird statue on the sidewalk to give any indication that something special was in the building.

"I always get Dragons Blood." Cohen loved the strawberry with coconut flavour, plus it was one of the only ones on the menu with an interesting name.

"I'll have mango."

"That's their best seller." Cohen probably shouldn't tell his potential new boss that his choice was boring. He ordered them both and gave the graveyard shift worker a decent tip. If he was about to get paid properly, he could pass it forward. Soon enough they were back in the car with their selections. Cohen put his in the centre console and began the drive home as he'd been instructed. Once he was on the freeway, he'd be able to eat some to keep him awake in this muggy, oppressive heat.

"It's sorbet." Paulo sounded surprised. Cohen kept the radio on low as he drove. Paulo didn't speak, just ate the water ice with little flicks of his tongue which made it hard for Cohen to focus on the road. Once he'd finished eating, Paulo pulled out his phone and called someone.

"Jaxxon. ... Yes, I'm fine. I need a favour."

Cohen heard a faint growl through Paulo's phone; whoever this Jaxxon was didn't like being asked for a favour at one in the morning. Fair enough.

"Nothing like that. Can you email me a copy of the standard Gamble Racing employee contract?" Paulo chuckled low under his breath. The sound caressed Cohen. Shit, if Paulo was going to be his boss, he really needed to suppress that response.

"Yes. I know the time, but I figured you'd still be celebrating with Ondrej. ... No, it can't wait until the team meeting. I want this sorted before then. ... Thanks."

After Paulo hung up, Cohen waited. It was still another forty minutes to his place. Normally Cohen drove with the windows open, eating his ice, and listening to loud music to keep himself awake after a night at work. A soft snore filled the quiet space. His new boss was fast asleep, and fuck, he looked so young and peaceful. He hadn't even signed a contract yet, but Cohen would protect him with his life.

———

The morning sun beat against the flimsy curtain of his room, and Cohen stood up to stretch after an uncomfortable few hours snooze on the chair beside his bed. Last night, Cohen had carried Paulo inside and put him in bed, carefully removing that giant heavy coat, and making sure everything was locked up tight. Lifting someone bigger than him without waking him had been a challenge, and there'd been a few moments when Paulo had grumbled but hadn't woken.

"What's the time?" Paulo's voice was husky.

Cohen checked his phone. "Nine-fifteen."

"Fuck. Team meeting at ten." Paulo leaped out of bed in a surprisingly athletic move for someone who'd just woken up. He grimaced slightly, then stretched out his shoulders. "Okay. Did you pack? You'll need enough clothes for a few days, and a passport. We'll sort the rest after Mexico." He grabbed his phone and flicked his thumb over the screen. "What's your email? I'll forward you this contract and we can use it as a base for the one we both sign. You'll be my personal employee, not the team, but this will be a good template. And text me your bank details and I'll sort out the signing bonus."

Cohen blinked at him. He hadn't had enough sleep for all this uncontained energy.

"Move. It's an hour's drive to the hotel, according to the internet, but I can make it in half that."

"What?" Cohen shook off the sense that he'd been left behind and grabbed his rucksack. He threw in some clothes, his meds, and hunted around his bedside table for his passport.

"I'll drive. You deal with the press when we get there. Read the contract on the way."

"Okay." Apparently, his life was going to operate at this speed now. He'd better get used to it.

"Give me your phone," Cohen said, and Paulo handed it over. "You'll need to unlock it. I'll add my contact details and you can email and text me what you need to get this sorted." Cohen added his information, then bolted from the room to brush his teeth. He'd need to leave a message for his house mates, not that they'd care if he wasn't around for a while as long as he kept paying the rent for his room. This morning, Paulo was so different to the man who'd walked into Horny's; suddenly more confident and determined. It was a good look on him. Fuck; Cohen really needed to NOT ogle his new boss. He returned to his room to finish packing, even though he had no clue what he was packing for; something about Mexico and international travel. He wasn't even sure exactly what Paulo did for a job —not really—or what his actual job would be in relation to Paulo's job, because he'd fallen asleep last night before he'd had a chance to do any research. A few minutes later, they locked Cohen's bedroom and walked out of the front door.

"Keys." Paulo held out his hand and Cohen tossed them to him.

"It's the grey Ford sedan." Cohen probably didn't need to say that, since they'd driven here last night in it. His car wasn't much to look at—old and cheap—but it was reliable and didn't chew through gas.

"This should be interesting. Buckle up tight." Paulo slid into the driver's seat, made a few adjustments, and turned on the engine. "Fuck. This thing has done over three hundred thousand miles."

Cohen threw his bag onto the backseat, sat down, clicked his seatbelt and pulled it tight across his chest. "It was cheap." He barely had time to close the door when Paulo slid the car into reverse and drove out onto the road.

"You'll have to direct me. Fastest way to the Austin Towers Hotel."

Cohen looked it up on his phone. "Turn right at the end of the street and then left, then you'll get on the freeway."

The car's tyres squealed on the road as Paulo hit the gas and Cohen grabbed the edge of his seat. He was pretty sure he'd yelped but he could pretend that hadn't happened. The car slid around the corner at the end of the road, and by the time they hit the freeway, Paulo had to have been going twice the speed limit. What the fuck. Cohen forced his fingers to release from where he'd been gripping the seat. He looked over at Paulo, who didn't seem stressed at all. His mouth was curled up slightly at the corners as if he was enjoying himself. How?

"This car has been in a crash. The chassis isn't straight, and the front left is slightly flat."

"Probably. I got it second hand, cheap, well, maybe third or fourth hand. Ha." Cohen babbled as they passed cars like they were standing still. He tried not to scream as they changed lanes and flew around a couple of cars. He was going to die.

"Which exit?" Paulo asked. How the hell was he so calm? And smiling...

"Um..."

"Well?"

Cohen grabbed his phone and immediately dropped it on the floor. His hands were slippery, and he wiped them down his jeans. As soon as he ducked his head down to grab his phone, he could pretend they weren't racing to their doom. A siren echoed. Cops?

"Ah, about ten miles to the exit." If he kept his eyes closed, he could pretend he wasn't in a car threading through traffic at speeds no one should go. Seriously, this was inhumanely fast. He opened one eye to check the map on his phone and gave directions without looking out the window.

Somehow they managed to get to the hotel without dying. Several cop cars had joined in a chase from various freeway entrances, but they'd left them all behind. If Cohen hadn't been so stressed that he was about to be killed in a dramatic car crash, he would've been impressed that his crappy old piece of shit car could speed away from the cops. Paulo eased the car slowly into the hotel driveway. Six people stood beside the front door under the awning with three of them holding very big cameras.

"Get me through the media. Ignore Freddy's questions. I'll answer one from Alicia Blasi."

Cohen nodded. Presumably the woman wearing jeans and a beautiful light green blouse was Alicia Blasi. He was good at his job—even if they hadn't exactly confirmed what that would be—so he could focus on the people waiting for them.

"Oh and don't worry about the fines. I'll pay them and get you a new car. The engine is cooked."

"Okay." What else could Cohen say? Fines? Cooked engine? It was a lot of information to take in, and his heart wasn't going to recover to a normal rate for months. He was just glad to be alive after hurtling down the freeway so fast. How could Paulo manage to think about all those details? It'd be a while before he could even think about reacting to the news that Paulo had ruined his car. Was he angry? Impressed? He shook out his hands. Work had to come first.

He stepped out of the car and immediately had to move as the six people were swamping Paulo, who emerged from the driver's seat looking unreasonably calm.

"Stop. Paulo will answer one question." Cohen used his body position to guard Paulo and prevent them from getting in his face.

"Blasi," Paulo said.

The woman grinned. "How are you after that crash?"

"Fine."

"And where were you?"

Cohen held up his hand. "He said one question. Thank you, that will be all." Cohen got Paulo past the six people, ignoring their loud questions and the constant flashes from their cameras, and they walked into the hotel. A wave of cool airconditioned air hit Cohen in the face, freezing the sweat still sliding down his temples.

"Who were they?"

"Media."

Of course. No wonder Paulo felt like he needed a bodyguard if he had a throng of media waiting for him at his hotel. From there it was a matter of following Paulo as he talked to the concierge, then they followed a staff member through the hotel until Cohen found himself walking into a meeting room, with his heart still racing as fast as his car had gone. A large Black man pulled Paulo into a hug, and Cohen automatically grabbed the man's hands and tore them from Paulo's body.

"It's fine. This is Jaxxon, the Team Principal." Paulo's relaxed frame should've told Cohen that he didn't need to intervene. He blamed the wild ride here. He'd never been so fast in a car in his life, and he really didn't like the danger implied by travelling so quickly.

"Jaxxon, this is Cohen. He's my personal bodyguard."

The room exploded with noise and Paulo held up his hand. "Quiet. It's no big deal. Let's get on with the meeting."

"He can't stay."

"Fine. Cohen. Sit outside the door. I'm safe in here with my team."

Cohen glanced around the room at the group of people seated around a long table, nodded, and left the room. At least he'd have time to calm the fuck down and figure out what the hell he'd agreed to.

CHAPTER 4

"WATCH SANCHEZ'S WILD RIDE. EXCLUSIVE POLICE FOOTAGE HERE."

"SERIES ONE'S NEW BAD BOY."

Paulo really didn't want the press to think of him as a bad boy. He didn't really want them thinking about him at all, but that was pure fantasy. All he'd wanted was an evening to remove some frustrations after crashing out at Austin, and he'd snuck out of the hospital to get away. Now he was all over the press, thanks to a fun drive to get to the team meeting on time. He had a new bodyguard, but still hadn't scratched that persistent itch to get pegged. If only he could combine the two. Hell no. He needed to maintain that separation. It was one thing to employ someone competent and get them out of a crappy situation; and quite another to take advantage by asking for a closer relationship. Or just sex. It was a misuse of his money and power. Speaking of that, he ignored the series of new texts from his father and tucked his phone into the pocket of his seat.

"What happens when we get to Mexico?" Cohen didn't look comfortable in the first-class seat of the commercial plane they were taking from Austin to Mexico. It was only a short flight, a couple of hours, and while some of the teams took private jets between races, Paulo felt that commercial first class gave him enough privacy, besides Gamble had a risk-avoidance policy of always sending their two drivers on different planes when they travelled, so he was used to travelling alone or with a few of the crew.

"I'll get Melati to email you the press and fan schedule for the Mexico race. She does all my social media and general PA stuff. Otherwise, I'll be training and setting up for FP1 on Friday."

"Okay."

"Brazil is going to be more intense." Paulo probably ought to get this out of the way now. He'd rather avoid talking about it, but now that Cohen had signed the contract to be his personal security, he needed the whole story.

"I like to be prepared." It was true. When they'd met after the team meeting to go over Cohen's employment contract, Cohen had shown that he'd spent the time waiting in the hallway doing a lot of research. He understood the season schedule and had asked plenty of logistical questions about how Paulo moved between countries and races. He wanted to know how each hotel dealt with media, and how they kept his location secret from overly keen fans. He'd obviously spoken to the team's general security manager too. Cohen's competency eased the swirling tension created by all the headlines over today's little freeway drive. People needed to calm down. He was one of the best drivers in the world. The cops and the press had easily tracked him via Cohen's number plate and the hotel, and he'd been able to pay all the speeding fines before they'd left for the airport. If only dealing with the headlines, and the implication that he wasn't the perfect obedient son, was so simple...

"Paulo?"

He glanced around the first-class section of the commercial plane and held back a sigh. "Fine. Brazil is going to be a complete fucking circus. If you think the media has gone overboard after today's little drive, they are going to be overwhelming in Brazil."

"I assume that's because you were born there?"

"You've done your research."

"Of course."

Paulo breathed out slowly. Excellent. "Obviously, there is the hometown hero crap, and I DNF'd last year in my rookie season in kind of sensational circumstances."

"I read about the sabotage scandal."

The relief at not having to explain things to Cohen reinforced that Paulo had made the correct choice. "Yeah, and my father and brother will want to show me off around town too."

"That'd be Enzo Sanchez, billionaire shipping magnate, and Enzo Junior, politician?"

"Yes."

"What do you mean; show you off around town?"

Paulo sighed. "Dinners with business acquaintances

and lunches with politicians, that sort of thing. Nothing like having a famous sports star as a son to show everyone important how great you are. Plus with a two week break between Mexico and Brazil, there is no excuse to say no." Paulo paused. He didn't want to explain his distant relationship with his parents; they weren't exactly hands on parents. He'd had nannies until he left for England and boarding school. Everything was transactional between them and him. Paulo got his trust fund and a seat in an S1 team, and in return, he showed up whenever his father needed to live vicariously through his famous son's sporting achievements. It was all a performance, and he had to play his father's game to keep his seat in S1. He wasn't good enough on his own merits to stay without his father's money. The expectations were huge because his life was a great marketing opportunity for his father. Luckily Cohen didn't push for more details. He simply waited.

"You'll need a tuxedo. Did we include uniforms in the contract?" Paulo asked, even though he knew the answer. Jaxxon wanted Cohen to wear a Gamble uniform, but since Paulo was paying him directly, well... they were still negotiating. Jaxxon would likely get his way—at a cost—and until then, Cohen would wear plain black.

"Yes."

"Good. I think we'll fly back to Austin after Mexico to finalise your things and we can get you set up with the right clothing then."

"Okay."

Paulo gulped. "Um, there's one other thing that you should probably know." He'd met Cohen in a gay bar; he was unlikely to judge him for the mess after Brazil last year.

"I can only protect you if I know everything." Cohen paused. "You are putting a lot of trust in me, and I promise to do my best to serve you and keep you safe."

Paulo nodded. "You stopped me from being robbed and you stopped Stanley from being stabbed. I can tell that you are diligent and observant and that's enough for me."

A soft blush painted Cohen's cheeks. "Thank you."

"After the race last year, I was upset and made some bad choices. My father paid off the hotel and kept it a secret." His father thought he'd been caught with some female prostitutes, and Paulo wasn't going to change that perception. Ever. His father had clapped him on the back and said a bunch of toxic masculine rubbish, going as far as offering to introduce Paulo to the escort service he used. The double standard between his father's behaviour and the expectations on his mother and sisters had Paulo wishing he could say something without losing all the Sanchez sponsorship money for Gamble Racing and his seat as an S1 driver.

"Oh? Do you think there's a chance the media will find out?"

Paulo shuddered. "I fucking hope not." He had a reputation of being a boring mid-field driver—just another rich kid who'd bought his seat, whose social media was filled with racing images and the occasional fashion photo shoot with gorgeous women models—and he needed that reputation to be able to keep his dream alive. The drive this morning had been ill-advised because it'd drawn too much attention to him; to the real him. If the press got any hint of last year's drunken night... He pushed away the rising panic. At least, the stewards at S1 weren't going to fine him for this morning. There was too much precedence with other drivers; S1 tended to ignore external speeding fines provided the drivers in question paid whichever authority without fuss.

"Do you want me to stop you making a similar choice?"

"I suppose so."

Cohen chuckled and elbowed Paulo. "I'm not the fun police. My job is to keep you safe. I'm not going to interfere with your private life."

"It was only once. Twice if you count last night which I don't really."

"You wanted someone like St.."

Paulo covered Cohen's mouth with his hand before he could finish that sentence. He shook his head. "You can't say that out loud. No one knows and there's too much at stake."

"I won't judge you. People visit my former place of employment to find what they need. I've seen it a lot. Now tell me what happened last year?"

Paulo shrugged, pretending to be casual about it while his stomach twisted into knots. "I don't remember everything. I was upset after the race... The fucking engine caught fire and my rookie season hadn't been great. There was a lot of pressure on me to perform, and the media were obsessed with whether I'd keep my seat for this season."

"You're only twenty-two." Cohen once again proved that he'd researched everything about Paulo, whose age was public knowledge, though what his age had to do with anything, he wasn't sure. He'd been the average age for a rookie. "You can forgive yourself for buckling under such immense pressure. From all I've read about your sport, it's very intense."

"Yes. Well, I should've found a less public way to let off steam. I went out drinking. It was annoying because people wanted to talk about work..." There had been huge speculation about the team's sudden loss of reliability. "But I eventually found a place where no one recognised me. I ended up in a cheap motel with a group of people." Paulo blushed and ducked his head low against his chest. "Things were a bit blurry, and then the cops arrived, and my father hushed it all up." When the cops arrived, he'd been getting fucked by an attractive man, and he was kissing a woman who had beautiful tits. They were probably quite ordinary looking, but he'd been very drunk, and he was happy to remember them as giving and gorgeous. It was the best and worst night of his life. He wished he remembered more details, and he really wanted to be fucked again. Women were everywhere in S1 and he was offered more sex than he wanted, but women tended to want him to fuck them. It was fine and fulfilled a need every now and then, but it wasn't his absolute favourite, and he really wasn't going to ask a hook up to use a strap on with him. He didn't need that detail being leaked to the press, so he'd stayed away from any sexual encounters since Brazil last year. His own hand and toys were safer.

"Were you arrested?"

"Technically no. Being gay is legal in Brazil and most people are fairly accepting. My family is not."

"Oh. Is that why you can't mention it? You aren't out to them?"

"And my father sponsors my team. If he knows, he'll withdraw the money and I lose my seat." He threatened to do that when Paulo didn't finish in the points; not wanting to have an embarrassment of a son. Most parents blamed the car, not the child, but not Sanchez Senior, whose expectations for positive results were impossible.

"That isn't great."

"I know." Paulo had been told multiple times that it was Paulo's responsibility to be a 'real' man, and that having a gay teammate was good for Enzo's political career as it made him look inclusive, but Paulo couldn't let the gayness rub off on him, or some such nonsense. If his father and brother knew how his heart skipped a beat whenever Cohen flexed his forearms, they'd withdraw their funding faster than he could get to turn one at Spa.

"What's the ideal outcome here?"

"Remind me not to fuck up again. I can't let the pressure get to me."

"Pressure always needs a release or it builds up."

Paulo rolled his eyes. "Thanks for the basic philosophy." He leaned back in his seat and focused on slowing his breathing. After a while, he turned his head. Cohen sat stiffly in his chair, staring out the window at the clouds.

"I'm sorry. I shouldn't have bitten at you like that."

"What do you do for fun?" Cohen asked.

Paulo shook his head. "Drive fast."

"This morning was fun for you?"

For the first time in forever, Paulo felt some of the tension across his shoulders ease. "It was wonderful. I drive much faster for work, obviously. I tend to obey the speed limit on public roads; mostly because it's not worth the risk to other drivers and because I don't need to." Paulo didn't like drawing attention to himself either. "This morning was brilliant because there were no expectations on me to perform. I needed to get to the team meeting on time, and I used my skills to do it."

"And that was fun?"

Paulo grinned. It'd been fucking fantastic to push a car to its limits, even if it wasn't a fast car. "When I get in the car on race weekends, there is a whole team of people relying on me to be as fast as possible. Everyone works so hard to get the car ready; the pit crew practice and practice so we can box without issues. And the team's success comes down to me and Ondrej and the way we drive. I love it, but it's still work."

"That's a lot to carry."

"Yeah, and if I fuck up, I could die." He shrugged because dying was in the lap of the Gods. He did what he could and that was that. Cohen gently squeezed Paulo's hand, then snatched his hand away before Paulo could react. He liked that—too much—having someone care about his well-being. Regret made his throat hot; talking about dying was an asshole thing to say.

"The odds of me dying are less than you'd think. We have a lot of safety equipment. I crashed at two hundred miles an hour on Sunday and I'm fine." He was a bit bruised; nothing serious and he'd be fine by FP1 on Friday. "The moment I start worrying about the risks is the moment I won't be fast enough anymore." And he was already struggling to be fast enough.

"Why mention it?"

"You should probably know the risks involved. Don't get too attached." Paulo already liked Cohen more than he should and needed to push him away. Silence fell between them for a while.

"What else do you do for fun? You must have a way of releasing some of the pressure of your job away from driving?"

"No. Mostly I'm focused on what I need to do to win." He breathed out. Winning was all he'd ever wanted to do, ever since his first kart race as a small boy. "Brazil will be a distraction. Not the country or the racing. My father and brother are the distractions. When I am away from them or when I am in the car, focus is easy. In Brazil, with them watching and commenting, it is hard to find the focus I need."

Cohen chuckled. "Well, if there's anything I under-stand, it's toxic families and not being accepted by them."

Paulo stared.

Several minutes later, Cohen scoffed quietly. "Don't stress about me. I only said that because I understand how tough it can be."

"Your family?"

"My mother disapproves of ... well, everything about me. My father ignores me. My sister—who is amazing—is the child he wanted. She's successful, a lawyer like him, while I'm..."

"Someone who saved the life of an ordinary man over a few hundred dollars. You have integrity."

"Thank you."

Paulo closed his eyes. He should be thinking over today's team meeting, the agreed strategy for the weekend, and how to approach the race in Mexico; not wasting energy being curious about Cohen. Cohen was here to protect him, to do a job, not to be his friend. Yes, they would spend a lot of time together, and Cohen was the only person other than Monica who knew he was pansexual, although technically, he hadn't been specific about his identity with Cohen. The only others who knew were those strangers who'd fucked him here last year, except—hopefully—they didn't know who he was.

He settled himself with a deep breath. "Monica, my race engineer, knows I'm pansexual. She's bi too." He breathed out. "Most of the core members of the Gamble team are queer in some way. The owner, Socrates, probably created that deliberately, although as far as he knows, I'm his token straight driver."

"It sounds like a very welcoming environment for you, if you ever wanted to come out."

"I can't. My father would pull the sponsorship and my results aren't good enough."

"What do you mean your results aren't good enough?"

"Last season, Ondrej scored 104 more points than me. This season, I have as many points as he had last season, but he's 180 points ahead of me. The car has improved, but I haven't. The gap between us shouldn't be that big and it shouldn't be growing."

"You believe that without your father's money, you aren't good enough to keep your job?"

"Yes." Paulo hated to hear it said out loud. It was nothing the press hadn't said a million fucking times, often enough that it was glued to his chest and wouldn't let go. No one cared that he'd left home at fourteen to pursue this dream; he wasn't quite good enough in a cutthroat world where there were hundreds of drivers as good as him desperate to take his seat. The problem consumed him.

"You could be out to your team without being out to

your family." Cohen didn't mention Paulo's racing ability. He didn't need anyone's philosophy or bullshit reasoning to convince him of something other than the truth; he wasn't a good enough driver. He already had trainers and a whole team of people working to make him as good as he could possibly be; if he wasn't good enough, it wasn't for lack of trying or resources. He was missing that spark that separated the very good drivers from the champion drivers.

CHAPTER 5

Cohen double checked that Paulo was safe in his hotel room before heading to his own room, right next door. Being rich was a freaky thing. Gamble Racing had a whole floor booked in this hotel and that meant there were a few empty rooms that had been paid for without being used. It made security for the team easy; they knew exactly who had access to this floor and it kept out the media and fans so the team could have privacy all week and during the race weekend. Cohen had naively assumed a race was just that, but it was a whole weekend affair with practises on Friday—FP1, free practice one, and FP2—and FP3 then the apparently exciting qualifying runs on Saturday, or at least that was the part everyone talked about the most in all the press he'd been reading for research. The actual race wasn't until Sunday.

He showered, then lay down on the bed staring at the ceiling. It'd been a wild twenty-four hours. Cohen checked his phone; it was just after ten and he hadn't eaten any dinner. He'd been too nervous and there'd been too much to organise. Since landing in Mexico, Paulo had been in meetings, so Cohen had spent a couple of hours working out how to get his phone to work internationally—because of course his cheap plan didn't do international coverage—and he'd spoken to Gamble's security team learning how the hotel set up would work and how he'd fit into the team's plans.

This time yesterday he'd been working at Horny's and texting with Lilly-Anne. She always got up early in Paris to work out, so the time zones meant they often talked around now. Now he lay in a fancy as fuck hotel in Mexico looking after one person and being paid more than his wildest dreams. He should tell Lilly-Anne; she'd be so pleased for him. There was only one problem. He hadn't told Paulo that he was a trans man and the longer he went without saying something, the weirder it might get. It would be better to tell him now, get it over with, and get sacked before he got addicted to his new pay cheque. Let Paulo be awful now before Cohen liked him too much and got hurt by the inevitable way that most people responded to him. Ergh, there was no reason to borrow trouble from the future. First thing in the morning. He'd tell him then.

His phone buzzed.

Paulo: You hungry?

Cohen stared at the message, then jumped up and shoved on some clothes. He knocked on Paulo's door and waited until Paulo let him in.

"I take it that's a yes. I skipped dinner and need to eat."

"And you want me to protect you while you go out?"

"No, room service is fine. Just wanted some company."

Cohen should stop this now. "We aren't friends."

"Travelling days are always lonely. Eat with me, Mr not-my-friend." Damn it, why did Paulo have to be funny? Cohen's job was to protect him, not to like him.

"Okay." Cohen stood awkwardly. He should say something now. He coughed. "One thing."

"You have allergies?"

"No. I'm trans. I should've told you before I signed the contract. Is that a problem?"

"I don't see how that's relevant. Will it stop you doing your job?" Paulo asked. Cohen had been watching carefully, but Paulo hadn't reacted negatively at all. What a fucking relief.

"No. And thank you."

"For?" *For being a decent person and making no big deal of it.*

"Just thanks. What's for dinner?"

"There's a menu on the side table." Paulo jumped to his feet. The man moved like a cat, or a gymnast, on the rare occasions when he wasn't still. Cohen had been in a car with Paulo with him driving at speed; he'd seen his reflexes in action, so it shouldn't surprise him, except that for most of the past twenty-four hours, Paulo had been stationary. Paulo tossed the menu at him, and Cohen caught it, then read through it. It all looked amazing.

"What are you going to have?" Cohen asked.

"I always have the braised brisket wrap with chipotle mayo when I stay here. Jaxxon likes the nachos, and Monica raves about the Oaxaca Cheese Quesadilla." Paulo tapped his fingers on his phone. "There's an app. Just let me know."

"Fuck, I don't know. I can't afford any of this."

"Food is paid for as part of your contract when we are travelling. Pick anything. Order the whole menu if you want."

Cohen scoffed because it was better than staring at Paulo. "I'm not doing that. Besides, what the hell is a cactus paddle?"

"Try it."

"Yeah, okay. That'll be the grilled skirt steak with chili pesto, green onion, and yeah, the damned cactus paddle."

"Taco or quesadilla?"

"Whichever." There were too many options and it all sounded incredible. Was this going to be his life now? Paulo tapped on his phone and Cohen waited. He'd read his contract thoroughly before signing and hadn't forgotten that all travelling expenses—accommodation and meals—would be covered by Paulo. It was just habit to think about how much things cost and stare hopefully at his bank account as if looking harder would magically make money appear.

His phone dinged with a message. A quick check on his phone told him it was four-thirty in the morning in Paris. His app that worked out time zones was going to get a lot of use in the next year with the travel that came with his new job. His sister always woken ridiculously early, even when they'd been teenagers, and now she usually went to the gym before work.

Lilly-Anne: Did you see that guy on the news in Austin?

She'd attached a video file of their drive down the freeway this morning.

Lilly-Anne: Must be the most exciting thing to happen in Austin in years.

Cohen: Ha

"What's funny?" Paulo asked.

"What?"

"You are grinning at your phone."

"My sister sent me the news clip of you driving."

Paulo flinched and rubbed his forehead. "Series One's new bad boy."

"That headline bothers you." Duh, Cohen. Obviously Paulo was irritated by it; his sarcastic tone and worried expression would clue anyone into that fact.

"Yes. I..."

Cohen tried not to gasp as he put it together. "You are worried that they'll find out about the hotel incident in Brazil last year and—"

"Obviously."

"But your father already knows." Cohen was missing something here. "Didn't you say he paid off the press?"

Paulo rolled his neck on his shoulders. "What if being seen as a 'bad boy' improves my popularity among fans? Then it'll be in his interest to leak some of those details, and he doesn't know everything... If some of it leaks, maybe a couple of the people who were with me

48

will recognise me, and then the actual truth will be known."

"And the actual truth?"

Paulo glanced up. His brown eyes were wide open with a slightly wild expression. "My father thinks I was with a woman."

"And you weren't?"

Paulo blushed and looked away. "It was several people."

"Oh." Cohen finally connected ALL the dots. "You said earlier that you weren't arrested because it's not illegal to be gay in Brazil. I get it. And while your father believes you were with a woman, he's happy to cover it up, or equally happy to tell people if it suits him, and that opens you up to the risk of being outed to him." Cohen completely understood the nuances in knowing who to be out with and who wasn't safe. It was a constant navigation for queer people.

"Yes."

Cohen was out of his depth. He knew how to keep Paulo's body safe in a crowd, how to watch out for anyone who might be a physical threat, but this ... slippery media related issue wasn't something he had any idea how to solve.

"You don't have to solve it for me." Paulo read his mind, or ... his expressions anyway. "It's just good to have someone to talk about it with."

Cohen was saved from having to answer by a knock on the door and their food arriving. Cohen stood, watching carefully as the staff set it all up on the little dining table in Paulo's suite, and then he followed the hotel staff person to the door as they left. It was probably unnecessary, given the general hotel security, and the poised way the staff member had ignored Paulo, but Cohen needed to feel useful.

"What is it about you? Why are you so easy to talk to?" Paulo stabbed his wrap with a fork.

Cohen's heart clenched at the sadness in Paulo's tone. He was a lonely young man under a ton of pressure who desperately wanted a friend. Cohen couldn't be that for Paulo, and he gently tried to ease Paulo away from that idea. "I have a theory that it's not me... not exactly. It's more a timing thing."

Paulo glanced up, raising one eyebrow, with a quizzical look in his stunning brown eyes. Fuck, Cohen would never get tired of Paulo's eyes. Neither could the internet, if the volume of memes and thirst images he'd found while doing his research about this job were any indication! Several fans had made dedicated accounts for photos of Paulo's eyes.

"You came to Horny's looking for something, and you didn't quite find it, but you found me. You made an instant decision to employ me. Maybe what you need is a confidant, not a bodyguard, but bodyguard is a good excuse to have someone with you all the time."

"Are you saying that I employed you because I'm lonely?"

Cohen breathed out. He'd need to be careful not to further upset Paulo's defensive tone.

"I don't think it's that simple."

"Good."

"What I do know is that you are quite young, and you have a lot of pressure on your shoulders. Some of it is external expectations; from your team, your fans, your family. And some of it comes from within. You seem willing to deny yourself—"

"Stop. I've wanted to be an S1 driver since I was fourteen. Nothing—not even my own desires—will get in the way of that. I have three races left this year to prove myself as a solid mid-field driver with the potential to get better. This is only my second season at this level."

Cohen didn't answer. If Paulo didn't want to admit he was lonely and that denying his own desires was causing him angst, it wasn't his business. His job was to be his bodyguard, not to analyse Paulo's reasons for his sudden employment, and he really didn't want to be Paulo's therapist as he dealt with what sounded like the weight of internalised homophobia.

Instead, he ate some of the quesadilla, which was delicious, like mouth-wateringly incredible. He'd never eaten such a combination of flavour and texture. The skirt steak melted in his mouth, while the chili paste added a zing, and the cactus paddle—presumably the tender, crunchy, small green diced cubes—had a slightly sour taste that made the whole dish amazing. He finished his quesadilla and wiped his mouth on a napkin.

"You should talk to your social media person," he said.

"Melati."

"Yes." Cohen couldn't remember her name among all the information he'd taken in today. "She'll know how to counter the headlines in a way that you are comfortable with."

"Like a social media video or something?"

Cohen nodded. "Yeah. I'm no expert on that..."

"You're right. Melati is the expert. I should utilise her skill rather than worry. Thank you."

"For?"

"The pragmatic advice."

"Okay. Well, I'll head back to my room, and you can sort that out. You don't need my skills for the rest of tonight." Cohen reminded himself that he was here for work—to protect Paulo—not to be his friend or his therapist. He stood up and scanned the room, although nothing had changed.

"Be here in the morning at six-thirty."

"Yes, boss." Cohen nodded and left the room. He pulled the door shut tight, satisfied that Paulo was safe, then swiped back into his own room.

> Cohen: Can I call?

He already knew Lilly-Anne was awake as she'd texted him a little while ago. His phone rang.

"What's so urgent that you are going to call me? You can't afford that."

"Well, actually—"

Lilly-Anne cackled. "You can't well actually me."

"Just did. And I can afford to call you now."

"You got a pay rise?"

"I got a new job."

Lilly-Anne's squeal nearly split his ear drum.

"Holy fuck, Lilly-Anne. Maybe wait until you hear what the job is."

"If it pays more than at Horny's, my excitement is valid."

Cohen laughed quietly. "Um, I got a signing bonus that was almost as much as a year's pay at Horny's, and my annual salary is like five times that, plus I get all my uniforms, travel and travelling expenses included."

"Wow. Cohen." Lilly-Anne paused for half a second. "What's the downside?"

His boss was hot and lonely, and he wanted to fuck him and make him feel better all at the same time ... which wasn't exactly in the job description. He tried not to choke. "I guess the biggest one is that I have to travel a lot?"

"What's the job?"

"Personal security guard for ... ahh—" Cohen wasn't actually sure if he could say.

"Someone famous?"

"Yes. I signed a confidentiality clause, so I'm not sure if I can say."

Lilly-Anne made a huffing noise. "You signed a contract without me looking it over."

Cohen rolled his eyes. "I thought you might say that. It's a standard employment contract."

"How do you know?"

"I might not have a legal degree, but I do know a few things about how the world works and how to protect my own interests."

"I'm sorry. I know you do. It's just that you are my baby brother and I'm really fucking good at contract law."

Cohen laughed. It always sounded good when she called him her brother. "I probably should've got you to look at it. Is it too late now?"

"You've signed it?"

"Yes."

"Were you under duress?"

"I don't think so."

Lilly-Anne hummed quietly. "Yesterday you were working at Horny's and you didn't mention that you were going for an interview or anything. This must've happened quickly."

"Yes?" It had, but why was Lilly-Anne asking?

"Would you say you were rushed into signing?"

Cohen paced around his hotel room, trying to work out what Lilly-Anne meant. "What do you mean?" Sometimes it was easier to ask.

"If you were pushed into signing in a hurry, I could argue that you didn't have time to consult properly and therefore were under duress when signing which would make the contract invalid. It's not easy to prove, but I could do it."

Cohen didn't doubt her. She earned a seven-figure income working for one of the biggest law firms in Europe doing complicated taxation law.

"Would it make you feel better if you read the contract?"

"Definitely. Let me use my skills to help you." Lilly-Anne's comment reflected his own advice to Paulo. It would be foolish not to make sure he hadn't signed anything he didn't want.

"Alright, but you can't tell anyone who I work for."

"I do understand how confidentiality works. And when I'm happy with the contract, then I'll be excited for you."

Cohen laughed. "Be excited for me now. This is my dream job."

"Soon. People don't pay that type of money and rush someone into a job without wanting to take advantage somewhere."

"So cynical."

"I'm a lawyer. Cynicism is my baseline." Lilly-Anne's laugh rang through the phone.

"I'll email you soon. I'm happy. It's a great job."

"How?"

"How did I get a job like this? I guess you could say that I saved someone's life..." It was technically true.

"Your new boss?"

"No. He witnessed it and offered me this job." Cohen had probably said too much already. "Hey, Lilly-Anne. You can't talk about this. My boss was never at the Dirty Sixth, okay."

"Understood. Plenty of people drive through there on the way to somewhere else."

"Yes, if it ever gets known, that's an excellent explanation." He should've thought of that, but he was glad his sister had an answer.

"Email me and I'll call you once I've read it."

"Okay." He hung up and sent Lilly-Anne a copy of his contract before he could talk himself out of it. It made sense to have her read it. Why did it feel like he was betraying Paulo by doing this? As she'd said, if anyone understood confidentiality, it would be Lilly-Anne. He flopped back on the bed and stared at the ceiling. He must've dozed off because when his phone vibrated with a text, he woke with a start.

> Lilly-Anne: The contract is fine.

> Lilly-Anne: Also. OMG. Does that mean you get to meet all the drivers?

Cohen: Only if Paulo meets them. I don't really know how much each team talks to each other.

Lilly-Anne: You'll have to binge watch that series now.

All day, Cohen had seen ads for the famous show on the streaming service; the downside of the research he'd been doing about his new job.

Cohen: We'll be flying a lot, so I'll have lots of time for watching it then.

Lilly-Anne: OMG. I sent you that footage of him driving and you said nothing.

Cohen sent a gif of someone saying 'what could I say?'

Cohen: It was my car

Lilly-Anne: How the fuck was I supposed to recognise your car?

Lilly-Anne: OMG, were you IN the car?

Cohen: Yes

Lilly-Anne: If you'd died, I'd be so mad

Cohen rolled his eyes.

Cohen: He was late to a team meeting and borrowed my car. I'm fine.

Cohen: He's one of the best drivers in
the world

Lilly-Anne: Fine. It must be late where
you are. Where are you?

Cohen: Mexico. Same time zone as
Austin. And yes, I have to be ready for
work early tomorrow.

Lilly-Anne: Good night. And hey, I'm
super proud of you. You deserve an
opportunity like this.

Cohen: Thanks

Now he just had to do his job without fucking his boss. Gratitude sex, or any type of sex, was not part of the job description.

CHAPTER 6

By the end of Wednesday, after two days on the simulator, Paulo started to feel ready for Mexico. Cohen had ignored his comments about taking time to explore the city and had instead stayed with him on both days. Cohen had made a good point. Series One was new to Cohen and he could learn more by watching Paulo's complete immersion in his work leading into a race. There would be time for tourism later.

"Hey Paulo. Good social media vid yesterday," Jaxxon said.

"Thanks. It was Melati's idea to counter the bad boy nonsense." Talking about road safety was a boring way to achieve that. He'd also apologised to his fans for being reckless by knowingly driving a car that didn't have the correct safety equipment at speeds beyond what it was designed for. He hoped that people wouldn't make the same mistake and that they would forgive him for it.

"We're all going out for a drink tonight. Freddy says

there is a bar that does tarantula venom margaritas. Want to come?"

"You know I don't drink during race week." The whiskey afterward Austin had been different.

Jaxxon smiled. "Then come and watch us drink them. You need to relax more."

Paulo had to work to keep his gaze firmly on his Team Principal's face and not glance at Cohen who stood quietly in the corner of the room. He had a bodyguard now. Going out in public, especially in this part of the world, was going to be better with someone to watch out for him. "Sure."

"Awesome. I'll tell Freddy." Jaxxon's boyfriend was a retired driver who was one of the most well-known race commentators.

"Tell Freddy I'm not going to talk to him."

"He knows tonight is off the record. Relax, Paulo."

Paulo breathed out slowly. The comment from Cohen about having more fun and finding friends to support him echoed in his head. "Okay."

"Great. Meet in the foyer in two hours." Jaxxon clapped Paulo on the back. Cohen pushed himself off the wall, then relaxed again as Jaxxon walked away. Cohen's alertness and attention to his job—to him—shouldn't be this enticing.

Nearly three hours later, Paulo sat tucked in a dark corner of a bar, themed for Día de Muertos, watching several important members of his team drinking the famous Aragog tarantula venom cocktail. Mostly orange, the main part of the drink was supposedly mango based, not that anyone could taste it once they'd sipped the thin black layer floating on the top.

"My whole mouth is numb." Freddy's normally posh British accent was a little slurred. "This is wild."

Paulo sipped his bottle of sparkling water and let the conversation flow around him. His teammate Ondrej sat across the table, staring at his phone, and occasionally grinning to himself and texting someone—probably his boyfriend Hudson. Cohen's comment on the plane flittered in his head; maybe he could tell his team about himself—not everything—and it would be alright. They'd guard his secret from his father because they understood the implications. Maybe.

He'd made the right decision to socialise tonight; even if he couldn't partake in the venom drink—as if he ever would—because he enjoyed listening to everyone talk. This time of year was the busiest for rumours, with most of the contracts for next year signed, but a few key spots still up for grabs. Freddy held court with all the nonsense he'd heard from different places; S1 loved gossip and with twenty teams filled with over six hundred people each, there were so many people invested in who was going to be the headline act for each team. Tomorrow was the last day for preparations before FP1 on Friday, when he'd finally get out on track in his car, and he couldn't wait. He'd be able to stop all this thinking and just drive.

The table jerked as a man slapped his hands on the edge of it. "Sanchez, you dog." The man leaned into Paulo's face, yelling. Paulo barely had time to gasp before Cohen hauled the man backwards.

"Give your seat to Letherbarrow," the man yelled. Cohen dragged him by his collar across the room towards the bar's security guard. Paulo's heart raced as if he were flying into a corner with cold tyres, unsure if he'd stop in time. He swiped his face with a napkin, removing the wrong feeling of the man's breath on his skin.

Jaxxon leaned over the table. "I was sceptical that you needed your own bodyguard, but that was pretty wild. Does that happen often?"

Paulo shook his head. "No. Usually only in Brazil."

"Ahh, makes sense."

Paulo's heart steadied with Jaxxon's acknowledgement. "People have opinions about my brother's politics and the way my father runs his business. It can get a little intense." It was why Paulo tended to avoid the real world as much as he could. Last year, when he'd been dragged to various events with his father, they'd used his father's security forces to keep fans away. This year, he would have Cohen to protect him; from fans and from his own need to escape this life and just be himself.

Jaxxon nodded. "Makes sense to employ someone before you get there so they can get used to the whole S1 circus first."

"Yeah." Paulo stared as Cohen pushed the man out the door.

"For a small guy, that was pretty fucking impressive too." Freddy said. "And it's clever too."

"What is?" Paulo asked. Cohen chatted to the security guard of the bar, standing in his usual casual way that hid his readiness for action. Their gazes met across the room, and Cohen lowered his chin slightly in a question; 'Are you okay?' Paulo nodded, then tried to focus on what Jaxxon and Freddy were saying.

"If you had someone huge, it'd be obvious that they

were a bodyguard, but someone like him is unexpected. It'll catch people off balance. You know, the surprise element." Freddy had that assessing look in his eye; the one that had made him an excellent driver and now an intrusive journalist who got to the heart of a story.

"Off the record." Jaxxon nudged his boyfriend who laughed. Everyone fell back into the conversation from before. Paulo didn't relax until Cohen walked towards him and leaned against the wall beside him.

"It's bullshit," Freddy turned towards him.

"What?"

"That your seat should go to Letherbarrow."

Paulo frowned. "How do you figure?" Letherbarrow was the obvious choice; he'd rushed through the lower grades and was likely to be the S2 champion in his second season at that level this year. He'd put out rumours that he was negotiating with four teams, but so far, nothing had been announced.

"There's no doubt that he's got plenty of talent, but he's also got way too much ego for this team. He needs a team that will give him their number one driver seat and I think the reason he hasn't signed with anyone yet is because no-one has offered him that. I wouldn't be surprised to see him miss out this year."

Paulo nodded. There was some logic in that.

"Ignore what that random man said. You are going to have a long and successful career. I can tell."

"Freddy. Paulo doesn't need his ego boosted by you," Jaxxon said. Paulo wasn't so sure about that. Having someone like former star driver Freddy Hiptonstall tell him that he was going to be successful was exactly what he needed to hear right now. He'd been struggling with doubt, especially after the crash at Austin, trying not to listen to everyone else's opinions on him. And failing. Far too many people thought he wasn't good enough. It was hard to ignore the weight of all that doubt. A gentle touch stroked the back of his collar then disappeared. It must have been his imagination to feel Cohen's reassuring brush of fingertips.

"Fuck, Freddy, you should be a politician. Letherbarrow is a bigoted asshole. Too much ego is the nicest thing you could possibly say about him." Ondrej looked up from his phone.

"I said he wouldn't fit in the Gamble team dynamic. Socrates and Jaxxon would never jeopardise the culture they've worked so hard to build up."

Jaxxon sent his boyfriend a sappy grin. Paulo stamped down the rise of envy in the back of his throat. Damn, everywhere Paulo looked there were happily paired up queer men, who were open about themselves.

"We have over six hundred people in our team with the highest number of women employees in any S1 team, the highest number of openly queer people, and we are the most racially diverse team. We are ruthless in getting rid of bigots in any form. Not every team is open to anyone. And that's why we are going to win the constructor's championship next season." Jaxxon glanced at Ondrej; because of course it would the team's number one driver who would get them the constructor's title, not Paulo. He was the support act.

Ondrej shrugged one shoulder. "You don't need to

convince me. Convince Paulo. He's the straight one at this table."

Paulo gulped and glanced over at Monica whose mouth was twisted around as if she were suppressing a grin. This was his chance.

"Hey, what about me? I can be a token straight person too." Ondrej's new race engineer, Theron, interrupted while Paulo was still deciding.

"You are straight?" Ondrej asked.

Theron nodded. "Yeah, my wife would be surprised if I wasn't."

"You could be bisexual. Just because you are married to a woman doesn't make you straight," Jaxxon said.

"True."

Monica elbowed Theron. "Come on man, you ought to know better while you sit at this table."

"Hey, I'm still learning this ally business."

"Ally. You don't get to call yourself that!" Freddy joked and half-stood up, the grin on his face making a lie of his outburst. Jaxxon touched him on the bicep, and he sat down with a wink to Theron. Paulo couldn't really believe they could all be relaxed enough in their identities to roast each other about it. He'd spent most of his life pretending to be straight and it was still a shock to be part of Gamble's open and accepting team.

"Settle down, Freddy. I wouldn't have this job unless I'd passed Jaxxon's bigot test. My sister is queer. I just forgot about the bisexual thing because it's not me, you know. I'm sorry." Theron actually sounded sorry, and Paulo nodded slowly.

"Having a queer sister doesn't make you an automatic

ally." Monica made a good point. "I mean, my sister has a queer sister, and she's fucking dreadful."

"Are you saying that you are dreadful, or..." Freddy grinned.

"Stop being a grammar pedant, Freddy." Monica laughed. "You know what I meant."

"I'm sorry that your sister is horrid. Chosen families are so much better than biological ones, don't you think?" Freddy's sigh was echoed by almost everyone at the table. Paulo's shoulders ached with tension, and it'd been ramping up throughout this conversation. He should be relaxed by the easy way everyone accepted each other and commiserated over their journeys, but every time someone mentioned being queer, or joked that he was the token straight person, his muscles pulled taut until he thought he might snap.

"I'm pansexual." He just blurted it out before he could second or third guess himself again. The rush of endorphins made him dizzy, just like the first time he'd stood on an S1 podium. "But you can't tell anyone outside the team. My father's sponsorship is conditional on me being straight."

"Our lips are sealed." Freddy rested his hand on Jaxxon's shoulder, who mimed zipping his lips shut.

"Thanks for sharing, Paulo. We won't tell your father." Monica's sincere tone created a little prickle in the back of his eyes, and he swallowed.

"I have an early start tomorrow. Enjoy the tarantula juice." Paulo needed to move, needed to get away from everyone's careful niceness to his awkwardness. Let them all talk about his lack of talent, his career, and his need to be closeted around his family without having to listen to it all. He stood up.

"Get plenty of rest, Paulo." Jaxxon shook his hand, and the others all waved.

"Okay. Bye." He walked out of the bar onto the street with Cohen trailing behind him. "Walk beside me." He couldn't deal with more weirdness right now. Cohen immediately shifted and walked alongside him, their steps in sync.

"Thank you for dealing with that fan."

"It's my job." Cohen's simple response helped calm the storm inside Paulo's head. There was so much happening in there. He wanted to get in his car and just empty it all out with his focus on the one thing he understood; racing. They walked a block in silence with Cohen just being there. His presence created a peacefulness that continued as they walked into the hotel and rode the elevator up to their floor.

"Are you alright?" Cohen asked.

Paulo wasn't sure. "Do you mind if I unload on you for a bit?"

"Yes boss."

Well, that didn't help. Paulo cringed. "Never mind. I don't want to overstep the bounds of your contract."

"Paulo. I know I've only worked with you for a few days and I'm still learning your job, but..."

"But what?" Paulo didn't need Cohen to bolster his ego right now.

"It's clear to me that your job is highly stressful and if it helps to unload a bunch of thoughts onto me, then please do it. Add therapy to the job description if it makes you feel better."

Paulo swallowed—Gamble Racing had a sports psychologist already—but he really did need a queer therapist or at least someone else queer who he could talk to and figure out himself.

"Fine. Come in and be my bodyguard slash therapist." He opened the door to his room, kicked off his shoes, and started to pace. "Okay, fuck. I don't even know where to start." He glanced over at Cohen who leaned against the wall with one hand in his jeans pocket and the other hanging loosely. As usual, he managed to look casual and alert at the same time.

"I haven't had sex for nearly a year. And damn, watching Jaxxon and Freddy be so fucking cute together makes me want that for myself."

"You want a boyfriend?"

"Yes. No. I just want someone to look at me like Jaxxon looks at Freddy, or how Ondrej stares at Hudson. I basically have no preference for gender ... like, I don't even understand how people can only want one type of genitals. Eww —" Paulo rubbed his eyes. Had he really said that out loud? He looked up to see Cohen holding his hand over his mouth, trying not to laugh.

"Was that super weird? I'm being weird."

"You really aren't. I get what you mean, even if the phrasing was a little awkward."

"It's an awkward topic and..." Paulo sighed. "I grew up avoiding everything to do with this topic."

Cohen nodded. "So you don't have the language to describe what you feel inside?"

"Fucking yes. That's exactly it." Paulo wanted to leap in the air. Yes.

"You are only twenty-two. You have plenty of time to figure this out."

The tension at the back of his neck started to relax. "When did you know?" Paulo pressed his hand against his forehead. "No, you don't have to answer that. Never mind."

"I don't mind. Everyone has their own journey and there are many things that influence self-discovery."

Paulo yearned to know more. "Like?"

"Gender and sexuality is a spectrum, you know, and the world forces heteronormativity on everyone so it can be very confusing..."

"I've always felt like I don't quite belong anywhere." Paulo hadn't known anyone who was openly queer until he signed with Gamble Racing. He'd gone from actively suppressing any thought that didn't fit the world around him to slowly wondering about himself—until he'd run wildly towards what he wanted last year in Brazil. And since then, it'd been a long series of questions without any answers.

"The thing about being queer is that most of us don't have family to teach us our own history. We have to discover it on our own. I was lucky to have a teacher at school when I was twelve who taught us about Stonewall..."

"Stonewall?"

"The Stonewall riot happened in America in 1969 when the police invaded an underground gay club. The retort against the cops was led by trans women like Marsha P Johnson, and it became the beginning of the fight for gay rights in America. The first pride march was held on the one-year anniversary. To learn about the amazing people who fought to be themselves was awesome, not just because I discovered there were people like me, but because I learned about intersectionality too. I have so much respect for trans women. They are so brave, living their truth in the face of so much antagonism."

Paulo's heart skipped a beat and he nodded to encourage Cohen to continue.

"It was lucky timing, learning about Stonewall just as I entered my teens because soon after that I experienced some strong gender dysphoria. I was able to explain it to my older sister Lilly-Anne, and she helped me find a doctor who helped me." Cohen's face was shuttered, and Paulo figured there was a lot of pain behind that story, a lot of misunderstanding. He'd mentioned on the plane a few days ago that he understood toxic families and a rush a hot guilt flew up Paulo's spine.

"I'm glad you had that teacher and your sister, and I'm so sorry that I asked about this."

Cohen blinked. "It's fine. It was a lot of words to explain that I understand."

"Thank you."

"Trust yourself and how you feel."

Paulo wished he could hang onto that statement and hold it tight. "But what if what I want is wrong?" He didn't know how to articulate this sense of wrongness inside him. It wasn't about his identity; he was learning to be comfortable with being pansexual. The biggest problem was about his specific desires.

"Wrong because you've always been told it's wrong, or wrong because it's unethical and will hurt someone else?"

He would never hurt anyone. What he wanted was the

opposite. Paulo closed his eyes. "Because I want someone to hurt me," he whispered. He couldn't look at Cohen right now, maybe never again.

"Plenty of people are into pain play." Cohen spoke as if it was no big deal and Paulo snapped open his eyes to stare at him. This whole conversation well overstepped the bounds of Paulo's role as Cohen's boss and made Paulo's stomach churn, but he had no one else to talk to about this either. From the moment that Cohen had leaped the bar at Horny's to defend Stanley, Paulo had trusted him with everything. Maybe it was illogical. Too bad. Tonight in the bar had only reinforced that his initial gut feel had been correct. Cohen had stepped in to pull away the overly zealous fan almost before Paulo had even noticed him.

"Okay. Well, good night." Paulo needed to be alone. He wasn't ready to explain that it was more than that. He wanted to earn someone's love. All his life, he'd been gifted everything. Money, a reasonable amount of driving talent and the resources to pursue his dream, fame; he had every-thing most people craved, and he'd never had to truly earn it. Even his seat at Gamble had been bought for him. He wanted to kneel at someone's feet and earn them, to let them take their pleasure from him, and give himself fully to someone. Anyone. He wanted to work hard for someone's care and attention until he hurt with trying. It was fucked up.

"Good night and good luck. You'll work it out." Cohen cast his gaze around the room then left, leaving Paulo standing awkwardly in a generic hotel room alone with his uncomfortable thoughts.

CHAPTER 7

"Five. Great drive, Paulo." Monica's voice was calm in the ear-piece Cohen wore. He'd been given his own set to wear whenever he was in the pit lane and had spent the whole weekend standing in the corner behind the engineers, out of the way of the mechanics, watching the whole process. It'd been a crash course in car racing. A staggering amount of work went into getting two cars on the track for the weekend. Paulo hadn't been exaggerating when he'd said there was a whole team relying on him to perform and race well. Now the race was finished, the real work—for Cohen—would begin as the media and fans all wanted a piece of Paulo.

"Yes." Paulo's squeal of excitement rang in his ear. "Fuck yes."

The mechanics were all slapping each other on the back and Cohen leaned on the wall to absorb the excitement in the garage. Judging by the hugs and shouts, fifth was an amazing achievement and Cohen's chest filled with warmth. A minute later, Ondrej crossed the line in tenth.

"Ondrej P Ten. Points for both cars."

"Awesome job." Paulo's voice was steadier this time. The race hadn't been without incident. Ondrej had been caught up in a skirmish early and lost his front wing, but he'd made his way back through the field to finish in tenth. The action didn't stop when the race ended. Cohen waited and watched as the cars were parked, waiting for the weigh-bridge, and eventually, Paulo walked back to the pit garage with a camera crew following him. He handed his helmet to his trainer, Heather, then congratulated all the crew one at a time.

"Cohen." Paulo wiped his face with a small towel. He was so sexy, all covered in sweat with a satisfied smile on his youthful face. God, he was so young; nearly eight years younger than Cohen and naïve about real life. Yes, if Cohen could keep that thought at the front of his brain, he might stop lusting after him. He had a lot more life experience than Paulo; it made things quite uneven between them.

"Congratulations. That was amazing." The whole experience had been incredible. When he'd sent Lilly-Anne a photo of himself in the pit garage on Friday morning before free practice one, she'd sent back a video of Felix laughing and saying how jealous he was. Only the team ever got access to this part of the garage ... which made Cohen part of the team. He wore the team kit now. Jaxxon had over-ruled Paulo in their negotiations and transferred Cohen's contract to Gamble Racing, something that made Cohen a bit more comfortable whenever he noticed how hot Paulo was, because now Paulo was merely his responsibility to protect, not his boss. A subtle change. It also gave Cohen more personal security because he was employed by a company, rather than an individual, something he hadn't thought about at first because he'd been so thrilled to have a job that paid decent money.

"Thank you. It feels great to be back in the points."

"Does this make you the fifth best driver in the world?" Cohen teased.

The smile that broke across Paulo's face glowed like the fucking sun had fallen into the pit garage. "Today, yes."

It took a few breaths before Cohen could find his voice. "Good."

"I have a few media things to do before we can leave the track."

"I know. I have your back."

Paulo nodded. "Yes."

Cohen woke early the next day, already adjusted to Paulo's schedule after less than a week. The post-race media, meetings with fans who'd paid for extra access to the drivers, and team meetings had taken a few hours, and Heather had made sure Paulo had eaten something between interviews. After the rude confrontation in the bar, Cohen had been happily surprised by the racetrack fans and how respectful they'd been towards Paulo and the other drivers. They'd flown from the track back to the hotel in a fucking helicopter. Everyone seemed to take it in their stride, as if this was their life every day, and Cohen had tried not to stare wide eyed at the luxury of flying over roads filled with traffic. He'd been warned by Paulo that he'd probably sleep in late after the race, and with no messages on his phone, Cohen got up and had a shower. When he was done, there was a message waiting for him.

> Paulo: What do you want for room service breakfast?

> Cohen: Something simple. Whatever you are having is fine.

> Paulo: Okay. Come here to eat. We need to plan.

Cohen responded with a quick thumbs up emoji, before locking up his room and knocking on Paulo's door. When it opened, Cohen tried not to gasp as Paulo stood there wearing only boxer shorts. His lean torso was on full display. He turned and waked back into his room with a swagger that hadn't been there before this weekend. Funny what success could do.

"So fifth is pretty good, then?" Cohen wanted to say that it looked good on Paulo, but he tempered it, softened the joke to avoid the truth.

"Not as good as first, but yes, it feels good to have finally driven well after three rubbish races."

Cohen frowned for a moment at the apparent backhander—not as good as winning—before he remembered Paulo had won a race earlier this year. "You won in Belgium?"

"Yes. At Spa."

"And you have the audacity to tell me you aren't good enough to be a champion? Look at you."

Paulo tilted his head to the side. "If I could drive like this weekend every weekend, then maybe."

"But?" Cohen was missing something.

"I'm not consistent enough. This was only my sixth top five finish this year."

Cohen waited, not quite sure what Paulo was trying to say. Car racing was still new to him.

"Come on, Cohen. There are twenty-three races in the season. To only get six top five finishes doesn't even make me a mid-field driver. To be one of the better drivers, I need to be in the top five for at least sixty percent of all the races and I need to score points in nearly every race. I'm a long way from that, let alone champion."

Cohen nodded. "Help me understand this. A one-off win or decent placing is nice, but it's not enough."

"Yes. Precisely that."

"What happened on each of those six times that was different to the other races?"

Paulo raked his hands through his short hair and Cohen tried not to stare at the way Paulo's lean muscles rippled and stretched. His chest was covered in curly black hair with a perfect line down his abdomen that disappeared into his boxer shorts. Fuck, Cohen's skin flamed with lust.

"I have a whole team of people who try to figure that out with me. Do you think we haven't invested time and money to try and understand this?"

Cohen grinned. "Yeah, but you've also told me that you can't be one hundred percent honest with your team because of your father. So... tell me."

The gasp from Paulo echoed in the room. "Fuck." By contrast, his whisper was so quiet it almost disappeared, absorbed by the luxurious carpet. "Fuck. You are right." Paulo's pacing was interrupted by a quiet knock on the door. Cohen answered and let in the staff member who served their breakfast on the table in Paulo's suite.

"Thank you." Cohen closed the door after the staff person left. He'd been the unseen worker, knew what it was like, so he was polite even as he wanted them to leave quickly and not see Paulo's distress. Paulo was still pacing the room and heaving out long breaths. Occasionally he'd stop and hold his hands in front of him as if he were holding the steering wheel of his car, and he'd turn it while staring straight ahead. Was he driving a racetrack in his memory? Cohen waited as Paulo puzzled out whatever was happening in his head.

"I don't have an answer."

"You don't need to know instantly. Come and eat. Didn't you say we have to do some planning?"

"Yes. I have a team meeting at ten, then—" Paulo sat down and started eating.

"Then what?"

"Normally I head directly to São Paulo and spend time with my family for a week before I have to be at the track for race preparations."

Cohen knew there was a two week break before the next race, although the break was for the fans, not the drivers and team who spent the entire time doing race preparations. "From everything you've said, Brazil is going to be stressful for you. What can I do to ease that pressure?" It was his job to get Paulo safely to his races; technically it was just the physical safety that was his jurisdiction, but he couldn't help but wonder if he might be able to help his mental state. Paulo obviously didn't have anyone else to talk to about being queer. Cohen rubbed his temples; now that

Paulo had told some of the key members of his team, maybe the best thing Cohen could do would be to encourage Paulo to talk to them too.

"When we first met, you left home with only a passport and a backpack of clothes. I always intended to spend some of this week helping you figure out your life now that you'll be travelling with me all the time. Can you do some planning while I'm in today's team meeting? Then we can head back to Austin and pack up your stuff or whatever you need."

"You don't need to do that."

"I do. I plucked you out of your life for this job. I ought to help you settle in."

Cohen nodded. It made sense, even if it was much more generous than Cohen expected from anyone. "Are you only offering to avoid your father and brother?"

Paulo laughed. "Of course. No. Yes. Fuck, I mean, it's a side benefit but I do feel some responsibility for the way I uprooted your whole life."

"You offered me my dream job. I get paid well, I get to travel, and I get to guard a celebrity." Cohen was the one who was gaining here, between his signing bonus and the regular pay cheque he was going to get, and the benefits in his employment package, this job would allow him to set himself up for a tidy future. He'd even have plenty of money to support his preferred charities, including giving back to the places that had supported him when he'd needed help.

"Celebrity?" Paulo scoffed.

"Yes, a celebrity. Honestly, have you seen your fans? How many followers do you have on socials?"

"I'm not sure. Melati will know exactly. Less than a million. Not as many as the champions." Paulo shrugged as if he hadn't just mentioned a number the size of a whole city.

"You are a celebrity. People like watching you drive. Look at how Stanley responded to meeting you."

"Okay?"

"I get to be the one who keeps you safe." Cohen rolled his neck on his shoulders to ease some of the tension. "Trust me. This is a dream job for me."

Paulo nodded. "Good. I'm still going to help you pack up or whatever you need. We'll fly to Austin this afternoon."

"Okay." Cohen probably should cancel his lease at his share house. He didn't care about his stuff, most of it was second-hand junk. He'd give it away to whoever took the room after him. There were a few things he wanted; clothes, photos, his favourite two sets of darts, and his collection of sex toys.

"Did you want to live in Monaco? I said I'd subsidise your rent, and I still owe you a car."

Cohen shook his head. "You don't owe me a car."

"I do."

"No, you owe me the cost of the car that you broke by driving too fast. Is that even a thing? How does that work?"

Paulo straightened in his seat. "Basically, I pushed the revs to the limit of the car's capability, which increases the heat in the engine, and because I did that for almost thirty minutes, the engine overheated and that softens the aluminium head, which means the head gasket will fail."

Cohen wasn't disappointed that he'd asked because the

passion for the subject made Paulo's face glow. He grinned. "I didn't expect so many technical details."

"Let me buy you a car. Please." Paulo brushed his fingers against Cohen's shoulder, then snatched them away quickly. Cohen wasn't going to say no to a gift like that. He wasn't one of those people who had any qualms about getting gifts from people; especially from someone like Paulo who could easily afford it. Maybe it made him a bit of a gold digger, or whatever the masculine non-sexual partner version of that was. The redistribution of funds from the rich to the poor was a good thing and he wasn't going to have an ethical breakdown over it.

"You can buy me a car and yes, I'll live in Monaco." Cohen had no idea what rent would cost there, but he earned decent money now and it would be almost in the same country as Lilly-Anne. They could spend time together in person, more than once a year when she visited Austin for Christmas.

"Excellent. I'll flick a note to my real estate agent and he can sort something out for you."

Cohen closed his gaping mouth. "You have a real estate agent?"

"Yes. Lawrence manages my property portfolio."

"Okay." Cohen had been fine with the idea that Paulo would replace his car, and he was going to make sure he didn't buy him something ridiculous, but sometimes Paulo said shit that reminded him that he wasn't just rich—he was super rich—and billionaires didn't pay nearly enough taxes.

"Good. How long do you think we'll need in Austin?"

"Couple of hours should do it." Cohen really didn't have that much stuff.

"Seriously?"

"Yes."

Paulo's face twisted in disbelief for a second, but he quickly schooled his features into a neutral expression. "If you say so. What about friends? Do you need to talk to people, let them know where you've been for the last week, that kind of thing?"

"I've already told Lilly-Anne. She's my sister." Cohen paused; Paulo probably knew that already. "And I left a note for my housemates. Dean and Stanley know, since they were there." There were a few others he should send a text to, but no one really close. Most of his friends lived on the internet and he'd been chatting in groups to a few people about his job change in the quiet moments of his job. People were very excited for him, especially after he'd cleared it with Paulo and was allowed to mention who his celebrity client was. His success had a positive impact on other trans people which really warmed his heart.

"Good. I'll book everything and let's do this." Paulo's excitement was nice, and Cohen let it wash over him. If Paulo could get excited about helping him, then Cohen would let him help. He just needed to find a way to pack his dicks without Paulo noticing. They were both ignoring the crackle of chemistry between them, and Cohen didn't want to upset that delicate balance. At least not so early in this working relationship.

CHAPTER 8

BRAZIL

"This is my son, Series One driver, Paulo Sanchez." Paulo's father, Enzo Sanchez Senior, introduced Paulo to the table in one of São Paulo's most expensive restaurants. Paulo's brother Enzo sat directly to Senior's right, while two grey-haired men—one balding, one not—filled two of the other three seats, leaving Paulo the empty space between Senior and one of his father's random guests. Hopefully he wasn't a complete clone of Senior's temperament.

Senior turned to him with a little glare. "You are late, but I suppose that is forgivable since you are so famous."

"Hello everyone." Paulo ignored the jab about his lateness, pushing away the need to explain that he'd been working. He was only here to appease Senior, something that would help his team retain the valuable sponsorship money Sanchez Shipping provided. With FP1 three days away and with Brazil being one of the few sprint races on the calendar, there was additional planning and strategy to figure out.

He sat down, careful not to glance over at Cohen who presumably had found somewhere to stand and watch. Cohen was wearing his Gamble Racing uniform tonight, and the tight black shirt with the team's logo on his chest looked amazing on him. Senior would be pleased to have him walk through the restaurant with Sanchez Shipping in big letters across the back of Cohen's shoulders.

"Of course my eldest son has the honour of my name." Senior nodded towards Paulo's brother Enzo who preened. Enzo was more than ten years older than Paulo, the son of Senior's first wife. Enzo was a politician who did all of Senior's backroom deals for him. "We named Paulo after this city, but he's not a saint. Ha, ha." Senior's forced laugh was an icy breeze and Paulo's sense of dread deepened. Would Senior continue his jest to talk about what happened last year? Paulo's palms were clammy.

Enzo sneered. "No, he thinks he's a star instead."

Paulo would've rolled his eyes at Enzo's interruption, except that it stopped his biggest nightmare from happening. Paulo had no retort to Enzo's nonsense, so he turned to the man seated beside him.

"Please excuse my brother's jesting, Mr..."

"Antonio Fonte. Call me Tony."

"Tony. How do you know my father?" Paulo relied on his British schooling to shift the conversation away from his brother's backhanders.

"I am the CEO of the Santos Port."

"Oh, I didn't realise this was a working dinner." Paulo knew his father would have invited everyone he wanted to impress, so it was no surprise to find the man who ran the local port here.

"It's not. We socialise frequently."

"Ah, I misunderstood." He didn't misunderstand at all but saying this would appease his father and brother who liked to keep him in his place as the sports guy without any aptitude for business. "I'm afraid the racing schedule doesn't allow me much time with my family, so I'm unfamiliar with my father's social circle."

"All you do is sit in a car for a few hours every weekend. It's hardly a stressful life." Enzo said.

Paulo raised one eyebrow. "Yes, it's so simple that only twenty people in the world are good enough to do it." Talking back was a rush of blood to his head. Paulo really wanted to glance over at Cohen to communicate how proud he was of himself, but he didn't dare. No one at this table would ever acknowledge their security staff, and there was no fucking way he could risk letting anyone realise he cared about Cohen. They wouldn't see how he was fighting an undercurrent of lust whenever he was around Cohen because they were so straight, it would never occur to them. At worst, they'd make a snide remark about awkwardness; but he still wasn't about to take any unnecessary risks. He'd leave his risk taking for the racetrack.

"Boys." Senior warned. "My guests didn't come to dinner to listen to two brothers bickering."

"Sir." Paulo's stomach churned at the scolding.

"Brothers!" The other man at the table spoke up. "I have a brother and I understand. He is always trying to one up himself over me; it is tiresome, but of course, that's the way of it. He is a mere schoolteacher, so it is nonsense." Everyone laughed with that meanness that Paulo hated. These men had everything; more money and power than any one person needed; and they still had to punch downwards. He benefited from some of that money and power, and it was a constant internal battle to play their game without losing himself to it.

"That is hardly worth the discussion of brotherly competition, Carlos." Senior said. "My two sons are always going to fight for dominance, given how successful they each are in their chosen profession. Enzo's career in politics will set him up well for his future as the CEO of Sanchez Shipping."

Enzo sent Paulo a smug look and Paulo ignored him. He had no interest in working for the family business, and he certainly didn't want to compete with Enzo for anything. Enzo's slimy approach to life and business was suited to politics; running Sanchez Shipping was merely Senior's way of dangling a carrot for Enzo, to get him to do what Senior wanted. Paulo almost laughed at the fleeting empathy for Enzo—they were both manipulated by Senior in their own way—Paulo with sponsorship funds and Enzo with the promise of CEO.

"Paulo has a different challenge. His star shines bright right now, but sports and fame are fleeting. He should be doing more to set up his future for when he retires."

"My focus is exactly where it needs to be. On becoming World Champion." Paulo earned every damned cent his father spent on sponsorship by telling Senior what he wanted to hear. Paulo might not believe that he had the necessary spark to be world champion. The technicality didn't matter. Senior wanted to see a display of confidence that would allow Senior to boast about his famous son.

"That would certainly be an amazing achievement." Tony said.

"Champion." The gloating satisfaction on Senior's face should guarantee funding. "What steps are you taking to get there? Is the team supporting you with the best car? A goal is no good without proper planning and commitment." Senior's comment stopped the breath of relief before it had time to escape. Fucking hell, he hadn't come to dinner to be quizzed by his father. Still, at least he hadn't said something snide about how much it would cost to be the best in the world in the world's most expensive sport. Building an S1 car didn't come cheap; the development costs each season alone were staggering, and that was without paying the wages of the six hundred strong team, or the logistical costs associated with racing all over the globe. Yes, there was a cost cap—which didn't include the driver's salaries and a few other key personnel—although many mid-field teams didn't have the funds to get right to the edge of that. Sanchez Shipping wasn't Gamble's only sponsor; just the biggest one that topped their funding up to the full cost cap amount, and companies willing to stump up that type of cash each season weren't easy to find.

"Consistency is the aim." Paulo didn't look at his brother. He didn't need to see the way his top lip would be curled up. "As successful businessmen—" Paulo deliberately gave Senior and his two friends a pointed look each. "—you'll all understand that a win, like I achieved at Spa..." Paulo saw the blank looks when he mentioned the track by its nickname. "...In Belgium this season, isn't enough to build a long-term career, just as a singular success isn't enough to build an entire business. The team is working hard to produce a car that can achieve consistent results. We aren't there yet, but as you know, in a highly technical complex sport, the pursuit of perfection can take time."

"A chip off the old block, Sanchez." Carlos—the balding man who Paulo hadn't been introduced to—raised his glass, and Paulo's father nodded as if he'd done all the work behind Paulo's victory.

"It must feel good to see your son on the world stage."

"Yes. I keep pushing him for further success. It's not great to rest on the minor victories along the way." Fuck, Senior took Paulo's sensible comment and turned it into an insult. His father couldn't even give him one little compliment.

"What will we see this weekend? Not a repeat of last year, I hope?" Enzo asked.

Paulo gulped. There was a chance Enzo knew about the hotel issue. "I take it you are referring to both cars not finishing the race because the engines were sabotaged."

"Sabotage?" Tony asked.

"Yes. It's been well documented in the media, and the culprit is currently serving his sentence in an English jail."

"Why England if it happened here? Our jails would teach him a lesson."

"The sabotage was spread across several races, so it became a global issue. Gamble Racing is based in England, near Silverstone, so the case was taken through the English courts. It's all in the media if you want the details."

"Son, these are my friends. They will appreciate the full story."

Paulo shrugged one shoulder. "There's not a lot to tell from my perspective. Most of the problems happened in the logistics and engineering department. It was frustrating to have the car continue to fail under me, of course, but once the reason was discovered, it allowed the team to move on to this season with a renewed commitment to success."

"And how is that going?" Enzo asked. Fuck, he just couldn't help himself.

"Are you saying you don't follow my races, dear brother?" Paulo smiled. Playing this mean game came too easily and when he arrived back in his hotel tonight, he was going to worry that he'd gone too far. Last time he'd had dinner with his father and brother, he'd lain awake most of the night replaying everything he'd said and being frustrated at his lack of kindness.

"No, I'm too busy."

"Enzo, it's only a few hours on a weekend. You could at least be across your little brother's results." Senior had a crack at Enzo, which wasn't nearly as satisfying as he thought it might be. His father was an asshole to everyone; how he managed to find two friends to come to dinner with him was a mystery. Like everyone else, they must also want something from Senior. What a way to live life, with everything as a transaction.

"It's fine." Paulo gestured with his hands to communicate the truth—he didn't give a flying fuck if Enzo watched his races or not. "S1 isn't a sport for everyone. It's highly technical and while I am absorbed by all the details, I don't expect others to have the same level of understanding."

"I think most men just like to imagine themselves driving that fast," Carlos said.

"Isn't that the appeal of being an S1 driver? The men want to be you and the women want to fuck you?" Senior continued to lower the level of the conversation, but his 'friends' thought this was the funniest thing anyone had said tonight. The mirth gave Paulo a moment to figure out how to respond. If he wanted to keep his father on side, he'd better give him more of the same toxic bullshit.

"Popularity can be a side benefit to success. It's not why I do it. Racing is a passion that is hard to explain; it's a thrill while also requiring technical ability and steady heart." Given the way Carlos and Tony leaned forward, that was exactly the right thing to say. He chalked it up to fulfilling the obligations to his father and ignored the twist in his stomach.

"That's my boy." Senior clapped him on the back, and Paulo refused to flinch at the jolt which was just that bit too hard to be as friendly as Senior wanted it to look. Cohen shifted slightly at the whack and Paulo realised he'd been completely aware of Cohen's presence without needing to look at him. Having his presence in the room had given Paulo the confidence to promote himself tonight.

"Will we see you with the championship trophy next season?" Tony asked.

"My team is certainly on an upward trajectory." Paulo faked a little laugh; all that media training was handy for situations like this. "When I came to Gamble, the team was in desperate trouble. They'd been last on the grid for two seasons in succession. My father's contribution has been key to lifting the team's results so dramatically from last into the mid-field." As he expected—and wanted— Senior's chest puffed out. "It will take more work to climb beyond the mid-field into championship contenders, however the results last season, and so far this season, demonstrate that it is possible with enough resources."

"But you didn't finish here last year?"

Paulo tilted his head towards Carlos in acknowledgement of his question. "Like I said earlier, a season isn't won or lost on one race. Before I joined, Gamble Racing was consistently the worst performed team on the grid. Having the Sanchez sponsorship allowed Mr Drayton to make significant changes that took the team from last on the grid to a reasonable mid-field option. To do that in one season—even with the issues we had at the end of the season—is a spectacular result in such a short time, and one that I think my father can be very proud of." He didn't have to pretend; all of this was true. Senior's money had been the key to employing Victor Tsui as the new chief engineer and allowing the expenditure on a brand-new design. Last year's car was fast, but difficult to drive, so the team's results hadn't been very consistent even before they'd been sabotaged. This year's car was less twitchy, and they'd been testing some innovations for next year's car that promised even more speed.

"I wasn't going to let my son drive for a team in need of funds when my business is more than capable of providing the support Paulo deserves." Senior's need to impress his friends with his billions was so reliable.

"I'd like to think I would've earned the seat at Gamble without the Sanchez sponsorship deal, however, I would've been driving in the slowest car, so it's fortunate that my father is able to support my team's success in this crucial way." This simple truth was why he attended dinners like this, because he would never be content to drive a slow car.

He'd rather have his own inadequacies to blame for lack of results than have a terrible car to blame. At least with a fast car, he would find his own limitations with every chance to be the best he could be.

"Next stop, world champion." Senior said with a smile that was almost genuine. Paulo was so glad he'd done a million media interviews because now he'd settled into all these questions, it felt the same as any other day at the races.

"This season, the car is faster and more reliable which has allowed the team to build on last season. If we maintain the same improvement each season, then a world championship isn't unrealistic. It all comes down to being able to produce a fast enough car and having the right systems and the right drivers to get the best out of the car."

"And if you never make it, you'll just blame the car?" Enzo asked, still smirking.

Paulo forced his smile to stay put. It felt like a grimace. "A driver isn't much without a fast car, just as a politician is no good without friends in the right places."

The nod from Senior shouldn't be so satisfying when he was really just scoring points off his brother. He didn't want to find satisfaction in this game.

"What makes a good car?" Tony asked.

Paulo glanced over. He couldn't tell if the question was genuine. Unlikely, given that nothing at this dinner was genuine. "We've already covered that. The car needs to be fast and reliable to let the drivers maintain peak performance across the whole year. It's in the final one percent; the difference between pole and last in qualification is often less than three seconds across a six or seven mile lap. At top speed, one second is about ten car lengths, which means the reality is that any driver and any car could win any race if the conditions are right."

Judging by the look on Senior's face, now was the time for Paulo to earn his sponsorship dollars. Senior would want to know what he was getting for his expenditure; more than being able to gloat to his friends that his son was in S1 or hear that his money had single-handedly lifted the team off the bottom of the grid.

"In my rookie season, the team had seven races where one or both of the cars didn't finish, which is a lot of missed opportunities for points. Many of those DNFs were due to sabotage. That's not exactly something a team can plan for, although the security has been increased since then, and the team does a lot more background checks on employees."

"It was an employee?"

"Yes. After the disastrous season prior to when I joined, and the team earned just the single point for the entire season, Mr Drayton sacked the chief engineer who was responsible for that season's slow design. My father's sponsorship allowed the team to invest in a better engineer, a better design, and ultimately a competitive car."

"So the sacked engineer was the saboteur?" Tony asked.

"Good guess. His son worked in the logistics department and sabotaged the cars as revenge for his father losing his job."

"He must've cared for his father," Carlos said. "I would hope my children would show the same respect."

"I would hope my children weren't so foolish as to be caught." Senior said and his two friends roared with laughter. Enzo's laugh was the loudest of all, but when Senior glanced at him, he stopped completely. Fucking hell. Paulo felt sorry for his brother, who had to put up with that toxic bullshit all the time. He would never tell him that, though, because Enzo was similar enough to their father that he'd use it for his advantage somehow. The wait staff came past and took their orders, and the conversation moved on to local politics and business. Paulo tried not to count down the minutes until he could leave; waiting for the pre-arranged phone call from Jaxxon that would give him the excuse to escape dinner before the cheese course.

It felt like hours of boring grandstanding conversation had passed before his phone rang with Jaxxon's name on his screen.

"Mr Loharani-Jones." Paulo had already told Jaxxon that he would name drop him in a formal manner to impress the dinner guests. "Excuse me for a moment." He spoke to Jaxxon, then held the phone away from his head and turned to the table. "I'm so sorry. It's my Team Principal. I have to take this." He put the phone back to his ear and stepped away from the table, remaining close enough that Senior could overhear his half of the phone call. Jaxxon had made him rehearse it and he was grateful to his boss for helping him navigate this dinner. Cohen followed discreetly, although Paulo could feel his presence as always.

Jaxxon cackled in his ear. "Here's your 'get me the fuck out of this dinner' phone call."

"Yes sir."

"Why couldn't the frog find his car? It'd been toad."

"Sir." Paulo clenched his teeth together.

"Are you laughing yet?"

"No, sir."

"Damn it. What do you call it when three billionaires go to space? ... A good start."

Okay, that one made him want to giggle and he pressed his lips together for a second. "Yes, sir. I will head back to the hotel immediately."

"Good. Let's meet in the bar for a drink. I'll drink and you can talk."

"Yes, sir. And thank you, sir. I'm sure my father will appreciate the gesture."

"He's paying royally for the massive sponsors tent above pit lane for fifty guests. You don't need to entertain his guests too."

"Understood." Paulo hung up and walked back to the table. One thing Jaxxon didn't understand was that he did need to entertain Senior's guests—he would do everything he could to ensure Senior's financial support, and this was the big weekend for Senior. The home-bred hero. The billionaire whose son was successful in one of the most difficult to access sports in the world.

Paulo leaned one hand on the table. "I'm so sorry, but my boss has requested an urgent team meeting. We've had some information come to hand that needs to be analysed and discussed immediately."

"So late at night?" Enzo asked.

"S1 is a global business. It never sleeps." Paulo shook the hands of everyone. Senior stood up and pulled him into a manly hug with a couple of thumps on his back.

"I'll see you on Friday."

"Yes. Once I've cleared my schedule with my team, I'll let you know what times I'll be in your sponsors tent."

"At least once a day."

Paulo nodded. "I will definitely be there after the race on Sunday, and probably after the sprint race and quali. It's trickier before and after the practice sessions as we have a lot of data to analyse."

"You?" Enzo just couldn't help himself.

"Yes. The feel of the car is an important part of the analysis. Data tells one story, I tell another. The team needs all the information to make the best strategic choices." Paulo hated the way the hairs on the back of his neck rose as he defended himself. It wasn't just sitting in a car and steering. "I can talk more about that interaction to your guests over the weekend, if you want." He directed that one to Senior who grinned like a Cheshire cat.

"Enzo. It's been good to see you again brother. Let's get some snaps for our socials over the weekend." A simple gesture of empathy for his brother who likely wouldn't appreciate, but damn, Paulo had to try sometimes because this negative vibe was tiring. He nodded to Cohen, then walked out of the restaurant with his head held high. As soon as they were near the front door, Cohen handed him a ball cap, and he kept his head bowed low as they walked outside.

"Your car is over here." Cohen touched him on the elbow. The briefest touch should send a sizzle up his arm, and he tried not shake out his arm as he followed Cohen towards a white SUV with a ride share sticker on it.

"Thanks." Paulo got into the backseat and sat quietly looking away from the mirrors. Cohen sat in the front by the driver, chatting about how it was Cohen's first visit to Sao Paulo.

"What brings you to Sao Paulo?"

"Work."

"Oh, what do you do?"

"Security for a car racing team." Cohen's bland response was charming. It gave Paulo something to focus on that wasn't overthinking the way he'd performed at dinner tonight.

"The Grand Prix is on this weekend. Do you know Paulo Sanchez? Did you know he's from here?"

Cohen glanced at Paulo. "Yes. I did know that he is a local. You must be proud to have an S1 driver from your own city."

"It's amazing." The driver didn't speak again for the next few minutes until they pulled up at the hotel. They probably could've walked, but Cohen didn't want to risk the exposure in the week before the race as the local media were very excited about all the drivers arriving in their city. Snaps of J-P and Ondrej having a beer together yesterday were all over social media, according to the daily report he got from Melati. Tomorrow at lunchtime, he had to do some tourist stuff with Ondrej as part of a local sponsorship deal that S1 had with the city; that'd be enough social media for him.

"Thanks." Cohen jumped out and Paulo eased himself out of the passenger door on his side of the car. He started walking into the hotel when the ride share driver called out.

"Mr Sanchez. Please can I have a selfie. No one is going to believe I had you in my car."

Paulo glanced at Cohen who didn't react. "I'm always happy to have a photo with a local fan."

The grin on the ride share driver's face was the second best thing Paulo had seen all night; second only to the way

Cohen had stared daggers at Senior when he'd thumped Paulo on the back. Soon enough, Cohen was given the driver's phone and was taking photos of Paulo and his fan.

Paulo smiled. "Pick the best one and put it on your socials. It's great to meet a fan."

"Thank you so much."

Paulo shook the man's hand, then turned and walked into the hotel. The hotel's concierge had been hovering throughout the selfie process, and now opened the doors for Paulo and Cohen.

"Welcome back, sir."

The walk to the elevators wasn't long and soon enough, Paulo stepped inside one of them, pushed the button to his floor and leaned against the wall.

"Your father is a piece of work." Cohen said.

"Yeah." Paulo was tired and just wanted a shower to wash off the whole evening, then go to sleep.

"I'm here any time you want to talk about it." Cohen brushed Paulo's hair off his forehead, but when Paulo opened his eyes, Cohen snatched his hand away and stood to attention with his hands clasped behind his back.

"I have a race to focus on." Paulo couldn't let himself be distracted by the handsome man whose job it was to keep him safe. If it felt like caring, it wasn't real, it was just Cohen's job.

CHAPTER 9

Wearing only boxer shorts, Paulo collapsed on the hotel bed clutching his third placed trophy. Holy shit. What a weekend. He'd won the sprint race, then finished third in the main race. The sprint race trophy sat on the table on the other side of his suite. Even hours after the race, through all the podium celebration, endless media interviews, time with fans, and the quick post-race debrief that they always did, the buzz hadn't gone away. This felt better than his win at Spa earlier in the season because he'd earned this one. Spa had been a bit of a gift when the three leaders had crashed after a restart and he'd managed to avoid the mess to grab the lead, then had stayed in front to take the win.

This weekend's results had been all because of him. He'd been super quick in quali, then won the sprint race—holy shit—and he'd driven a smooth race to finish on... The... Fucking... Podium. Cohen leaned against the wall, the same way he always did, with one hand in his jeans pocket.

"Congratulations."

"Only one thing could make today better." Paulo sat up. He probably shouldn't ask, but this opportunity might never happen again.

"What's that?"

"If you fucked me with one of those dicks I saw you pack."

Cohen blushed, so charmingly. "You saw those?"

"Sure did. Please."

"No." Cohen's retort reminded Paulo of the way Cohen had brushed his hair from his forehead in the lift after dinner with Senior.

"But?"

"Paulo—" The way Cohen said his name seduced him and filled his chest with bursts of heat. "—this is just a response to your success."

"I know that." He flopped back on the bed. "Fine. Whatever."

After a long silence, Cohen sighed. "I'll do it."

"Fuck. Don't sound so put out about it."

Cohen laughed. "We've been skirting around the chemistry between us, not talking about it because we have to work closely together."

"It won't change anything if we don't let it."

Cohen's chuckle was low and rough. "Life isn't a romance novel. We can't fuck the chemistry out of our system and move on."

"Why not?" Paulo could. After today's race, he could achieve anything, even believe that one day he'd be the World Champion.

"Have you ever read a romance with that trope?" Cohen looked amused.

Paulo had no idea what he meant, so he simply shook his head. "I don't have time to read fiction. Books aren't a guidebook for real life."

"What a politician you are. I swear you could convince me of anything. Work for me. Get in this car. I'm one of the best drivers in the world."

Paulo sat up again and stared at Cohen. "What is the matter? I thought you liked this job."

"I do. It's my dream job."

"You are worried that I'll sack you if we do this and things turn out to be weird afterwards."

Cohen coughed. "I wasn't worried about that until you mentioned it." After a pause, Cohen shrugged one shoulder. "Technically you can't sack me since my contract transferred to Gamble Racing. You'd have to ask Jaxxon to do that."

The change put all the power in Cohen's court, at least from Paulo's perspective, because there was no way in hell that Paulo would ask Jaxxon to sack Cohen for sex reasons... Hell no. Paulo sucked in a deep breath. He needed to fix this awkwardness between them before it grew legs and ran away.

"Um, please fuck me. I'd be so grateful." Fuck, that sounded weird as hell. "I mean, shit. I fucking got a podium today and I want to celebrate. I'm not going to sack you." He clamped his hand over his mouth because he could feel too many words about to fly out, as if he was drunk with his own success today and couldn't stop himself from blurting out his real feelings. He wouldn't sack Cohen because he really, really, liked him, maybe too much. Over the last three weeks, they'd just fit together, working easily, and Cohen was so easy to talk to about things he'd never been able to say to anyone else. He wanted more than to be fucked and to feel valid in his desires; he wanted to thank Cohen for being there for him and listening to him figure himself out.

Cohen plucked Paulo's trophy from his fingers and placed it on the bedside table. "It's all sticky."

"Champagne. Someone in the crew will wash it later before it gets sent home."

"Are you sticky too?"

Paulo gulped. "No. You know that I had a shower after the podium."

"Yeah. I was there." Cohen shoved his hands back in his pockets.

"You are uncomfortable." Paulo had already made a mess of this.

"Not for the reason you think."

Paulo rolled over and buried his face in the pillow. "I shouldn't have asked. Sorry." This was why he never talked about what he wanted. Now he'd made Cohen uncomfortable for some unknown reason. A sharp sting dragged down his spine. He gasped.

"You like that?"

Paulo could hardly speak. "Yes." His whole body was drawn tight, every nerve concentrated on the line of Cohen's fingernail, or whatever he'd used to scratch Paulo's back. "Please can you do that again?"

Cohen's low chuckle rang in his ear, and a whisper of his breath skated over his shoulder. "I like teasing you."

"But you were uncomfortable?" Paulo really didn't

want to ask Cohen to do something he was weird about.

"It was a moment of doubt. You are so young, beautiful, talented, and you could have anyone in the world."

Paulo turned his head. "I want you." No one else would do. No one else had listened to Paulo as he'd poured out his problems. No one else walked with such natural confidence. No one else protected him. No one else was Cohen. It was the easiest thing in the world to reach up, cup Cohen's cheeks and pull him closer for a kiss. Their lips met and Paulo wanted to roar with joy. Nothing—not even winning a race—felt as good as this. He'd wanted this kiss from the first moment he'd seen Cohen and the yearning had grown with every hour they spent together. Which was a lot of hours. Paulo loved the sensation of Cohen's goatee against his own clean-shaven chin, loved the touch of their lips together, and when Cohen pushed Paulo onto his back and straddled him, Paulo gripped Cohen's face harder. Fuck. This was so much better than anything; better than being fucked while drunk in a grubby cheap motel room, better than his imagination, because this was real. Cohen was real. He was here. Kissing Paulo. Paulo kissed him back with everything he had. He wanted to earn this attention, earn this kiss, and he gave everything of himself to the kiss. Paulo wanted to live up to those words Cohen had said; he was young and talented and could have anyone in the world. Except. Only Cohen would do. He stroked Cohen's tongue, played with him, savoured him and his taste—rich like vanilla butter cookies—loving the way Cohen used his weight to push Paulo into the bed.

"Roll over." Cohen's voice was all husky. Paulo obeyed with a whimper—rolling onto his stomach—as Cohen took each of Paulo's hands and spread them wide across the bed. Gooseflesh broke out along his arms as Cohen trailed his fingers along his skin.

"Please."

"Please what?"

"Fuck me. Use me." Paulo wanted more than he knew how to ask for. Cohen chuckled against Paulo's shoulder blades, then scraped his teeth across the tendons in Paulo's neck.

"Bite me."

"No. You'll do as I say now."

Paulo didn't think his cock could get any harder, but that did it for him. He whimpered, unable to speak.

"Will you do what I ask?"

"Anything." Paulo pleaded. How did Cohen know exactly what he needed?

"Good." Cohen did that thing with his teeth again, and Paulo shivered.

"You are so responsive."

Paulo frowned. "What?"

"It's a good thing. I'm just playing with you."

"Do you like it? Playing with me?" Because if Cohen stopped, Paulo might die dramatically from unreleased need. His blood was hot, boiling in his veins, and his cock ached with desire. His body spun with more G-force than a high-speed crash.

"I could certainly get used to having the world's third best driver between my thighs."

"Jesus, Cohen." Paulo shuddered. Cohen's confidence had been on display during his work, and the potential for this had always been there. Experiencing it was better than he could have hoped for. For three weeks, they'd pretended this wasn't here between them, so they could co-exist while ignoring this searing chemistry. It'd been too fucking long. Cohen's weight disappeared.

"Don't move. Don't look."

It took a herculean effort to keep his face buried in the pillows. But it was all worth it when Cohen pulled the elastic of Paulo's boxer shorts and released it back onto his skin with a ping. Paulo gasped, lifting his head slightly to suck in some air.

"Take these off, and you can arrange the pillows if you need too, but don't look." Cohen's command had that cocky tone that was Paulo's favourite.

"I want to see you."

"Not yet."

"Soon?"

"Yes." Silence filled the room with a heavy air. Paulo was sorely tempted to roll over and look around for Cohen. Was this part of the game? The waiting and the not knowing where Cohen was or what he was doing? Paulo hoped so, because if it was, he would lie here obediently doing what Cohen wanted. He could earn this by doing as he was told, no matter how uncomfortable it was, or how many of his thoughts rushed to stressful ideas. Like what if Cohen had left the room and was calling the press? Breathe, Paulo. Cohen would never betray him, that's why Paulo was here —willingly waiting—trusting him. Paulo stripped off his boxer shorts. It was awkward from this angle because his cock was hard and he had to wriggle his hips to figure out how to extract himself from his own clothing. He wasn't usually this uncoordinated.

"I hope you aren't allergic to anything." Cohen's voice sent a wave of relief down Paulo's spine. Of course he hadn't left. Paulo could trust him, and he didn't want to think too hard about why it felt so good to know Cohen was still here.

"Nope." Paulo didn't have to time ask why as Cohen placed his hands on Paulo's butt cheeks. The bed shifted slightly as Cohen dragged his hands down Paulo's thighs, slowly pushing Paulo's knees apart, until Cohen could place himself between Paulo's legs. Paulo wished he could see, but his face was pushed against the pillows, and his nostrils filled with the scent of the hotel's laundry soap. Cohen pushed Paulo's thighs, guiding his knees forward, so his ass lifted into the air. A cool rush of air covered his naked cock as he bent to Cohen's requirements.

"You look great." Cohen traced his fingers slowly over Paulo's thighs and lower back and ass until Paulo shook with need.

"Please."

"What would you like, Paulo?" Cohen asked.

Paulo squeezed his eyes shut. It was one thing to ask Cohen to fuck him when Cohen was dressed and standing away from him. It was a lot more difficult to wrap his tongue around the specific words—to beg for one of Cohen's dicks—when he was prone like this with his skin on fire and his cock so very hard and untouched.

"Paulo. I will give you exactly what you ask for. Nothing else." Cohen made it sound like Paulo was in control of this situation. As if. If Cohen as much as touched his cock or his hole, Paulo was going to come so fucking hard...

"Paulo..." Cohen paused and just as Paulo swallowed away the dryness in his throat, Cohen tapped him on the ass. Paulo groaned. He had to focus very hard so he didn't come. Yet. He needed to hold the base of his cock to stop himself but he wasn't sure he was allowed to move his hands.

"Again?" He begged for another tap, somehow getting the word out between his shallow breaths.

"How many points did you earn today?"

"Fifteen." His fingers curled against the blanket, clinging on tight. Eight on Saturday, fifteen today. Season total; seventy-three. He'd moved from tenth on the table to eighth.

Cohen laughed and rested his head on Paulo's lower back. "Fuck. I was going to slap you for each point, but nah, that's too many. You'll be too sore to drive in Abu Dhabi on Friday."

"It's not. Cohen." Paulo needed him now. "Please slap me fifteen times."

"No. But I will fuck you with fifteen slow thrusts."

"Please." Holy shit. Paulo needed that more than anything else. He'd earned his podium today and he was going to get a reward in the very best way. He gasped. "Cohen. Do you want to do this? I'm not making you..."

"Paulo. If you knew how fucking gorgeous you look with your ass up in the air, open for me, and your cock so hard and untouched and leaking, you wouldn't ask that question. It's no hardship to fuck you."

"Okay." Paulo hoped that was true because he really wanted this. A cool liquid dripped onto his crack. All Paulo's attention focused on the way Cohen's fingers worked the lube into his ass. He had barely any time to adjust when the blunt end of Cohen's silicon dick pushed inside. Paulo eased out a long breath, relaxing his body to accept Cohen's dick until he was seated deep inside him. Fuck, he felt so full and incredible. This was better than the first time. Mostly because it was Cohen, but also because Cohen had been so careful with him. Tender.

"Count with me."

"Huh?" Paulo couldn't think. He was so full and riding the edge of his orgasm.

"Count." Cohen pulled part of the way out and waited. How the fuck did he have such control? God, Paulo was going to explode. He couldn't make his mouth work and his lungs heaved.

"Fifteen." Cohen thrust once, sliding slowly against Paulo's prostate.

"Fuck."

"No. Fourteen." Cohen thrust again, and the same shot of heat flooded Paulo's body. He had to earn these by counting properly.

"Thirteen." Paulo's voice was all hoarse—an unrecognisable croak—and his lungs emptied with a jolt as Cohen thrust again. Softly, almost too gentle.

"Twelve." Paulo found the rhythm of it and counted down. Cohen wasn't thrusting hard—just a slow rhythm that built and built the tension. With each thrust, Paulo's balls tightened and he was sure he was leaking all over the bed. He didn't care anymore.

"Four." Nearly there. Soon he could let go. Cohen rested one hand on Paulo's lower back, an anchor under the onslaught of so much pleasure.

"Three."

"A nice long one for the third best driver today." Cohen's sultry comment made Paulo bite the pillow. He was going to last. He could do it. His competitive nature overrode the glorious pressure on his prostate. He shuddered; clinging to the bed with his hands, desperate to make it all the way to the end.

"Two." His voice was strangled.

"Good boy. Nearly there."

"One. Fuck." The praise from Cohen sent him spiralling over the edge. Paulo couldn't hold on anymore. Stars filled his vision as he came hard, simultaneously barely aware of the final thrust as Cohen's dick caressed his prostate again and he felt nothing else. The whole world shrunk to the connection between them, to the way Cohen held Paulo's hips and the way Cohen's thighs pushed up against his hamstrings.

Cohen kissed him between his shoulder blades and slowly pulled out. "Come and have a shower and get cleaned up."

Paulo collapsed on the bed, right into his own mess. He could just lie here, completely sated, but he hauled himself to his feet and followed Cohen. Cohen stood in the hotel bathroom naked—except for the harness around his hips— waiting for the water to heat up.

"Please let me wash you." Paulo had to give back. His legs were unsteady and he knew he was about to sleep better than he had all year. Cohen tested the water—lean muscles rippling as he reached forwards—then he adjusted the temperature, stepped under the stream, and beckoned Paulo to join him.

"You want to wash me?" Cohen held out the bar of soap.

"I would like that. Just let me know if there is anywhere you don't want me to touch."

Cohen closed his eyes for a moment.

"Am I intruding?"

"No. I'm fine."

"Good. I ... Please let me care for you like you just did for me." Paulo didn't know how to explain how he felt. Dazed, happy, sated, like he wanted to fall on his knees for Cohen but he didn't want to overstep and do something off-putting.

"Okay. Just not between my legs."

Paulo could do that. He lathered up the soap and spread it all over Cohen's body, worshipping him, enjoying the way Cohen's bottom lip started to sag and his breath sped up as Paulo washed Cohen's torso, arms, and legs. He skirted over the thin scars on Cohen's chest, unsure if Cohen would be comfortable with Paulo's touch there yet. As Paulo washed each of Cohen's fingers, Cohen grabbed his hand and wrapped it around the silicon dick strapped to his body. Together they stroked the dick with a harder down stroke.

"Just like that."

Paulo copied, and quickly picked up the technique that pushed the dick against Cohen's body in a way that made him gasp and pant and grip Paulo's hand tighter.

"Like that?"

"Yes. Harder." Cohen commanded. Paulo obeyed, and with the other hand, he reached up and pulled Cohen's head closer until they were kissing desperately. Paulo drank in Cohen's cries as he came with a shudder against Paulo. Somehow they managed to rinse off the soap, unbuckle Cohen's dick, get dried, and strip off the dirty quilt from the bed, before collapsing onto the mattress. Paulo slept, unaware of the world around. Cohen would keep him safe.

CHAPTER 10

Cohen had always known he preferred to top and to have Paulo offer exactly what Cohen loved the most had been too tempting. Part of his capitulation was the awkward—completely real—conversation they'd had, and Cohen let himself pretend all the reasons why they shouldn't have sex suddenly didn't exist. This morning, they'd slept in, having a lazy Monday morning together, enjoying kisses in bed but mutually agreeing to no more sex, mostly because by the time they'd woken, they were running late for the post-race team meeting between the drivers, strategists, and engineers.

Cohen had chatted to Lilly-Anne and a few other mates online while he'd waited outside the door. The team guarded their race security carefully with only core team members allowed access to the information, and since the room was secure, Cohen didn't have anything to do while they analysed the race. Over the past ten minutes, most of the mechanics had arrived in the hallway and he'd been chatting to a few of them.

"Everyone please come in." Paulo opened the door and leaned out.

He waited until the others had filed inside. "Do you want me as well?"

"Yes. We are about to have a whole team meeting. Come in. You are part of Gamble's wider team."

Cohen walked into the room. Several people were seated around a long table, each of them with laptops—all showing blank screens with the protected team data hidden —and a big screen showed a lot of faces, all in a large online meeting format. Most of the mechanics leaned against the wall, so he joined them, standing behind Paulo's seat. The room was filled with people from the pit lane and the logistics team. It must be important if they'd pulled everyone away from the task of getting everything packed up for the next race.

Jaxxon stood at the front of the room and when he nodded, the room fell silent. "Welcome everyone to our pre-Abu Dhabi meeting. Those of you who have been with Gamble for more than one season will know what this meeting is all about." Jaxxon paused. "For those of you who have joined us this year, there is one thing you need to know about Abu Dhabi. Being queer is illegal there."

Cohen held his breath. When he'd agreed to this job and been told he would need to travel, he hadn't anticipated travelling to nations like that.

"As with every year, the logistics team will have already talked to all our mechanics and have put together a team of people who feel comfortable travelling to that region of the world with all their unwelcoming laws. Series One has an agreement with the local government that ensures the safe entry for everyone on a racing team, and this has worked well in previous years. Regardless of the privilege we have from being part of a major international sporting event that promotes their oil industry and brings in tourist dollars to this nation, we still have several members of our team who are at risk from the local laws. Everyone—gay or straight—at Gamble Racing has the responsibility to ensure the safety of our fellow teammates. This is not a nation where we can relax or be tourists outside of working hours. Be careful with your actions and the words you say, and don't put anyone else at risk. As usual, Gamble Racing will cover all legal costs if anyone finds themselves on the wrong side of the law, however, with the penalties being so harsh, please be careful. If anyone has any questions, or concerns, please come and talk to me."

Jaxxon handed over to someone else who went through all the details and laws and the practical ways people could stay safe. Once that was done, he reiterated that they would stay in the team group for the whole weekend of racing, moving together from the airport to the hotel and race-track, and keeping away from the public.

"Focus on the racing. Let's have another result like we have in the last two races, then we'll head back to headquarters in England for a proper end of season celebration."

The room cheered and slowly emptied out.

"I'll be fine without you." Paulo stood up awkwardly in front of Cohen.

"You are not going to Abu Dhabi without me. I've been employed to keep you safe. You are going to need me."

"But you heard what Jaxxon said. You won't be safe."

Cohen breathed out between clenched teeth. "It's my

job. I'll—" Well, he couldn't precisely say that he'd be completely safe. If they did a body x-ray at the airport, things could get horrible very quickly. "Didn't Jaxxon say this sport gets a special pass?"

"I'm allowed to be worried about you."

Cohen nodded. "You are, and I'm thankful that you care."

Paulo's eyes widened. "Of course I care. Cohen."

"Are you two okay?" Jaxxon asked.

"Yes." They both answered tersely.

"I don't think Cohen should come to the next race." Paulo shifted from one foot to another.

"Cohen?" Jaxxon asked.

He breathed out; Jaxxon already knew he was trans because they'd had that discussion when they'd transferred his contract from Paulo to Gamble. "It's a concern. It is my choice to continue to do my job as Paulo's bodyguard and attend the race in Abu Dhabi. My passport is valid. There will be no issues provided the team and the sport is as supportive as they say." Cohen's passport had him noted as a man and all his change of name and gender documents were safely stored in France with his sister.

"Gamble will support you in your decision. Ondrej and Paulo are booked to fly there on Wednesday, with the team spending the least amount of time there as we can manage."

Cohen frowned. "I thought we were leaving this afternoon?" He'd already become used to the constant travel and hadn't read the plane tickets that had been emailed through to him from Gamble's headquarters a few days ago.

"We are flying to Monaco tonight, then will head to

Abu Dhabi as late as possible before FP1 on Friday." Paulo's voice was quieter than usual.

"Cool." Cohen probably should reassure Paulo a bit more, especially because his sense of identity was so new and he was worried about the impact of him having to head back into the closet when he'd barely left. Or perhaps the brilliant sex they'd enjoyed last night was having an impact on Cohen's own perceptions. Shit, that was the most likely reason he was feeling so much today.

"Sounds like you guys have plenty to talk about," Jaxxon said. "Don't sweat too much. Every year, we travel to nations that aren't welcoming and everyone in the team remains safe. We have to be careful and we need to plan, that's all. Being part of a big event like this helps a lot; it gives us a lot more leeway and privilege than we'd otherwise have."

"Okay." Cohen hadn't been part of a team of people who went out of their way to make sure he was safe and protected, and it was odd having the shoe on the other foot. He was used to being the protector.

"I'm heading to England tonight. Paulo, we'll talk on the phone tomorrow. I want more of the same energy we've seen in the last two races. Let's get you another podium to end the season." Jaxxon shook their hands, clapping Paulo on the back for good measure.

"I'll do my best." Paulo's solemn response was enough for Cohen to usher him out of the room quickly. If he'd learned anything watching him for the past month, Cohen knew that Paulo was overthinking this whole interaction and he'd need some reassurance. One thing about having been out and queer since he was a teenager—literally a queer elder by most measures—was that Cohen had strong coping mechanisms. They walked in silence back to Paulo's hotel room, and they'd barely made it inside when Paulo turned around.

"I'm so fucking sorry. I was so worried about you and I shouldn't have made a decision for you without asking first."

"Apology accepted."

"That's it?"

"Yes. Jaxxon had made it clear, back in Mexico, that Gamble Racing is a safe place for me." And for Paulo too.

"Are you sure?"

"Yes. I am pleased with the efforts the team is doing to ensure everyone's safety, not just mine. Now stop thinking too hard, and let's get you ready for the next race." Cohen avoided the real issue; how it made him feel to have Paulo decide to go into a dangerous place without him. His job was to protect Paulo. He wasn't about to abandon him, especially not in a place where they were both at risk.

Paulo's breathing slowed down. "Okay. Are we good?"

"Yes. We are good."

CHAPTER 11

Cohen stood back, leaning against the rear wall of the pit garage, as Ondrej and Paulo walked inside. Ondrej had finished the final race of the season in third, with Paulo just behind in fourth. Every team member swamped the two drivers, hugging them and laughing, slapping each other on the back. It was loud and glorious, and Cohen ended up in the middle of everyone as he tried to push through the crowd towards Paulo. The swarm of people spilled out of the garage into the pitlane. Joyous shouts filled the air. Finally, Cohen stood in front of Paulo. His hair was all slick with sweat, stuck out at strange angles after he'd wiped his face with a towel after taking his helmet off. Cohen grinned up at him.

"Congratulations."

"Cohen. How good is this!" Paulo grabbed Cohen around the shoulders and swung him around. A few flashes registered in Cohen's peripheral vision. Cameras? Paulo was laughing as he put Cohen down and leaned down to brush a kiss against Cohen's cheek. What the fuck?

"Careful." The spontaneous kiss was amazing, but obviously Paulo had forgotten where he was. At Cohen's warning, Paulo stiffened. With jerky movements, he grabbed the person standing beside Cohen and hugged them too. Cohen stood there, still surrounded by people and noise, just blinking and breathing. Had Paulo just kissed him on the cheek? In public. In Abu Dhabi. Fuck. And worse—those flashes had definitely been cameras. He pushed through past all his teammates and marched up to the cameraman standing at the edge of the pit garage.

"Cohen Wright. Security for Gamble Racing. I need to look at all your photos."

"No."

Cohen knew he had no ground to stand on here. He had no legal reason to make his demands. "Look, can we talk about this?"

"Why?"

"Do you understand the local laws around homophobia?"

"No."

Cohen had to make this sound generic. "If you've been following S1 for a while, you'll know that a few members of the Gamble team are openly gay."

"And?"

"It's illegal in Abu Dhabi."

"Seriously?" The cameraman was obviously straight if he was oblivious to the bigoted laws here.

"Yes. The consequences are very serious. All I'm asking is that you are careful about the perceived way any photos of team members might be taken, given the local laws and the common knowledge about some of our team. We would appreciate your assistance in keeping people safe."

The cameraman nodded. "Of course. I had no idea. I'll talk to all my colleagues too. No hugging photos from this race."

"Thank you. We appreciate it. It's something that shouldn't be an issue. Teammates enjoying a good result shouldn't have to come with a worry that they might be seen as breaking an unfair law."

"Of course."

"Thank you. I didn't catch your name?" Cohen glanced down at the big press lanyard the man wore.

"Alan Hickwater."

"Alan. Thank you so much for your consideration."

"I appreciate the heads up. Ondrej D'Grieg is a fantastic driver. It's a terrible shame that his sexuality makes him unsafe. Love is love, you know."

Cohen pinched his lips together. "Yeah, except not here in Abu Dhabi."

"I'll talk to everyone I know and make sure they are careful." Alan cast his gaze around the garage. The team was still celebrating wildly. "Perhaps you could arrange some exclusive photos with both drivers?"

Cohen grinned. "I'll see what I can do. Wait here." He turned towards the crowd, looking first for Paulo who was still handing out congratulations to each team member. Jaxxon clambered up on a large box at the back of the pit garage.

"Hey everyone."

The crowd stilled at his command and turned towards

him. Cohen spotted an opportunity and quickly walked back to Alan.

"Come." He guided Alan into the pit garage—somewhere the press weren't usually allowed—careful to guide him away from any confidential items like their massive bank of computers that processed all the data. "You can stand here and take a few photos of Jaxxon's end of season speech as an exclusive." Not having permission to bring a cameraman into the garage was probably a breach of his contract. Cohen gulped; it didn't matter. This would ensure the safety of everyone in their team, and most importantly, if any photos of Paulo kissing his cheek existed, they'd never become public.

"Ondrej and Paulo; get up here."

Alan lifted his camera to his face. The huge lens didn't hide the grin on his face, as the two drivers made their way through the crowd to stand next to Jaxxon.

"Two seasons ago, this team stood in the pitlane here at Abu Dhabi with just one point for the whole season. We were last by a long way, and it looked like everything Socrates had built up with Gamble Racing since the nineties would fail. Two seasons ago, this race was a disaster. Now we stand here as a team with drivers who finished today's race in third and fourth."

The cheer that rang out was loud with a capital L.

"And most importantly, Gamble Racing finished third in the constructor's championship. Third."

Cohen wasn't sure how the cheers could get any louder, but they did.

"Third, third." The chant began somewhere near Jaxxon and soon the whole team was jumping up and down in time, repeating that single word. Third. After a long time, Jaxxon raised up his hands and everyone stopped.

"Next season. Number one."

Fuck. The noise was deafening. Incredible. Eventually, things quieted down enough for Jaxxon to remind everyone there was plenty of work to do to pack up. "Once we are back in England, we'll have a proper party. Until then, let's get everything packed up and sent home. Stay safe, everyone."

It was satisfying to see Alan's smile disappear with the reminder from the Team Principal.

"Thank you for that." Alan dropped his camera so it hung around his neck again.

"No problem. Just remember what we talked about, and I hope it goes without saying, that even the straight members of our team are at risk by association, so please be careful with every photo." Cohen could protect Paulo from his father with that excuse. It was true anyway. If the authorities here in Abu Dhabi had the inclination to arrest Ondrej, they'd have no conniptions with widening their noose to everyone else in the team, simply by association. Alan thanked him again and walked back out into the pitlane, back to where he was allowed to be. It wouldn't be until they were safely back in their hotel, hours later, that Cohen could let himself touch his cheek and remember the spontaneous press of Paulo's lips against his skin.

———

Paulo was so fucking glad to be back in Monaco. Cohen was safe again.

"What happens now?" Cohen stood in Paulo's apartment staring out the glass windows overlooking the sea. The weather was terrible today with wintery grey skies and a misty fog rising off the Mediterranean.

"We have about a week to find you an apartment, then we have to be in England for the end of season stuff. After that, it's the winter break."

"The winter break?"

"Yes. If you need to take leave, it's a good time as I'm going to sleep and play games in my apartment for a few weeks, then probably head to São Paulo for Christmas with my family unless I can avoid it. There's nothing much on during December. In January, we usually have a pre-season fitness camp for the team, then in February, I'll be getting into pre-season testing."

"Okay."

"Are we good?"

"Of course." Cohen's answer wasn't exactly helpful.

Paulo sighed. He needed to clear this up. "The sex in Brazil was amazing and I don't want it to be a once off. I know I've been distant this week—"

"You've literally been working."

"Yes. I also don't want to be that rich guy who takes advantage. I'm stressed about how your job takes you to places where you might not be safe. I'm having a lot of feelings." Ergh. Paulo wanted the floor to open up and hide him, but he'd had this spinning in his head whenever he wasn't behind the wheel of his car, so...

"Those places aren't safe for you either. Besides, you aren't taking advantage of me. If anything, I'm the one doing that."

"How do you figure?" Paulo stared at Cohen, unable to work out how he'd come to that conclusion. Paulo had money and was essentially Cohen's employer; not technically anymore but naturally he had more power in this situation. Or was it a relationship? Whatever they were.

"I've been openly queer for years. I know exactly who I am. You, on the other hand, have only told a few people. You have trusted me and your team with knowledge that could make your life incredibly difficult, and, for me, that evens out any power imbalance created by your wealth. I think we are uneven in an even way."

Paulo replayed Cohen's words a few times. "That makes some type of sense. What now?"

"I think we need to decide if Brazil was a one-off, or if we are going to keep having sex, and if that sex will be part of a closer relationship."

"Are those the options?" Paulo had plenty of feelings for Cohen; more than just physical attraction to his confidence. He took a punt. This felt the same as the moment in a race when a gap opened in front of him, and he was going fly through it. "I want everything with you. I employed you because the minute you kicked that guy to save Stanley, I knew I couldn't walk away from you. I had to have you; not just as a bodyguard—that was just an excuse—but with me. Every minute we've spent together since then only reinforces that I'm safe with you. I can be me, and you'll support me even when I fuck up. I—" Could he say this? He gulped. "I think I might be falling in love with you?"

From the way, Cohen covered his mouth, it was too soon to say that. Then a long moment later, Cohen removed his hand and nodded.

"Paulo. I have no idea how you've managed to not tell people you are pansexual until now. You just blurt stuff out all the time." He shook his head, but he was smiling at Paulo as if he liked it.

"Only with you. I've always been comfortable to be myself around you."

"There are lots of reasons why I shouldn't agree to this..." Cohen paused and Paulo's mouth went dry.

"But?" Please let there be more.

"You are under my protection. You are so young."

"Not that young. I'm twenty-two."

"And I'm twenty-eight. Maybe in a decade those six years won't matter. Right now, there is a vast difference in our life experience." Cohen shifted his weight from one foot to the other. "Damn it. There's something about you that I can't resist. I want to be with you and all the reasons why it might be not sensible or might not make sense... well, none of those reasons matter when I'm in the same room as you."

"Oh." Paulo couldn't have hoped for a better answer. "Should we try and have a relationship?"

"I think so. You are honest enough that I know you'll talk about it if it starts to feel weird."

Paulo laughed, a puff of relief more than a joyous noise. "It feels weird not to kiss you." He walked towards Cohen who reached out and pulled him closer for a kiss.

"Feels like home." Paulo murmured against Cohen's lips before he let himself sink into the kiss. Cohen's signature vanilla cookies taste surrounded him; somehow unique and comforting and fucking sexy all at once. The prickle of Cohen's beard added to the swirling sensations that settled the unsteady thump in Paulo's chest.

Cohen pulled back. "I still want my own place."

"Anything." Paulo needed more kisses.

"Not forever. But if this is going to work, and we are going to work together, it'll be good to take it slowly."

"We can still have sex though?" Paulo's face flamed.

"Absolutely. In fact, if you don't let me fuck you now, I'll reconsider this boyfriend business."

"What?" Paulo gasped, but the grin across Cohen's face had him shaking his head. "You are the fucking worst. And also the best."

"I do like to tease you."

Paulo made an embarrassing mewling sound. "Please."

"I wonder..."

"What?" Paulo would say yes to almost anything if it made the man in his arms happy.

"I wonder where your limit is."

Paulo wanted to know too. "Could we find out together?"

"Patience. We have a whole lifetime."

Paulo's body filled with a wonderous warmth. A whole lifetime with Cohen sounded fucking amazing. "I want to try it all now."

Cohen leaned closer, then sucked Paulo's bottom lip into his mouth. Hard enough that it stung a little. Just hard enough to send delicious shots of electricity through his body into his ramrod hard cock. He gulped.

"Are you always in this much of a rush?"

"I drive fast for a job. Yes."

Cohen tilted his head for a second. "Can you do three things for me?"

"Yes." Anything.

"One. Get undressed. Two. Kneel on your bed. Three." Cohen paused.

"Three?" Paulo's breath was hot in his throat.

"Well, I was going to ask you to wear a smoky eyeshadow on those gorgeous eyes when you take me out to dinner…" Cohen paused again, but this time, Paulo didn't bite. He just growled a little.

"Get your favourite lube and I'll fuck you."

"Please. Yes. And thank you." Paulo kissed Cohen hard on the mouth, then stepped away to strip off his clothes.

CHAPTER 12

Cohen couldn't believe he was paid to do this. Aside from one quick trip to England, and a week at Nungwi Beach in Zanzibar—with the whole team to celebrate coming third in the constructor's championship—they'd spent the entirety of December hanging out together, mostly in Paulo's apartment in Monaco, never bothering to rent one for Cohen since he woke up in Paulo's bed, spent the whole day with him, then went back to bed with him. Every morning, they'd both work out in the gym in the apartment complex, and while Paulo said he was only doing off season maintenance, Cohen had pushed himself harder than ever before. He was getting really buff, and he loved it. It was a thrill to see Paulo loving how much stronger Cohen had become lately. Back in Austin, he hadn't had the time or money for a gym and had used various free resources on the internet to build up his body. It was funny how being rich just made things easier; not that he was rich, but Paulo was rich and that meant Cohen had access to the same things now.

The whole month had felt like a honeymoon, just hanging out together, going to the gym, driving around France and Italy in Paulo's rare sports car, and lots and lots of sex. Everything was wonderful. His phone rang.

"Lilly-Anne. How are you?"

"I'm good but not as good as you."

"What do you mean?"

"You sound happy. It's awesome."

Cohen frowned. He didn't think he was unhappy before he started working for Paulo. He hummed a non-response.

"I mean it, you sound great. Must be that man of yours. I. Can. Not. Believe that you two are thing. Seriously?"

"Lilly-Anne. As if you hadn't worried about this from the start when he plucked me away from Horny's to work for him. And you need not have worried. He's cool. We're cool."

"Okay. Then I'm doubly sorry for this news."

Cohen gasped. "What's the matter?"

"Felix and I have decided to have our wedding in Texas."

"To appease our mother?" It had to be. Only a week ago, Lilly-Anne and Felix had both come to Monaco for a long weekend to meet Paulo, and they'd had a great time, exploring the city, going to the casino, and eating amazing expensive food. Cohen thought Lilly-Anne had decided to get married in Paris—the city of love—not this.

"Basically yes. She keeps going on about grandchildren and how—"

Cohen had heard this often enough. "Let me guess.

How I'm not going to give her any, so it's your responsibility. Blah blah."

"Yes. I'm not going to give her any either." Lilly-Anne's taut response was enough.

"Well, she can jump in a fucking lake or something." He'd blocked their mother years ago, and refused to have anything to do with her, but Lilly-Anne's journey was different and she had to make her own decisions about her relationship with their shitty parent.

"Cohen. She's still our mother. If I get married over there, she gets to have the big show off thing to her friends, and then I can come back here and hang out with you and Felix's family who are amazing."

"Why not just have the wedding with them here? It'd be cheaper to fly our mother over here, plus there's the added benefit..."

"Of having her away from her comfort zone. Yes. That's the other option."

"Lilly-Anne." Cohen realised he didn't need to solve this for her. "I'm okay with whatever you decide. I'll be there for you to support you."

"Okay." Lilly-Anne paused, and Cohen rolled his eyes.

"There's something else too, isn't there?"

"No. I don't know. I ... How can I get to thirty-fucking-seven and still want to please her when she's basically horrible and can't be pleased?"

"I don't think you should try."

"So I just say no to her? No babies. No wedding in Texas. Just like that."

"Yes. Lilly-Anne. You are good at saying no to people."

"That's work though. This is ... her."

"Copy me. No, Mom. I won't do that."

Lilly-Anne laughed, but it was high pitched and off-balance.

"Or have a wedding in Texas if it will make you happy, but don't you dare do it to make her happy. You should put yourself first."

"Thanks, Cohen. You are the best baby brother anyone could ask for." Cohen always got a thrill when Lilly-Anne called him that. He'd forgive her for unwittingly bringing Mom's toxic crap back into his life because she had to deal with a version of that toxicity too.

"It's a wedding, Lilly-Anne. It's supposed to be about the bride. Celebrate the things that make you and Felix happy."

"It's hard."

"I know. Trust me, I know. But look at what can happen when you do put your own needs first. You could end up in France—" Or Monaco, "—with a supportive partner who loves you."

"But what about Mom?"

Cohen wanted to say that he didn't care, but Lilly-Anne obviously still did care. "She's going to have to learn to deal with the fact that she's not going to get her society wedding to show off her successful daughter."

"Yeah." Lilly-Anne sighed. "Thanks for listening."

"Look after yourself and let Felix look after you too."

"God, when did you become the one with all the advice, little brother?"

"Ha. Maybe you should listen to me sometimes."

"Maybe I should. Are you two coming here for Christmas?"

Cohen frowned. "I'll let you know." He hadn't talked about Christmas plans with Paulo yet.

"Cool. It was such fun to see you guys. Let's totally do it again." Lilly-Anne hung up and Cohen let out a big sigh.

"Hey, are you alright?" Paulo stood behind him and wrapped his arms around Cohen's waist with his hands resting lightly on him.

"I think so. I'm just worried that she's going to make herself unhappy trying to please Mom."

"Some people will never be pleased."

Cohen grinned and leaned his head backwards onto Paulo's shoulder. "Look at you, coming to terms with life."

"You helped me. Without your support, I would still be pretending I wasn't pansexual. I would've spent the evenings alone until I did something self-destructive again, like find a bar like Horny's where some big top would fuck me senseless. And instead, I found you." Paulo's blush was everything.

"You want me to top you again?"

"Always and forever."

Cohen was completely and utterly in love with Paulo. The speed of it should scare, but it didn't. Paulo was his lover, his companion, and most importantly, Paulo was someone he'd protect with his whole life. Cohen had had a taste of life on the S1 circuit and he was looking forward to the new season with his boyfriend. Only a few months ago, he'd been bored, working an ordinary job at a trashy pub for basic financial survival, and now he had the best fucking life with full medical coverage. Paulo's gift of a job had turned into the gift of a wonderful life together.

"Being with you was my very best idea."

"Your idea? I'm the one who asked you to be with me."

"And I'm glad you did." Cohen spun around in Paulo's arm and kissed him deeper. This was how he wanted to spend the rest of his days.

CHAPTER 13

The problem with hazy honeymoon days was that they eventually came to an end. Nearly a month of spending every day fucking each other in every possible way was about to be interrupted by reality. They'd barely left the apartment after returning from the team party at Nungwi, except for Christmas in Paris with Lilly-Anne and Felix's family. Felix had a huge family with tons of aunties, uncles, and cousins, and all of them were so welcoming in a very French/Cote d'Ivoire enthusiastic kind of way. Cohen had the best Christmas of his life. No wonder Lilly-Anne wanted to marry the slender soccer player who was being touted as a potential for the French soccer team this season. At twenty-five, he was more than ten years younger than Lilly-Anne, but the perfect foil to her overly anxious workaholic tendencies. Felix got her out of her head and helped her find fun in her life, and for that alone, Cohen would happily call him brother. The fact that he obviously adored and loved Lilly-Anne was the icing on the cake.

It was only couple of days after New Years when they arrived back in Monaco and Paulo received an email.

"Pre-season training starts in a week with a ski camp in Austria."

"Back to work then." Cohen opened his new laptop— purchased for him by the team—to find the same email. The two drivers would be there, as would the Series E drivers, some of the younger development drivers, and the team of physical trainers. Cohen did some quick research on the location. Galtur was a village near Bielerhöhe Mountain and ski resort. The email outlined how they'd meet at Innsbruk and would take helicopters to their hotel—what a life these people led! From there, the trainers had a fitness program that involved a lot of cross-country skiing. Cohen had been to the snow just once; a trip to Tahoe as a ten-year-old kid, just before his parents divorced. That single day of lessons was about to become useful.

"You will come, of course." Paulo didn't ask it as a question.

"Yes. It's my job to protect you."

Paulo chewed his bottom lip. "We will have separate rooms."

"What?" Cohen had assumed that they were a couple now and would stay in the same hotel room. It made zero sense for Paulo to insist on separate rooms. A sudden rush of blood to the head that came with rejection, of not being accepted as himself, something that was always present, reared its head and he struggled to breathe. He'd literally signed a contract to ensure that it would be very difficult to be sacked, that it would make it impossible for Gamble to get rid of him without giving him more options; and the fact that Jaxxon, the CEO, had understood that need and agreed made Paulo's response just now feel worse than the reality of it.

"I'll be at work. It would be weird to stay together."

Cohen wanted to press his hands against his stomach to quell the rising hurt. "You are already out to your team. Surely, they won't mind if they knew we are a couple?"

Paulo didn't answer and Cohen didn't want to push it because he couldn't risk his job and his security and his life. A fear of being discarded was ever present for trans people, not just him, it was something they talked about in their online community with too many examples. He gasped for air, his lungs aching. He'd let himself hope that love was enough and the shock of this change from Paulo came out of the blue, making it harder for his usual defences. He'd imagined that Paulo would want to be with him when they were together in the safest of places. He swallowed. It wasn't like him to have such a shaky response. He couldn't stay here; in Paulo's house; with Paulo rejecting him as a lover and not even having the decency to look at him right now. Instead of talking about how Paulo's rejection made him feel and the sudden doubt in their love—they'd jumped into this too quickly—he grabbed his phone and his jacket, slipped on his shoes, and left. He didn't really want to leave, but he needed space and perspective before tackling this conversation.

He walked and walked, all the way up the big hills surrounding Monaco, until he found a quiet spot to sit overlooking the city and the water. Up here, he was alone with his thoughts and the view.

Part of him knew it had all been too good to be true.

Paulo was so young, and only cautiously out to a few people, and Cohen had been ignoring that it might all come crashing down around them. He'd also ignored the way it felt to have Paulo assume he'd head to Abu Dhabi without him; citing Cohen's safety as the excuse, but maybe that'd been just bullshit all along. It sunk in, deflating Cohen completely. His lungs burned ... from marching uphill or from hurt? Paulo's need to be in the closet in public would be fine if it was only Paulo who was affected by that decision. It would be fine—fine, fine, fine—if Paulo was open to showing people who knew about him that he was in a relationship, but the dismissal of the option of staying together in a space where they'd be safe was too much for Cohen.

Cohen was left with no option except to support Paulo's decision to pretend they weren't together, or to break up with Paulo and do his job from a distance. Either way, he'd keep his job but ultimately, he wouldn't want to keep the relationship if he had to pretend everywhere. It was for the best; Paulo hadn't been able to stop himself kissing Cohen in public after the excitement of the last race of the season. If he won a race, adrenalin and Paulo's blurting instincts meant it was likely Paulo would do something cute and accidently out himself to the whole world. Maybe not being with Paulo was the right thing for Paulo and his career.

The panicking gallop of his heart started to slow down. He had options; not great ones, but options were better than the very real possibility of nothing. There was no need to panic. He'd spend the rest of his days knowing Paulo's taste and the feel of Paulo's muscles under his palm without ever touching him again. Again, it wasn't the most catastrophic option. He breathed out. He could live with this ... because it meant being alive. In another few months, he'd have a solid nest egg saved up and that would ease this ever-present anxiety too.

So that took him back to the actual problem; not the fundamental one of being discarded, but how to deal with Paulo's needs. Cohen wasn't being tossed aside by Paulo, but the outcome was the same if Paulo refused to acknowledge their relationship even in the safest of places.

Paulo wasn't a mean or calculating type of person. All he wanted was to hide his feelings for Cohen away from the world. Paulo was quite literally putting his job above Cohen, putting his dream of being the world champion ahead of his love—lust?—for Cohen. Was Cohen being the mean one here by hoping they'd moved beyond that?

Paulo was under a lot of pressure with his job and Cohen would never really understand the drive and commitment it had taken Paulo to get this far. He understood the desire to stay safe and choose where to be out and where to stay closest, but he also didn't want to be in a secret relationship, hidden, ashamed, away from the everyone in the world. He'd survived as himself for too long to hide again.

He stood up and leaned on the railing, staring down the cliff to the city below. Gah. Only a few months ago, he could never have imagined standing here—in fucking Monaco—worrying that Paulo's reticence to be out meant that he didn't care enough for Cohen. That fucking little voice in his head that told him Paulo must be embarrassed to be with him wouldn't shut up. He wanted to scream and push it away. If he wasn't out to anyone, it might be different, but for Paulo to not want to be with Cohen around people who knew Paulo was pansexual... Fucking hell, his thoughts cycled around and around until he barely knew which way was up.

"Fuck." His voice was whipped away by the wind. It felt good, so he yelled it again and again until his throat stung and his lungs begged for relief. Now he just needed to put on his big boy pants and get on with the job. Regardless of his own feelings and expectations for their relationship, he was employed to be Paulo's bodyguard and he wasn't going to shirk on his duties just because Paulo had a different view of them than he did.

> Cohen: Two rooms is fine if that's your preference

He sent the text before he changed his mind, then tucked his phone back into his jean's pocket. It was time to walk home—no, not home, to Paulo's apartment—and figure out how they were going to work together now. Perhaps it was time to find his own apartment, his own space, where he could focus on his job without being in Paulo's place all the time. They'd kept putting it off, but suddenly it felt necessary because if this was how Paulo wanted to do this, Cohen would figure out a way to survive. He was good at surviving and finding ways to thrive in less-than-ideal circumstances. He could deal with disappointment and a broken heart.

———

Paulo read Cohen's text and invented all the subtext. His brain was spinning. It wasn't his preference to have a separate hotel room to Cohen. Or was it? He'd basically freaked out on reading the email and blurted it out. Yes, he was out to his team, but telling them he was pansexual was a baby step compared to staying in the same room as his boyfriend during the fitness camp. No one else would be bringing their partners. Would people think he was wrong to be in a relationship with his bodyguard? Would they judge him? He wasn't sure Cohen had it correct when he talked about Paulo not taking advantage of him. He'd grown up watching his father take advantage over everyone. It came with money and power, two things he had in spades around Cohen.

Last year's winter break fitness camp had been incredibly hard work. He'd slept and ate and skied until his hands and feet were blistered and his muscles ached. The idea of fitting Cohen into that was too much. No, that was a lie. The idea of telling his team that he was in a relationship with Cohen, and they wanted to share a hotel room made him physically ill. He pressed his hands hard against his guts, as if he could keep down the bile that rose into his throat. He couldn't even let himself contemplate how nice it would be to walk into his hotel room and have Cohen care for him. Nope, it couldn't happen, so it wasn't worth even letting his brain hope for it. He hadn't expected Cohen to leave before they could talk about it. Talking about the most awkward things was one of the things Paulo loved about Cohen.

Love. Yes. Hope wormed its way inside his heart; cheeky fucker. There had to be a way he could fix this. He might be able to figure out how to keep his secret safe and not mess things up for Cohen. Cohen was the type of person who stuck around for him, and the fact that he'd bolted out of their apartment was a clue—a huge glaring one—that Paulo had fucked up. He knew exactly how he'd fucked up too; he just didn't have a solution.

> Paulo: Please come home and we can talk about this

> Cohen: Home? You mean to your place.

Paulo's stomach sank. Yeah, he'd really fucked this up. It was time to be honest.

> Paulo: I want to be with you. I just don't know how.

If he was open with his relationship with his team, it was a slippery slope to being open everywhere, and there was too much at stake for that. The team relied on the sponsorship money from Sanchez Shipping, a notion rein-forced by spending time with Senior in Brazil. It wasn't just about him and his seat, especially now with the season approaching quickly, and all the expense that had gone into developing the new season's car. The reveal was only six weeks away, and pre-season testing—with the public watching—was only two months away. Paulo knew how fast that time would go. He sat on the floor, head in his hands, wishing there was a simple answer. If he was a better driver, his performance would naturally bring other spon-sors to the team. But he wasn't. Seventh out of twenty was the middle of the mid-field; good enough although it made a mockery of his claim to Senior that he'd be vying for the world champion trophy in the upcoming season. Perhaps if he could drive like the last three races of last season, there was a chance he'd score enough points to show the racing world that he deserved to be an S1 driver. Keeping his seat was such a low benchmark compared to the real, unachievable, goal of champion.

His eyes prickled and he pressed his fists against them. He'd driven well in those three races for one reason—Cohen. Having his steady presence around him constantly and knowing that Cohen would keep away all the distractions and noise on race weekends, was the one of reasons he'd driven so well. The biggest reason was having Cohen believe in him; the removal of doubt over his capabilities was so enticing and attractive, he wanted to keep that feeling forever.

He pushed himself up off the floor and did a few star jumps to get the blood flowing back into his legs. If he told Cohen all of this, it wouldn't help. No one wanted to know that they were only kept around because they were useful. Ergh. There was too much of Senior in that thought; what a dick he was sometimes. He paced back and forth. It was time to face facts.

One – he drove better with Cohen around to keep the world at bay.

Two – he wanted to be in a relationship with Cohen.

Three – it felt impossible to do that during the racing season with everyone watching. For all the reasons he'd spent too many hours stressing about. There was pretty much only one person who could help, and even then,

Paulo doubted talking to him would help but he was out of options. He pulled out his phone and dialled.

"Hi Paulo."

"Ondrej." Gamble's number one driver was openly gay and married to his adorable husband, Hudson. They were so cute together, the perfect type of queer that the public approved of.

"Um, can I ask you a question?"

"Sure, kid." Ondrej's answer was like being slapped by a wet fish.

"I'm twenty-two and..." Paulo paused. He'd been living independently since he was fourteen, hardly the naïve kid everyone seemed to assume. It always surprised him when he could pull out a mean, dickhead, comment just like Senior because they hadn't spent much time together in Paulo's formative years. Paulo knew his responsibilities and what was at stake here, and how much he was potentially giving up by saying this. "...I didn't call up to be teased about my age."

Ondrej chuckled quietly. "Don't tell me. You are queer too?"

"Were you not paying attention when I told everyone that in Mexico?" Paulo had assumed everyone on the team knew.

"No. I was texting Hudson."

"Okay. Well, I'm pansexual."

"How is your bodyguard, by the way?" The teasing note in Ondrej's voice sent a cold shiver across the back of Paulo's neck.

"He's ... That's why I was calling."

Ondrej barked out a short laugh. "I knew it. You've been fucking him, haven't you?"

"Is it that obvious?" Paulo was going to die of embarrassment.

Ondrej breathed out heavily into the phone. "Most people aren't that observant."

Paulo's tight shoulders relaxed, not all the way, but a little bit. "Okay?"

"I assume that's why you called. Because you want relationship advice from me, and you don't want to ask Jaxxon because he's our boss."

"Yeah." Paulo swallowed. "Also, I'm not out to my family. My father would pull the sponsorship if he knew."

"Are you sure? The rest of Gamble Racing is quite queer. He must know."

Paulo grimaced. "My father isn't happy about those aspects of Gamble Racing. He tolerates you because my brother says it makes his politics look more inclusive to have a brother who drives alongside a gay driver."

"It's interesting that you say that, because I remember having several conversations with Socrates about this and he mentioned that your father is incredibly proud of you and will support whatever team you want to drive for." Ondrej confirmed what Paulo had suspected for years; his father was unable to praise him directly but talked positively about him to everyone else. Paulo was part of Senior's image and only important to Senior if he maintained that level of positive perception for the family name.

"As if I had a choice. Gamble needed the money and they had a spot for a rookie; it was a good fit." It was the only fit for him. Paulo had been only one of several rookie options that Gamble had been considering for their second driver when Lucien Grenville moved into Gamble Racing's Series E team. Paulo's billionaire father put him at the top of the list for the new rookie in the S1 team.

"Tell me something, Paulo…" Ondrej paused.

"What?" Paulo breathed out slowly, annoyed that he sounded like a sulky petulant child.

"Is your father one of those people who will praise you to everyone except you?"

Paulo laughed, a slightly maniacal strangled noise that didn't sound like himself. He'd literally just thought that. "I'm not aware of what he says to others. He certainly never tells me that I'm worthwhile."

"He sounds like a right dickwad."

Paulo spluttered, trying not to choke on the rush of air that Ondrej surprised out of him. "He's a billionaire. People don't gain that type of money without trampling on others."

"Well, there is that. Look, I hate to be the bearer of this news, but your father was obnoxious in his praise of you for the whole race week in Brazil. I'm sorry that he doesn't share that with you."

"Yeah, well." Paulo hadn't lived in the same house as his father since he was fourteen and had gone to England for a driving specific boarding school. Short holiday breaks didn't really count, especially when he spent more time with his family's staff than with family members. He didn't exactly have a close relationship with his family.

"I think it would be okay to tell the team that you and Cohen are together. They are all going to guess given the fucking heart eyes you have around Cohen, anyway. You may as well stop the rumours before they start."

"Heart eyes?" Paulo asked as innocently as he could manage.

"I recognise a bit of lust when I see it." Ondrej laughed. "Also when I asked if you were fucking him, you changed the subject."

"Ondrej. It's because you can't ask me that."

Ondrej chuckled. "I can and I did, and you confirmed it by avoiding the question."

"This fucking sport and it's love of rumours." Paulo still couldn't bring himself to confirm Ondrej's guesses were on the money.

"So that's a yes, then." Smugness dripped through the phone. "Is Cohen coming to Galtur next week?"

"Of course he is. He's my security."

"Security blanket?" Ondrej's teasing note made Paulo's nostrils flare and he wanted to hide his head under a pillow and make it go away.

"Come on. I'm the famous son of a billionaire. My father has been bugging me about getting a bodyguard since I drove in S2. He used to have his own people trail around after me."

"Without your consent?"

"Of course. Who is going to stop a billionaire?" Paulo tried not to sigh. At least when he'd been racing, his father's employees couldn't get too close to him as they didn't have the team access. "I didn't see the point for ages because the team's security is tighter than one person could provide."

"What changed your mind?"

Brazil in his rookie season and meeting Cohen. "I don't need to explain anything to you."

"Hey, I'm your teammate."

"Yeah. A bloody nosy one."

"You called me." Ondrej's chuckle kept things light. "Look, your secrets are safe with me. I know we compete on the track, but we are still teammates, and I appreciate you calling to talk about this. I think everyone at Gamble would be okay if you told them about you and Cohen." Ondrej repeated himself, echoing what Cohen had said and Paulo wished it was fucking true. He needed the constant reminder before he made a decision, that was for sure.

"Not my father."

"People won't tell him if you ask them not to."

"You think so?" It was Paulo's biggest nightmare, that once people knew, they'd assume that everyone in his life knew, and it would only take one person to mention it without thinking and it'd become public knowledge. He'd have to talk about it when that was the absolute last thing he wanted to do. No one needed to know that he was pansexual, and they certainly didn't need to know that he loved being topped by Cohen. He breathed out slowly. He could probably mention the first part without mentioning the second.

CHAPTER 14

Cohen typed in the code for the front door of Paulo's apartment and walked in. Paulo was on the phone, pacing back and forth in front of the huge glass windows that overlooked the Mediterranean. The mild winter weather matched the confused expression on Paulo's face; as if neither Paulo or the weather knew what it wanted to do. Would it rain, or just stay vaguely cloudy? Would he make a choice in favour of Cohen or against?

"You think so?" Paulo sounded scared, worried, upset, and it took all of Cohen's self-control not to rush over and comfort him with a hug. But Paulo had made it clear he didn't want that anymore.

"You make it sound so simple," Paulo said into his phone. The person on the other end of the phone's response made Paulo blurt out a gasping laugh, as if he wasn't sure whether he wanted to laugh or cry or scream in frustration.

"Well, I guess ... I could talk to Jaxxon and take it from

there." Paulo's face was pale, so Cohen bent down and focused on taking off his shoes to give Paulo all the space he needed.

"Yeah, maybe. .... Thanks Ondrej. I really appreciate being able to talk to you about this. ... I'd rather you kept calling me rookie than kid. Fuck." Paulo laughed again, and this time the sound was a bit freer. It made a lot of sense for him to talk to his teammate about how he was feeling. Warmth blossomed in Cohen's chest; maybe there was hope for them after all.

"Okay. See you next week." Paulo hung up and stared out of the window for a while. Cohen straightened up and waited quietly until Paulo turned around.

"Hey Cohen, I'm so glad you came back and I'm super sorry."

"It's okay."

"It's really not. We decided to try and have a relationship and I failed at the first hurdle." Paulo closed his eyes and Cohen was reminded that Paulo's young shoulders carried so many responsibilities. In a sport where drivers were often accused of putting themselves first, Cohen was struck by how often that was perception created by the media who loved to talk about the drivers as the stars of the show, while the drivers understood the responsibility they held. Their performance made the final difference as to whether a team won or lost. A team could have a fast car and a perfectly run pit garage, but if the driver wasn't on song, it wouldn't matter because the end result depended on the driver alone. One tiny mistake could lead to a huge crash, no points for the team, and a lot of work for the mechanics. Cohen was astounded at the precision the drivers showed, driving so close to the edges of the track, often with an inch or less between the car and a concrete wall. One tiny touch of the car against another or anything else would result in disaster. The need for precision was the difference between S1 and every other motorsport; their cars were faster, more delicate, and required the highest driver ability and precision. Cohen had spent enough time in the pit garage now that he'd absorbed the information from listening to all the mechanics' chatter about it. On the other hand, if the car wasn't good enough, no amount of driver skill could make it win without a decent amount of luck too.

"Yes, you did fail." Cohen was glad Paulo acknowledged the cause of this current problem. He breathed in deep because... "I also failed you. I should've stayed to talk about how I felt, not run away, leaving you to worry about me and us."

Paulo's mouth twitched at the edge. "Relationships are so hard. Why does anyone do this?"

"Great sex whenever you want?" Cohen shrugged one shoulder. A blush spread across Paulo's cheeks as he opened those gorgeous golden-brown eyes and stared at him.

"I'd like that."

"What?"

"Sex with you instead of talking. I'm all talked out for the day."

Cohen knew he should mention that talking to someone else didn't really resolve the communication between them, however, it was apparent that Paulo needed time to figure out what was going on in his head and pushing him for answers might not result in open communication.

"Besides, once we get to ski camp, I'm going to be way too tired for sex, so now is good." Paulo's blush deepened.

"I'm not going to punish you for this." Cohen wanted to be clear on that one.

"What do you mean?" Paulo's deep frown marred his brow.

Cohen didn't want sex to be ruined by the complicated living situation between them. "Simply that. I want you to come to me and show me that you want me. I don't want to punish you for not wanting to be with me in Galtur."

"Oh." Paulo blinked a few times. "Are you saying that because I like to play at being punished?"

"Yes."

"Are you saying that you don't want an apology or a performance from me, you want to me to show you how much I care?"

"Yes." He wanted Paulo to be open with him, not misguided by guilt into doing something they'd both regret later. Paulo loved it when Cohen took charge, and normally that worked wonders for Cohen too, but right now, after this disagreement, he didn't want to add a complicated game to the tension between them.

"But what if I can't do that outside this room?"

"Paulo. You just said you didn't want to talk about this yet."

Paulo ran his hands through his hair, a distractingly sexy action that made Cohen's fingertips tingle, which wasn't exactly helpful.

"I know, but I'm not sure I can stop thinking about it

all. Ondrej made some really good points, but he doesn't know my father, not really. They've met a few times at sponsors dinners and in Brazil, but... well, I'm so confused."

Cohen wished he could wrap Paulo in a blanket and protect him from having to make this decision. It wasn't logical to want to protect Paulo from having to choose if he wanted to be with Cohen, but Cohen's need to protect Paulo overrode any emotional logic. He shook his head. As if emotions were ever logical!

"What's the matter?" Paulo asked.

"Apart from all of this?"

"Yeah. You shook your head. Did I do something wrong? I mean, like more wrong than wanting to stay, um, private?"

"No." Cohen ignored the unsteady thump in his chest. "I only shook my head at this situation. It's not fair for your father to expect you to put his reputation above your happiness."

Paulo ran his hands through his hair. "No one is ever going to tell a billionaire no."

"I would. If you wanted me to."

The shocked intake of breath from Paulo echoed in the room. "I always knew you were braver than me. No. Please don't antagonise him. It's not worth it."

"Okay." Cohen hadn't been joking. He knew his place in the world and that gave him an odd type of power because people couldn't knock him any lower than he'd already survived. The fear never disappeared, sure, but when he took a moment to think carefully, the knowledge he'd made it this far reminded him of his source of confidence. His only advantage in the world was being white—

admittedly a huge advantage, especially back in Texas—and that he'd grown enough of a beard to pass around people who weren't very observant. Ergh; this line of thinking was distracting and unhelpful.

"I mean it."

"Paulo. My job is to protect you and your interests. I would never put you into a situation that might jeopardise you or your goals."

"Your job?"

"Yes. My job." Cohen couldn't ignore the pained expression that flashed over Paulo's face. "And as your lover and someone who cares for you, I will always put your well-being first."

Paulo nodded. "Thank you." He walked over to Cohen and held out his arms. Cohen stepped against his body, and let Paulo hug him. He breathed in deep, pulling the warm familiar scent of Paulo's cologne into his lungs. The press of his lithe athletic body amazed Cohen. This man—this confused young man—wanted to be with Cohen, although it would be much better when Paulo understood his fears and became brave enough to step beyond them. Could Cohen wait long enough? As he hugged Paulo, he believed he could wait. Sure, the daze of being touched by Paulo probably made his brain spin with lust and not with good sense... He didn't care. This was a slice of perfection in an awful world.

"And..."

"Yes?"

"Please don't sacrifice your own safety to look after me. I want to put your well-being first too."

Cohen raised one eyebrow. "Risking myself for your

safety is literally the definition of my job." If he did his job properly, the risks were low, but he didn't want to get into that argument right now. It would derail them from what mattered; the negotiation on how to go forwards. Together. Or apart?

"You know what I mean, Cohen. I don't want to see you get hurt."

Cohen closed his eyes—he didn't want to argue anymore—and relaxed against Paulo's tense body. He'd fought against a lot of emotional hurt from his parents over the years, but that paled in comparison to the amount of hurt Paulo could unleash if he... No. Cohen was not going to hug Paulo and worry that he already loved Paulo too deeply and Paulo didn't—or couldn't—love him the same way in return. He nuzzled his mouth against Paulo's neck, loving the way Paulo's stubble scratched at his lips.

"Cohen." Paulo tilted his head backwards, exposing his strong neck further. Cohen slid his hands up Paulo's back and threaded his fingers into Paulo's hair. He'd been growing it out over the winter break, and now it was almost long enough to pull back into a ponytail. It curled loosely around his collar. Cohen pulled Paulo's face towards him and kissed him, taking his time to savour his lover. If this was going to be goodbye or if it wasn't going to be a continuation of their current path, it didn't matter because Cohen adored kissing Paulo. He greedily wanted one last kiss before they separated.

He couldn't get enough of Paulo's lips, the way he stroked his tongue along Cohen's tongue as if he loved the taste of him. Usually Cohen didn't like kissing someone taller than him—being a medium height man who worked in security was a sore point for him—but Paulo wasn't super tall, or maybe it was nothing to do with height, and everything to do with the way Paulo willingly followed Cohen's lead in this realm.

"Come with me." Paulo walked backwards to the couch, with his hands resting lightly on Cohen's hips. As Paulo lowered himself to the couch, using that incredibly honed body to control his descent, Cohen widened his stance so he stood with his legs either side of Paulo's knees.

"Sit." Paulo pulled him down so Cohen straddled Paulo's thighs. From this angle, he was taller, in control, and exactly how he liked it. And judging by the little grin on Paulo's face, he loved this too. Cohen reached out and held Paulo's chin, tilting his face upwards, before he leaned down and kissed him again. Paulo grabbed Cohen's hips and pulled his pelvis forward, grinding him against Paulo's hard cock.

"Is it me, or is it hot in here?" Cohen's shirt was sticking to his skin.

"Well, you still have your jacket on, and I have the heat on because it's..."

"Winter. It was bloody cold outside." Cohen sat up straight and pulled off his jacket, flinging on the floor behind him, then pulled his shirt over his head, enjoying the way Paulo's eyes widened as Cohen revealed his bare chest.

"I love your nipples." Paulo leaned in closer and sucked one into his mouth.

"Should I get a nipple ring?"

"Fuck, Cohen. Yes." Paulo licked all the way up Cohen's pectoral muscle and along his collar bone. "I can't get one because of the way the safety harness sits against my chest."

"You want one?"

"I ... It might make a fun toy?"

Cohen didn't like the uncertainty in Paulo's voice. One day he was going to learn it was okay to have desires, and that his desires weren't hurting anyone, so they were perfectly fine. The fact that Paulo liked a little bit of pain with his pleasure was his own business; it didn't make him ... well, Cohen wasn't even going to let himself think of all the frustrating ways heterosexual society was prudish about sex. Paulo was exactly right for himself.

"There are lots of other toys you could get that don't interfere with your job."

"Maybe the team will make a butt plug with my head on it." Paulo's face flushed bright red, as if he couldn't believe he'd said that out loud.

"Paulo. What a wonderful imagination you have. But seriously? You wouldn't want that. It'd look like your whole body was up someone's ass."

Paulo's mouth slowly turned upwards in a sly smile. "I know. Can you imagine?"

And with that, Cohen decided he didn't care if Paulo was planning to stay in the closet forever. He'd happily jump in there just to be with him. "I'm sorry I ran off before. It was a shock, that was all. I'll wait for you. I want you to be safe and happy. That matters more than—"

Paulo frowned and poked him in the chest. "Don't you dare say that my happiness matters more than yours. I thought this was a partnership?"

"Yes." Cohen leaned forward and kissed Paulo with all the lust and force that, hopefully, told him how much he meant to him. He kissed him like he'd arrived home from a long quest to prove himself, and he was finally here, mouth against mouth, lips against lips, chest against chest, and beard against stubble. It was messy and rough and absolutely everything. He lifted his head, dragging in a deep breath.

"Fuck, you always kiss like it's a competition." Cohen's voice was ragged and husky.

"I'm an athlete who likes winning. Plus I love it when you sound wrecked afterwards."

"I thought I was supposed to do the wrecking." Cohen licked his bottom lip on purpose, enjoying the way Paulo's gaze tracked his tongue.

"You wreck me just by being in the same room."

Cohen shifted on Paulo's thighs, moving backwards just enough to give him access to Paulo's jeans. He flicked open the buttons on his fly, carefully and slowly. Not just because every little touch made Paulo suck in a sharp breath until he was panting, but because Paulo's cock was hard and it made his jeans taut and difficult to undo. Practicality was sometimes a pest.

"You should've worn those sweatpants of yours."

"You don't like my ... ahh..." Paulo gasped as Cohen dragged his fingernail up Paulo's cock. His underwear would soften the sharpness—this time. "Um, jeans?"

Cohen kissed Paulo, a quick peck on the lips. "I like watching you walk in them. I don't like taking them off when you are ..." He traced a circle on the tip with his thumb. "...all hard."

"Gah." Good, he'd reduced Paulo to unintelligible noises.

"You like that?"

Paulo nodded, his eyes bright and glowing. Fuck, his eyes were fucking beautiful and talented; he was able to drive at speeds that made no logical sense and take in all the information needed to react quickly. Not just the reflex of his vision and his hand-eye coordination, but the way he could do all of that and race other drivers in close proximity without crashing. Paulo's ability in a car was at the limits of human capability for reaction time and visual processing.

"Cohen." Paulo whined a little. "I'm dying here."

"And I'm not?" Teasing Paulo always made him wet. Cohen slid off Paulo's legs and knelt on the ground between his legs.

"Cohen. You don't have to."

"I want to."

"Oh God. I'm going to die." Paulo lifted his hips and tugged his jeans and underwear off, somehow managing to make it look smooth and not the awkward argument with his clothing that Cohen would have. It was easy to fall into the trap that because Paulo's job was done sitting down that he wasn't an athlete. He was so athletic, it was sometimes intimidating. But then, all those worries went away as Paulo sat on the couch with his cock bare and hard and leaking.

"Moan for me."

"Now?"

"Yes. Moan and then I'll touch you."

"Fuck." Paulo wrapped his hand around his cock and Cohen flicked him on the wrist. It had the expected effect because Paulo let out a sinful noise from low in his throat.

Heat rushed down Cohen's spine. "No touching."

Paulo unfurled his fingers, one at a time, and much too slowly. Cohen allowed it. Eventually, Paulo lifted his hand off his cock and Cohen grabbed him by the wrist. He placed his hand, palm up, on his own thigh.

"Leave it there." He gave Paulo no warning, no time to protest, as he rose on his knees and sucked Paulo's cock into his mouth. The noise Paulo made was deliciously desperate, vibrating into Cohen's body. Fuck, if he could record that noise, it'd keep him happy on lonely nights for the rest of his days. Whatever. He wasn't going to have any lonely days because this incredible man was in love with him. Cohen was going spend the rest of his life with his mouth filled with cock, clean, slightly salty, hard cock. People always thought that sucking cock was an act of submission. Presumably it was for the right person. For Cohen, it was an act of power. He controlled all of Paulo's body now. If he'd told Paulo to stand on his head and eat spiders, he'd do it just to keep Cohen's mouth in place. Cohen wouldn't because he wasn't a sadist. It was enough that he knew he could ask and that he'd be obeyed. A delicious heat raced down his spine.

He just adored the way Paulo's hands trembled as he tried to keep them where Cohen had put them; he loved the noises Paulo made, and he fucking wanted to be the one who made Paulo fly to the heavens. He licked and sucked until Paulo couldn't keep his hands still anymore. Right at that moment when Paulo shouted out a warning and grabbed Cohen on the shoulders, Cohen flattened his tongue and took Paulo as deep as he could. Paulo's knees gripped Cohen's sides, his fingers dug into Cohen's shoulders, and he shouted out a stream of profanities as he came into Cohen's mouth. The salty come almost made him gag, but he swallowed it down.

"Fuck me, Cohen. That was amazing."

"Okay." Cohen stood up with one last lick that made Paulo groan. "I want you to kneel on the couch, arms outstretched across the back." They'd done this a few times in the last few weeks, so Cohen knew the couch was strong enough to cope. Paulo moved languidly, his gaze all hazy and sated. It was Cohen's favourite look. Paulo relaxed and obedient, with his naked ass in the air.

———

Paulo rested his chin on the back of the couch, spreading his arms wide, like Cohen requested. Cohen had asked for this pose several times; he must really like it. Paulo closed his eyes for a moment. He'd come so hard, he could fall asleep just here.

"Wake up sleeping beauty." Cohen tapped Paulo on the ass and he jolted awake with a grunt. Nice. Way to impress anyone. Hopefully he hadn't been drooling too. Cohen soothed his ass with a kiss and Paulo's sated cock twitched again. Hell. He cursed his need to keep this private. Right now, with Cohen's lube-covered fingers prepping his ass, Paulo wanted to shout it to the world that he loved this man and his talented mouth and hands.

"I have a treat for you."

Paulo tried to talk but only a groan came out.

"It's thick, purple, and ribbed."

"Please." He'd seen that dick among Cohen's collection

but every time he tried to hint that he'd like to try it, Cohen had chosen something else. Like many of Cohen's dicks, it had a clit stimulator that pressed against Cohen's body whenever he thrust. He lay in place as still as he could. Waiting. Cohen walked around the couch and grabbed a fist full of Paulo's hair and pulled. His head lifted up, tugged by Cohen's grip, pain prickling through his scalp.

"Open." Cohen held the purple dick against Paulo's mouth and he gasped as he opened his lips for Cohen. Soon the silicone dick filled his mouth and he sucked it as Cohen guided it in and out, past his lips. The combined pressure of the dick in his mouth with Cohen's other hand still holding his hair tight was ... fucking everything. Cohen pushed the dick in just far enough to make Paulo want to gag, but not so far that it hurt. Tears formed at the corners of his eyes and he gazed up at Cohen, wanting more. Pleading as much as he could while his mouth was being used so perfectly thoroughly. Just as it was almost too much and he almost wanted to ask Cohen to stop, he stopped. Cohen released him and his head fell forwards without the support of Cohen's hand.

"Paulo? Are you okay?"

"Yes." He was more than okay. "Please fuck me now." Paulo didn't have to wait long before Cohen spread lube over his hole, gently opening him up with his fingers before he guided the thick end of the purple dick inside him. Fuck it stretched so much. Paulo shivered, a whole-body shudder, as Cohen's purple ribbed cock filled him up. It wasn't going to take long before he was a mess, not with each stroke past his prostate sending heat flying across his skin.

"Fuck. Fuck." He clutched the couch and managed to shout out the word Cohen loved the most. "Please."

Cohen grabbed Paulo's hips and thrust—short quick thrusts—until Cohen cried out, coming hard, then collapsing onto Paulo's back. Slowly, Cohen pulled out, they cleaned up quickly, then they collapsed onto the couch. Every inch of Paulo's skin felt like it belonged to Cohen. Paulo loved this part the most, just lying in Cohen's arms, completely relaxed. He'd earned this by giving himself completely to Cohen's control and it was glorious. Together was where he wanted to be, and he'd been a fool to push Cohen away. His eyelids were very heavy. He'd tell him that; soon; after he'd snoozed for a bit.

CHAPTER 15

After two days of cross-country skiing, Paulo's body had done enough. Everything ached. Today, their trainers had pushed them to do the entire 21km trail, and it'd pushed his fitness and stamina to the absolute limit. He'd leaned against the wall in the shower afterwards, too tired to do much more than hold himself up and let the warm water heat him up. Cohen had helped wash him, which was weirdly nice even if he'd been too exhausted to get an erection, and now he'd forced his legs to take him downstairs to where the hotel staff would have a trainer-approved meal for him. This was his third time doing this pre-season fitness trial and it didn't get any easier. He collapsed into one of the huge leather chairs near the fire-place in the common area of the boutique hotel the team hired every year. With only twenty rooms, the team hired out the whole hotel for the week, which kept their fitness testing nice and private, and gave them all free run of all the facilities without having the worry about dealing with fans or other people.

"Why do we do this?" Lucien, Gamble's number one Series E driver, stretched out his legs with a groan.

"To win races." Paulo thought it was obvious. No one would put themselves through this without the promise of victory at the end. They needed to build up enough stamina to be able to drive fast for the entire length of a race.

"Fuck. I forget how young you are. Wait till you've been doing this for ten seasons, then you'll ask the same question."

"Hopefully when I've been doing this for ten seasons, I have more wins under my belt, and it'll still be worth it." He gave each of his legs a shake. Hopefully he would get to do this for ten seasons, and without the constant worry that he'd get sacked for non-performance at any time.

"Good attitude kid."

One of the hotel staff came over and offered them both a warm mug of soup. "Today's soup is tomato."

"Thank you." Paulo took the soup and sipped. It was the perfect temperature, warming all the way down his throat into his torso.

Lucien lifted his mug. "To another season of improvement. Victor is pretty excited about your new car." Lucien's partner Victor was the chief engineer at Gamble. Victor wasn't here this week; it was just the drivers and physical trainers. It was a good start to the pre-season testing, just hanging out with the other drivers who all understood the pressures of racing, even if they were in the lower grades or in Series E.

"I'm excited about it. The new suspension change should be a huge aero boost. How's your new car?" Paulo asked. The Series E team was run out of the same engineering office at Gamble's headquarters in England, but they had a different team of people designing the technology and running the race team.

"I haven't seen it yet, but it's apparently been performing well in the wind tunnel."

"Us drivers are the last ones to know anything."

Lucien laughed. "So true, kid. Not like the old days when drivers like Lauda had more say."

Paulo sipped his soup. S1 had always been a highly technical sport and now with the amount of computing power that ran the cars, it was hard enough to learn how to drive the complicated machines, without being involved with the design outside of reporting to the engineers about how the car handled in different conditions.

"Do you regret moving?" Paulo wasn't quite sure why he asked, but he felt like he needed to keep the conversation going. It was a bit awkward because Paulo had basically taken Lucien's S1 seat.

"From S1 to SE? No. I hated coming last every fucking race."

Paulo nodded. It made sense to move on when Lucien had been beaten by his teammate Ondrej in nearly every race; both of them in slow cars, but one of them was obviously better.

"I know a little bit about that." He'd only beaten Ondrej twice in his rookie season; and six times last season.

"What is your record with Ondrej?" Lucien asked.

"Two to nineteen in my rookie season and six to nineteen last season."

"My record in my last S1 season was five to sixteen, but

there was only one race where the team got points, and Ondrej got the single point, not me."

"You couldn't expect points from that car. It's not all you." He'd had the benefit of stepping into S1 with a decent car, while Lucien had struggled with Whitehall's career-worst designs.

"I would've loved to have driven Victor's car, but I made my choice with the information I had at the time. No one could have predicted the sudden success that Victor brought when he started." The pride on Lucien's face for his partner charmed Paulo. One day someone—Cohen—might have the same look when Paulo did well.

"I jumped from a terrible team, the laughingstock of S1, into a successful team and got a podium in my first race. I really don't miss the memes. Fuck." Lucien chuckled. "Besides, Series E is the future; you guys might get all the glamour now, but you are driving old-fashioned, out-dated tech."

Paulo grinned. "That's a fair point, although I think petrol engines will still be around until I retire."

"Enough boring shop talk. What's this I hear about you and your bodyguard?"

Paulo's face warmed. "What have you heard?"

"I heard he hasn't slept in his room since you both arrived here." Lucien winked.

"No one gossips as much as a car racing team." Paulo sipped his soup.

"So that's a yes then. This fucking team!"

"What about this team?" Paulo jumped on the opportunity to talk about anything that wasn't him and Cohen.

"Where have you been? Look at our key staff." Lucien obviously referred to all the queer members in Gamble Racing. Paulo loved the idea that Cohen was seen as being one of the key team members, but he stopped himself blurting that out and telling Lucien the answer he was trying to tease out of him.

"Did you have to do a lot of stuff, like with admin and stuff, when you... um?"

"Hooked up with Victor?" Lucien's whimsical expression was a thing of beauty.

"Um, yeah." He swallowed.

"Technically we aren't in the same team; he's S1 and I'm SE. Socrates just shrugged and said that if we fucked it up, he'd keep us away from each other."

"Okay?"

"We got the whole, 'well you two are grown men who understand the business and our goals here and I'm sure you won't let your relationship get in the way of those goals', talk."

Paulo nodded. He could probably deal with that from the team owner. It was the wider issues around his father's sponsorship that was the core problem.

"Really?" Ondrej grabbed another chair and pulled it closer. "What talk is this?"

"Socrates about Victor and me."

"Oh, that talk. I got one too."

Paulo was desperate to know but didn't know how to ask. Ondrej leaned over and clapped him on the shoulder.

"Look at how big your eyes are, kid. Just wait until you get the whole, 'keep having sex, it makes you drive better' chat."

Lucien threw his head back and cackled. "Oh my god. Socrates is a menace."

"Yes, but we all love the old fucker." Ondrej laughed too. "As you can imagine, he wasn't overly discreet either."

"Oh?" Lucien asked.

"He said that to my face in front of my agent and father."

"Fuck." Paulo would've died. All the air in his lungs disappeared. He hadn't even contemplated that Socrates might be the one to out him to his father; he really shouldn't have done any of this. Shouldn't have employed Cohen, shouldn't have fallen in love with him... Shit.

"Speaking of driving better after sex, Paulo. Your results improved out of sight after you 'employed' Cohen." Ondrej's emphasis on employed increased Lucien's mirth.

"I knew it. I fucking knew it." Lucien held out his mug of soup towards Paulo, who tapped his against it awkwardly.

"Fine. Yes, you already know that I'm pansexual. And Cohen and I are..." Paulo paused, not sure how to categorise their relationship. "Um, boyfriends, I guess."

"Awesome." Lucien's enthusiasm felt good. Everyone was silent for a while, and Ondrej waved to the hotel staff who brought him some soup too.

"I told you everyone would be cool if you said something." Ondrej winked at Paulo.

"Yeah. Just don't tell my father."

Lucien frowned. "Is he a bigot?"

"Yes."

"But he sponsors our team. He must know."

Paulo winced. He hated having to discuss this and have

people know how his family acted. If he wanted to ask how Lucien and Ondrej's family had reacted to their queerness, he'd have to give a little first, so he drew in a deep breath. "It is good for my brother Enzo's political career to be seen to support diverse interests, like having a brother whose teammate is gay. I am quote to show you all how to be a real man unquote."

"Well, shit."

"Yeah." Paulo sighed. "So you can't even hint to anyone outside the team that Cohen is anything more than just my bodyguard. The world can only know that I need a bodyguard because I'm famous and my father is a fucking billionaire and he's worried that I'm going to be kidnapped and ransomed."

"Are you?"

Paulo shrugged. "I haven't been yet, but I've spent my life surrounded by security, so maybe there hasn't been the opportunity for someone?"

"I guess it's just lucky that your personal security guard is always with you." Lucien paused dramatically and winked. "Even when you sleep."

"Speaking of which, he's not doing much of a good job now. Where is he? He wasn't out on the trail with us yesterday or today." Ondrej asked.

"No one would do this if they didn't need to." Lucien rolled his eyes at Ondrej.

"He spent the day watching the security cameras of the trail with radio connection to our trainers, and since we've been back, he has been sitting over there watching the room." Paulo waved towards the bar where Cohen leaned against the wall.

"Invite him over. It's still an hour until dinner."

"Please don't interrogate him." Paulo had enough nosy uncles to know exactly what his teammates were about to embark on. He'd seen the way his family talked to his sisters about their relationships to understand that he didn't want Cohen to be roasted in the same way.

"Wouldn't dream of it." Ondrej laughed in that way that told Paulo he was about to do exactly that.

Lucien stood up. "Well, would you look at that? There's a dart board over near him. Shall we all play?" The bar was a horseshoe shape in the middle of the room, and the dart board was on the far side of the bar away from the fireplace where they had been sitting.

"Great idea." Ondrej put his soup on the table and jumped to his feet. For someone who'd skied an entire trail today, he was still very energetic. "Lucien and I will be a team, and you and Cohen can be a team."

"Hopefully we'll be better at darts than we were driving Whitehall's shitty slow car." Lucien laughed, and walked off with Ondrej, leaving Paulo no option but to follow along unless he wanted to let them tease Cohen alone.

"Cohen. Time to clock off. We need you for darts." Ondrej called out. Cohen pushed off the wall and walked towards them. With every step, Paulo's fingers twitched with the need to touch him. They'd showered together after Paulo's ski work, so it hadn't even been that long since they'd touched. Fuck, Paulo was obsessed and he was starting to stop caring who else knew how he felt about Cohen, which was dangerous. He'd already snuck in a quick kiss to Cohen's cheek after Abu Dhabi when he'd finished fourth and the team had ended the season in third on the constructor's championship. Cohen hadn't mentioned it which ... kind of ... made Paulo stress that he was worrying too much or not enough and he couldn't decide which was the right option.

"I'd be up for a game of darts," Cohen said.

"Do you know the rules?"

"Yes. Do I get to choose my teammate?"

Lucien laughed. "No. Of course you will pair up with Paulo. You two are basically living in each other's pockets now. Let's see how you go under stress."

"It's just a game of darts." Paulo tried to communicate to Cohen with a glance that his fellow drivers knew about them.

"Oh come on, Paulo. There's no such thing as just a game. Let's test our accuracy." Ondrej teased and marched over the dart board.

"Do you guys want to be red or blue?" Ondrej came back, holding out two sets of darts in his hands. Cohen leaned a little closer but didn't say anything.

"Paulo?" Lucien asked.

"We'll have the red ones." Cohen's voice was authoritative, the tone sending a flash of heat down Paulo's spine. He loved it when Cohen demonstrated his confidence.

"Red it is. Since you picked, we'll go first." Ondrej stepped up to the line to throw.

"Hey, that's not fair. You told me to pick." Paulo shook his head as he teased.

"Serves you right for being so young, rookie. Now watch this."

"Wait." Cohen's authoritative command had everyone turning towards him.

"Yeah?" Ondrej asked.

"501 or around the clock?" Cohen asked.

"What do you mean?"

"We need to determine the type of game and how to score before we start. Traditionally pub darts is 501; everyone starts with 501 points, then you reduce your score by what you throw, including doubles and triples, with bullseye worth fifty points. And you have to end on a double to win. Around the clock is easier to score. You just have to hit each number in succession until you get to twenty."

Paulo loved the way everyone's eyebrows raised up.

"I grew up in Texas and I used to work in a bar." Cohen answered everyone's unspoke question about how he knew so much about darts without really answering it.

"I like the complex version." Lucien said. He wandered over the bar and talked to the young woman working there. She looked up from her phone and handed him some paper and a pen.

"Are you good at darts?" Paulo whispered to Cohen.

"I'm okay."

"Right. Because you used to work in a bar?" Paulo couldn't remember if Horny's had a dart board. He hadn't been paying much attention to his surroundings, firstly, he'd only cared about escaping his life for a while, and then Stanley had chatted to him about racing. And of course, Cohen had been there, pulling Paulo's attention towards him.

Cohen nodded. "Yes. Something like that." His mouth kicked up at the corners and Paulo couldn't wait to see how good 'okay' was.

"Right. You can do the scoring." Lucien handed the paper to Cohen. "I'll go first." He took the three blue darts from Ondrej and walked up to the line. His attempts at bullseyes all landed wide.

"Twenty-two points." Cohen made a note on his paper, then picked up the three red darts. He stood at the line, tested the weight of the first dart, then threw it. All three darts landed in the same place on the board; not the bullseye. "One eighty."

"What the hell? How?" Ondrej demanded. Paulo hung back watching.

"Triple twenty is sixty points. Each of my darts hit triple twenty. That's one hundred and eighty points."

Ondrej squinted at him, "Okay. Feels like cheating."

Cohen laughed. "Triple twenty is more points that a bullseye and easier to hit. I'd recommend it as a strategy."

Lucien elbowed Paulo. "He's good."

Paulo's cheeks hurt from grinning so hard. "Just okay, huh?"

Cohen nodded, then walked up to grab his darts from the board.

"You've stitched us up, Paulo. Did you know he was this good?"

Paulo shook his head. "I knew he'd worked in a bar, so I figured he knew the points and stuff from that."

"This makes things interesting. Now we have a proper contest on our hands." Ondrej took the blue darts from Lucien, waited until Cohen walked back, then took his place at the line.

"That was impressive." Paulo whispered to Cohen. Cohen nudged him with his shoulder.

"Yeah. I'm happy with that. These are nice tungsten darts. Expensive. Well-weighted and nicely consistent to throw."

"Hold up. You are more than okay, aren't you?" Paulo whispered. Lucien was leaning on the bar, watching Ondrej's throws.

Cohen smiled slowly. "Texas Under 14 Champion."

"Wow. That's amazing." The last time he'd been a champion at anything was back in his karting days. Once he'd stepped into single seater racing, he'd always been in the top few—before S1 anyway—but hadn't been an outright champion of any division.

"Thanks. I stopped playing competitively after that for a while, and then after I started taking T, it took a while to get used to my balance again."

"Thirty-two. Your turn, Paulo," Ondrej said.

Paulo took the darts from Cohen. "Just a warning. I haven't really done this before."

"You'll be fine. Just keep your elbow steady and throw from your wrist." Cohen demonstrated and Paulo nodded and walked to the line for his turn. Afterwards, he turned around with a shrug.

"At least they all hit the board? Nine points."

"I'm pretty sure you are still winning with Mr 'I used to work in a bar' over there." Ondrej teased. It didn't take long for Cohen to win the game without Paulo helping much at all.

"I'm not sure I like getting whipped like that." Ondrej said. "Congratulations."

"Thanks." Cohen shook Ondrej's outstretched hand, then Lucien's hand too. "It was fun."

"I'll guess I'll see you both at dinner soon. I'm going to my room to call Hudson. Laters." Ondrej wandered off, and Lucien nodded.

"Yeah. I might call Victor." He walked off too, leaving Paulo and Cohen alone at the bar.

"Holy shit, Cohen. You wiped the floor with them. It was amazing."

Cohen blushed. So freaking cute, and Paulo wished they weren't in public so he could kiss him. "It's just a hobby of mine now."

"You don't want to compete anymore?"

Cohen sagged a little and Paulo knew he'd asked the wrong question.

"What did I say wrong?"

Cohen shook his head. "Let's go to your room first." They walked in silence and Paulo's stomach churned. He'd done something wrong, hurt Cohen somehow without knowing how. He needed to listen and learn, so he could prevent himself doing it again.

"I'm sorry." He blurted it out as soon as the door shut, and they were alone in Paulo's hotel room.

"You don't need to be sorry." Cohen shook his head. "I don't compete because I'm not welcome."

"What?" Paulo gasped, then realised from the look on Cohen's face that he'd made it worse. Again.

"Sports tend to be classified by gender and trans people don't fit into traditional binary patterns. I'm not welcome."

"Well, that's not fair. They should let you compete in the men's competition. You are a man."

"I know. And yes, it's not fair."

Paulo felt faint. He'd fucked up. "Oh. I am sorry. I'm

sorry for asking about it. I'm sorry that I reminded you, and I'm sorry that I—"

"It's okay. Please don't apologise for being angry on my behalf. I don't mind that. I'm used to this."

Paulo wanted to say that Cohen shouldn't have to get used to it. But he nodded instead because he didn't want to make things worse by talking. He focused on listening.

"I usually compete in the LGBT competition at Pride each year, and I make darts and sell them online."

"You are amazing." Paulo stuck to the basic truth. Cohen was amazing.

"Thank you. It's ironic, really. There aren't many sports where the human competitors compete without gender."

"Why is that ironic?"

"Car racing is one of them and I've ended up working in it. Horse racing and other equine sports are another. A few gun sports, but almost everything else is split by gender."

Paulo breathed in slowly. "My own sport and I'd forgotten. My engineer, Monica, was a rally champion. Racing is such a male dominated sport that it's easy to forget that we don't have gender divisions, only divisions by car type."

"Perhaps one day there will be a trans S1 driver."

Paulo grinned. "There's nothing in the rules to prevent it."

Cohen's smile was everything, and so there was only one thing for Paulo to do. He threw his arms around him and kissed him. Paulo put everything into the kiss that he didn't have right words for; how much he adored Cohen and how he wished the world was more welcoming for him. How much he wanted to tell the world how fucking amazing his darts championship winning boyfriend was, and how thrilled he was to discover that fact, and how fucked up it was that Cohen couldn't continue to show the world how great he was. Paulo put all of these thoughts into his kiss and when Cohen threaded his hands through Paulo's hair, he knew they'd figure out how to do this together.

CHAPTER 16

Cohen shoved his hand onto the lens of the camera. "Move. There's nothing interesting here." The last thing he needed to deal with was the press standing on the front steps of Paulo's apartment building in Monaco. The week of pre-season training had gone well and now they had a week before they needed to be in England for simulation work, and the pre-season launch, before travelling to Spain and then Bahrain for the formal pre-season testing. He'd read the schedule so many times and still found it hard to believe that this would be his life; travelling to all these different countries and places. He couldn't wait to get through the next six weeks and get started with the new season in the middle of March.

Right now, his responsibilities were immediate. He had a journalist to deal with. Seeing the man on Paulo's doorstep was a good reminder to quit dreaming about love, and do his job.

"Just one comment, please."

"It's okay, Cohen. Daisuke is a colleague of Freddy's at

Inoue Media." Paulo held out his hand and the man put away his camera and shook Paulo's hand.

"Paulo Sanchez. I'm looking for a comment on the Jean-Pierre Lavigne news."

A frown crossed Paulo's face. "What news?"

"He broke his leg in a skiing accident yesterday." Daisuke's comment sent a chill across the back of Cohen's neck. It could've been Paulo. Cohen had stayed in the hotel, watching security cameras, rather than go out on the trail with him. At the time, it'd seemed logical. Cohen wasn't a great skier, having only done it once, and Paulo's trainers would be with him all the time. But logic didn't matter when the reality of what might have happened to Paulo on the ski trail suddenly became a real possibility with this news.

"Oh. Is he alright?" Paulo's worry for his fellow driver was apparent in his tone.

"He's out for at least four months, with some news agencies reporting six months. If it's true, we won't see him race until after Silverstone."

"I hope he heals quickly. It is an honour to race against him."

"Do you have a comment on how that will affect the upcoming racing season?"

Paulo shook his head. "No. No comment other than to hope J-P heals quickly. He's a champion driver and a good friend of my teammate Ondrej, and I'm sure everyone at Gamble Racing wishes him the very best in his recovery."

"There's a rumour that Letherbarrow is going to be offered J-P's seat."

The name sent a shiver down Cohen's spine, but Paulo just shrugged one shoulder.

"There are always rumours in S1. I have no comment."

Cohen took that as his cue to get Paulo away from the press. "That'll be enough for today. Thanks." He swiped the door to their building and held the door open for Paulo. Cohen nodded to the driver of their ride share who been hovering in the background and he helped them with their small carry-on luggage, and soon enough, they were inside away from the media.

"Poor J-P. That sucks." Paulo pulled his phone out of his pocket and turned it on. It dinged with a several incoming messages. "Oops, I should've turned my phone on at the airport. Everyone is telling me about this." Paulo tapped a quick message; presumably to J-P. All the drivers seemed to have each other's numbers whether they were friends or not. Cohen assumed it was because there weren't many people who understand the pressures of their job, so they formed a unique type of support club even though they were fierce competitors on the track.

"Yeah." Cohen didn't elaborate as they both stepped into the elevator. He wanted to hug Paulo right there and tell him he was glad he was safe, but Paulo rolled his eyes.

"Bloody journalists. Always hunting for that controversial quote."

"Like?"

"With J-P out for some of the season, it opens up the championship for everyone else. He's so good, and now he'll go several races without points."

"And the Letherbarrow comment?" Cohen only knew

the name because it'd been yelled by the fan who'd spat that name in Paulo's face in Brazil.

"He's a very good driver. He won S2 last year and is the backup driver for J-P's team. It's a big step up, but he's the obvious choice to replace J-P. I'm not threatened by him, or the rumour."

"Do you think the journalist—"

"Daisuke."

"Yes. It's amazing that you remember all their names." He still had a lot to learn about this sport that he'd been thrown into four months ago.

"S1 is a small world, and I talk to the main media people every week all year. Daisuke is very ambitious and he needs to be, because he doesn't have the advantage of being a retired driver, like Freddy does. It's no surprise that he'd make the time to visit me for a comment."

"Do you think he was fishing for you to say something feisty?" Cohen wasn't sure what Paulo might say, but he did tend to blurt out his feelings.

"I'm sure he was. I've had lots of media training, so I'm not going to say anything."

"Thank fuck for training!"

"Yes."

"Want to talk about it?"

Paulo breathed out. "About JP or Letherbarrow?"

"Which ever you need."

"Whenever I'm not going well, people talk about who might take my seat. For most of the second half of last season, there were rumours that Letherbarrow would be the one because he was doing so well in S2, but they were baseless." Paulo shrugged again. "It's just rumours and gossip."

"Baseless. How did you know?"

"Senior bought my seat. Unless I'm coming last in every race or costing the team a lot of money by crashing a lot, then my seat is safe."

"Fair enough." Cohen couldn't imagine how it would feel to have people talking about you all the time and be able to brush that off as irrelevant. He watched Paulo carefully, in case he needed to vent.

"Daisuke is probably right about Letherbarrow. It's logical as JP's team signed him as their backup driver for this season, so he's waiting and ready to step into that seat. Stranger things have happened in S1 though." Paulo's maturity around the media and his job shouldn't surprise Cohen. He'd been working with him long enough that he saw how Paulo's professionalism in his job overrode his youth. Paulo was about to begin his third season at the peak of his sport. It was hugely impressive.

The elevator doors opened and Cohen stepped half-out to check the hallway. Clear. He grabbed the luggage and they both walked along the hallway to Paulo's apartment.

"Home." Paulo pushed open the door and Cohen followed him inside, closing it carefully behind him. The whole building had excellent security, so he really didn't need to check, but it was a good habit. They took off their shoes, and Cohen was about to offer to make a snack when his phone dinged.

> Lilly-Anne: Did you get it yet? You haven't said anything.

> Cohen: Get what?

Lilly-Anne: Check your mail. I posted you a thing.

Cohen: Okay. We've been away for a week, but just got home.

Lilly-Anne: Where? Why didn't you tell me?

Cohen: None of your business. :D

Cohen: Just work stuff. I'll go and check now

"I'm going to pop down and grab the mail." Cohen called out.

"Okay."

Sure enough, there was a crisp thick white envelope in the mailbox with Cohen's name on it among the other pieces of junk mail. He carried it all the way to Paulo's home and joined Paulo on the balcony before he opened it. The fresh air held a wintery chill, although it was quite warm compared to Galtur.

"What's that?"

"An invitation to my sister's wedding." Cohen stared at the gorgeous invitation with its embossed gold writing. "It's in early March, on the weekend before the season starts."

"Am I invited?"

Cohen's stomach flipped. "Hold on. A week ago you freaked out about us staying together with your team who you are out to, and now you are keen to go to a wedding as my plus-one with random people? I don't understand."

Paulo rubbed his forehead. "True. I guess I didn't really think about it, beyond wanting to make you smile. I loved hanging out with Lilly-Anne and Felix, and I guess I forgot about all that other stuff."

He wasn't sure he could let this go. "You just forgot?" Cohen loved the way Paulo was comfortable enough around him to just blurt out his thoughts, but it also reinforced that the person most likely to accidently out him was himself.

"I always relax around you and yeah, I forgot."

"We've just walked into your apartment after talking to S1 media and you forgot?"

Paulo frowned. "Are you accusing me of something?"

"No. I'm confused, that's all. Before your fitness week, you could barely talk to the most trusted people on your team about being queer, and now you want to go to a wedding together."

"Yeah?" The expression on Paulo's face, a throwback to the uncertainty he'd shown when they'd first met, was like a shot to the chest for Cohen. He took a moment to settle his heart rate and control his breathing.

"I'm not doubting you. I'm thrilled that you want to come to Lilly-Anne's wedding with me. It's awesome."

"But? It feels like you want to say but something."

"All those things you said about your father and your sponsorship, those are still true. And there's one thing that people do a lot at weddings that you should think carefully about."

"Are you advising me as my boyfriend, or as my security?"

His mouth was dry, so he walked to the kitchen and poured them both a glass of water and handed one to Paulo. "Let's separate those for a second."

"Okay?"

"As your boyfriend, I'm thrilled that you want to come to Lilly-Anne's wedding with me. As your security who understands the pressures of your job, you should make your decision based on the knowledge that people take a lot of photos at weddings."

Paulo's gasp told Cohen that he hadn't thought about any of the consequences of attending, only that'd he'd wanted to support Cohen. Which was amazing. And terrifying.

"Shit. I suppose we can't ask the guests not to take my photo?" Paulo whispered.

"We can ask for anything. You are famous. Felix is famous in some circles too. It might help, or it might make things worse because you might have fans there. It could be that everyone agrees to no photos, and people ignore that courtesy and take your photo anyway."

"Right." Paulo leaned on the balcony fence, staring out across Monaco towards the sea.

"I'm not saying this to stop you from going. It's my job to ensure that you understand the risks around your decision to attend or not."

"Could you ask about the photos?"

"Yes." Cohen picked up his phone to text Lilly-Anne when he noticed a small piece of paper still in the envelope. He pulled it out and read it with a shake of his head. Naturally, his legally minded sister had already thought about this. "Here's your answer. It's a social media free event. People will be asked to leave their phones with the concierge at the venue. The concierge will notify them if someone calls so they will be contactable during the event without having access to their phone camera. Everyone will be gifted a photo pack in the weeks following the wedding. There are several guests invited who prefer not to have their photos posted to social media, and everyone is asked to respect that."

"Did your sister do that for me?" Paulo stared at Cohen.

"Maybe." He grabbed his phone.

> Cohen: What's with the social media ban at your wedding?

> Lilly-Anne: I assume that means you got the invite.

> Cohen: Yes. Thank you. We should be able to come.

"We can go, yeah?" He asked and Paulo nodded.

"Yes. It's the weekend between the final pre-season test and the first race."

> Lilly-Anne: I know. I checked the race schedule before booking the venue.

Cohen pressed his hand against his chest. Wow.

> Cohen: The best sister ever

Lilly-Anne: I know. Btw, the social ban isn't just for your Paulo. Felix is inviting some of the French soccer team.

"Fuck." Cohen exhaled. He'd forgotten that his sister was likely going through the same odd sense of displacement as he was, although she'd always worked with the super wealthy and famous in her job, while he'd gone down a very different—poorer—pathway. Their middle-class upbringing hadn't prepared him for the prospect of attending a wedding with famous sports stars. He showed the message to Paulo who laughed.

"Am I your Paulo?"

"Absolutely."

"Good. Now we need to work out what to wear. You'll look amazing in a tailored suit. Let me buy you something."

"Thank you. I'd appreciate that."

"You can't be attending a wedding with half the French soccer team in an off the shelf suit."

He didn't need convincing. He'd already decided when he took this job that he would enjoy every benefit offered by his rich client. "Yes. Buy me a suit."

"Excellent. Shall we drive to Milan tomorrow?"

Four months ago, he could barely afford his T, let alone travel or buy new clothes, even his visit to see Lilly-Anne in France had been paid for by her as a gift. And now he was being invited to Milan to get a tailor-made suit. As much as he'd said yes, the dissonance still took a moment to process.

"And you'll get me anything I want?"

"Yes. If you want to wear one of those wild high fashion outfits that look like art on a catwalk, I'll get it for you."

He leaned back against the wall with his eyes shut, reminded of a meme of some fashion show with men wearing oversized balloon shaped pants.

"Are you okay?" Paulo came over and cupped Cohen's face. It was the easiest thing in the world to stand up tall and kiss Paulo.

"I'm definitely okay. I have an amazing boyfriend who wants me to look good when he walks beside me at a wedding." Life couldn't get better than this. He kissed Paulo again, putting all the joy and love into the kiss. Soon Paulo groaned in that perfectly delicious way of his, and he slowly marched him backwards across his apartment towards his bed. With every step, Paulo relaxed in Cohen's arms and those incredible golden brown eyes of his went hazy with lust. He was about to blow Paulo's mind.

"You have too many clothes on." They'd just been travelling, not far and in luxury, but a shower wouldn't go astray. Or not. He wanted his hands all over Paulo first. He pushed Paulo down onto the bed and straddled him, loving the way Paulo's eyes flashed wider.

"Get undressed."

"You are on me." Paulo's protest was cute, and rather the point.

"Yes. And you are apparently a world class athlete. I'm sure you can manage to undress yourself while constricted."

The sound Paulo made was obscene and burned like a streak of fire in his core. Fuck. And when Paulo wriggled under him as he took off his clothes, Cohen held himself still, knees tight against the outside of Paulo's thighs, and arms bracketing his chest. Paulo managed to get his shirt off, and when he lifted his hips to shed his pants, his hard cock brushed against Cohen's stomach. Hell. He wasn't sure who was seducing who here. Paulo bent his legs up as he contorted to try and get his pants off, and the way his stomach muscles crunched was a sight to behold.

"Done."

He had to blink for a second because he was so distracted by Paulo's lithe athletic form that he forgot what he was doing, except the way Paulo stared at him with such expectation and awe. There was such heat between them, familiar and yet ready to ignite if Cohen moved to close the gap between them. He didn't. Instead, he leaned back, resting on Paulo's naked thighs with Paulo's hard cock eagerly waiting for his touch. Cohen spread his hands over Paulo's ribs, slowly caressing him until he found the tight nubs of his nipples and pulled.

"Cohen." The rough edge to Paulo's voice thrilled him, so he did it again and again until Paulo writhed under him, pleading for more.

"More, like this?" Cohen dragged his fingertip down the length of Paulo's cock, making sure the end of his fingernail skimmed his skin. The hunger in Paulo's eyes flashed, then he closed his eyes and gasped when Cohen gripped Paulo's cock tight and stroked.

Paulo hissed. "Fuck me, please."

"My pleasure."

"And mine." Paulo growled low in the back of his throat. Cohen leaned forward and kissed Paulo, taking his time to savour him, loving the way Paulo purred and moaned. This incredible athlete wanted to go out in public with him. He rolled off the bed.

"Don't move."

Paulo whined and Cohen regretted getting up, but it was necessary to grab a dick and give Paulo what he desired most of all. He got himself ready and in the few moments that it took, he figured out what he wanted.

"Come with me." He beckoned his finger and left the bedroom, not waiting to see if Paulo would follow, and sat on the couch with his arms spread out wide.

"Cohen."

He threw the bottle of lube in Paulo's direction, unsurprised when Paulo caught it easily. "Get yourself ready, then sit on me and fuck me." His voice trembled a little on the command, just as needy as his lover, who was eagerly getting himself ready. Paulo straddled him and slowly sank down on the dick. Love and desire filled his eyes with a glow that warmed Cohen all the way through. He traced patterns all over Paulo's skin, enjoying the way Paulo's torso and stomach muscles moved as he fucked himself on Cohen's dick. With a little push against Paulo's pecs, he shifted the angles, so Paulo arched his spine and his head fell backwards. Cohen dragged his tongue over Paulo's collarbones, pressing it hard against his throat.

"Oh fucking hell. Cohen."

He kept up the kisses, tasting the sheen of sweat that had broken out across Paulo's skin, all salt and need. Paulo's hands tightened on Cohen's shoulders as his breathing turned ragged, and he still kept up the rhythm that pushed Cohen's dick against his clit and made him equally as breathless. Hell, he might come before Paulo did at this rate. He reached one hand up and grabbed a fistful of Paulo's hair, tugging.

"Fuck." Paulo came in long streams all over Cohen's

shirt and Cohen followed him into bliss, rolling his hips to chase the last vestiges of pleasure.

"Welcome home." His voice cracked as Paulo collapsed on top of him, tucking his head against Cohen's shoulder and neck. It was the easiest thing in the world to stroke his hair off his face and caress his cheekbones and jaw as they lay there together, just breathing in time with each other.

CHAPTER 17

The hotel in Edinburgh had a gym and Cohen did a quiet workout on the exercise bike while he watched the space to ensure Paulo could continue his pre-season training in peace. There were two other people using the equipment, but they hadn't reacted to Paulo's presence, so hopefully that meant they didn't know who he was. Being here was a little surreal; it was just another hotel gym, very similar to the ones he'd seen in Mexico, Brazil, Abu Dhabi, Paris, Galtur, and even in Paulo's apartment building. Just listing out the places they'd been in the few months since Cohen accepted this job was wild. Stanley had meant it when he'd said they would travel the world. He opened his phone to send him a message.

> Cohen: I haven't forgotten you. How's Horny's?

Paulo had purchased the pub, as promised, and Dean had retired with enough funds to keep him happily drunk for several years. Well, it was none of Cohen's business how an addict spent their money. Paulo had offered to pay for rehab, but Dean declined. Cohen checked the time zones and chuckled. Oops. Hopefully Stanley had his phone on silent while he slept.

"Ready?"

Shit. Cohen had been looking at his phone, not doing his job, and he hadn't noticed Paulo had finished his workout. "Yes. Shall we go?"

"Definitely. I need a shower and then we can go out for a walk before our appointment with the tailor."

Cohen couldn't wait to meet Isabella Wallace. After Paulo had mentioned that he would buy him a suit from anywhere in the world, he jumped on the internet to research queer fashion designers and someone in his discord chat had shown him a photo of Isabella modelling a dress she'd made for Pride week. The statuesque trans woman wore a stunning gown in tartan with a massive feathered headdress that reminded Cohen of a Roman toga but in blue, pink, and white Scottish tartan. He'd immediately imagine a suit made up in that tartan, and now they were about to have an appointment to make it a reality.

"I can't believe you managed to get an appointment so fast." The wonders of being rich.

"Enjoy it, please. My money is your money, Cohen." Paulo leaned closer and Cohen breathed in his sexy workout scent. It was funny how fresh sweat smelled so good, and how quickly it turned dank as the person cooled down. Paulo whispered, nice and close to Cohen's ear, "I might not be ready to share myself completely in public yet, but please let me share my money, and all the things that come with it, with you."

Cohen grinned. "Since you asked so nicely. Yes."

The glow in Paulo's smile was worth it. Cohen wasn't bothered by spending Paulo's money; it was more the way Paulo spent it that took some getting accustomed to. The idea that he could just travel to another country to get the very best of whatever product he felt like was fucking wild, and Cohen couldn't help feeling guilty about the climate miles, or how easy money made life. It wasn't many months ago that he was driving a piece of shit car to a crappy job and dreaming of a better job. Like, not this type of better, his ambitions had been much smaller, basically the same job but at a nicer pub with slightly better working conditions. Health care for one. And now he was jet-setting around the world so someone could buy him a hand-made custom suit just because he wanted one, and he never had to stress about whether he could afford his meds.

"Are you okay?" Paulo wiped his face with his towel as they walked out of the gym towards the elevator.

"Yeah. I have no complaints."

"But?"

Cohen went to touch Paulo on the chin but stopped himself by crushing his hands into fists at his sides. They were technically in public. "Um, my life has changed a lot in a short amount of time, and I guess I'm just thinking about that."

"With no complaints?"

"No. It's good. Just a lot."

"Okay." Paulo pushed the button, and they rode up to his penthouse suite in silence. It wasn't until they'd walked into their room that Paulo pulled him into a hug and kissed him on the forehead.

"If it's too much, please tell me. I don't want to railroad you into anything."

"Thanks." Cohen understood the comment was more to do with Paulo's relationship with his father than anything else. Paulo was so careful to make sure he didn't act like his billionaire father who dominated people and took whatever he wanted. "I'm good. Shall we shower?"

"Yes." Paulo stripped off his clothes and dumped them into the laundry basket. Yeah, that was something else extra. Their suite came with a laundry service that picked up his dirty clothes in the evening and returned them clean and pressed in the morning. Being rich meant that all these little details were just sorted out without having to think about them, like a laundry service that meant not having to take dirty clothes home. When Cohen had visited Lilly-Anne in France, he'd brought home a suitcase filled with souvenirs and dirty clothes; and the end of the holiday meant a lot of work to sort everything out. Not for Paulo, he came home, and unpacked his suitcase of perfectly laundered clothes directly into his drawers. He wasn't complaining, just incredulous that this was his life now. It was the unexpected details that often made the change seem the starkest.

"This place can't be real." Cohen stared up at the ancient buildings as they walked along the Royal Mile towards the Isabella Wallace's shop and the appointment they'd booked. It didn't take much to remember where he'd been a year ago, and it sure as shit wasn't flying into Edinburgh for a couple of days to buy an outfit for a wedding. Holy crap, his life had changed so much. He'd been so worried it'd be a scam and the offer from Paulo was a load of bulldust. Stanley had pushed him to take a chance and now look at how amazing his life was. The warmth inside his chest was a good contrast to the chilly winter wind whipping between the tall buildings.

"It's probably a similar age to the older buildings in Monaco?" Paulo pulled out his camera. "Look over here." He took a photo of Cohen, then tucked his phone back in his pocket.

"Why?"

"You look nice."

Cohen scoffed. "I'm literally wearing the same clothes as I always wear." Standard black t-shirt, black jeans, and paired with a heavy warm overcoat today, because late January in Scotland was fucking cold, especially compared to Texas, or even Monaco's more temperate climate.

"Yes." A puff of cloudy cool air emitted from Paulo's lips. Paulo's simple statement implying that he thought Cohen always looked nice added to the balmy warmth inside him.

"Come on. It's cold."

They walked quickly along the street. A couple walked past them, and Cohen overheard them whisper, "Isn't that Sanchez? The S1 driver?"

He glanced at Paulo who didn't seem to have noticed. Cohen dropped back a little to keep an eye on the couple who were following them with their phones out and were taking sneaky photos of Paulo. After a few more strides, the couple got bored and stopped following them. Paulo waited for Cohen, then crossed a side street.

"Where were you?"

"People were taking photos of you."

"Oh. Ignore that. It happens quite a lot."

"Okay." It was a good reminder that he was here to do a job because Paulo was actually famous.

"Most fans are respectful."

He nodded. "I'm here in case they aren't."

"It's usually worse during the season. I don't expect to see a lot of fans out at the moment."

"It's too cold for most people to be walking around." He would've laughed, but the streets of Edinburgh were reasonably busy. People didn't seem too bothered by the freezing air, carrying on their business.

"Here we are." Paulo pushed open a big glass door and Cohen followed him into Wallace and MacDonald Designs. Warm air made Cohen's cheeks hurt, and he reached over to help Paulo with his jacket. The shop was primarily filled with kilts, although there was a display of other fashions made from the tartan cloth that Wallace and MacDonald were famous for.

"I can deal with my own clothes."

"I know." Cohen moved his hands away from Paulo and took off his own jacket instead.

"Can I help you?"

"Yes. I'm Paulo Sanchez. I have an appointment." Paulo had made the appointment, using his famous name to remove any waiting time.

"Of course, Mr Sanchez. Please come this way." To his credit, the shop assistant didn't react to Sanchez's name, but if the understated luxury of the shop was anything to judge by, he probably dealt with the rich and famous all the time. Paulo followed the man. Cohen spent a couple of seconds checking their surroundings, standard stuff, then followed along at an appropriate distance.

"Cohen. You aren't at work now."

Cohen nodded, holding back an acidic comment about doing his job properly. Paulo was out in public; it was Cohen's duty to keep him safe from over-excited fans and any other potential threat to his person that might arise. The fact that Paulo was buying him a suit—a gift to a lover —complicated things. It didn't—and shouldn't—stop Cohen from doing his job. The shop assistant opened a door and waved them through. The back office was the opposite of the neatness of the luxurious shop front. One wall was covered in an array of different fabrics, while another had shelves filled with cardboard boxes. A man sat at a large table, paper and sketches spread everywhere, with a computer perched on one edge of the table.

"Mr Sanchez, please meet Mr MacDonald, our tailor."

"Hi." Paulo shook Mr MacDonald's hand. He was so perfectly Scottish looking; broad and brawny with a shock of red hair and enough freckles to paint a whole beach. It was like walking into a movie set where they'd deliberately picked the most Scottish looking person they could find; and of course—Cohen nearly burst out laughing—he wore a kilt. He swallowed. It was a kilt shop. What did he expect?

"Please call me Mac. I'm sorry that Ms Wallace couldn't be here today, but she is very excited to create a suit from our tartans for you."

"The suit isn't for me. It's for my bodyguard, Cohen

Wright." Paulo waved his hand in Cohen's direction. "I mentioned this in my email."

Mac clicked his mouse and raised his eyebrows. "This is for the wedding in a month's time?"

"Yes. Money is no object."

"That is true for most of our clients. A three-piece suit made from one of our Pride tartans?"

"Yes, that's exactly what I want." He jumped into the conversation with a glance to Paulo, who stepped back.

"We have two options." Mac pushed his computer screen around and showed them the two different options. Both had the light blue, light pink, and white of the trans flag woven together. "This one is called 'Finally Me' and this one is called 'Carefree'. Which one do you like?"

Cohen wanted to bathe in this moment and how simple and accepting Mac had made this process. There had been no discussion about Isabella or himself, or anything, just a simple question about which tartan he liked the most.

"I like 'Finally Me' the best." Carefree had smaller squares and was busier, while Finally Me had a more relaxed pattern.

"Okay. I'll check our supplies to see if we have enough quantity, and if not, I'll send an urgent order to our factory. Now, let's get you measured up." Mac stood up and moved to the back of his office. Cohen tried to breath softly.

Paulo slung his arms around Cohen's waist and whispered in his ear. "I can't wait to see you naked again."

"I'm not going to be naked for a few measurements." Cohen sincerely hoped not.

"I wasn't talking about now. I'm not a complete fool. I know this process might be stressful for you. I—" Paulo swallowed. "Think of it as a promise for later. A reason to get this done quickly, so I can get you back to our hotel room and shower you with all the kisses you deserve."

"Do I deserve them?" Cohen winked, tipping his head back towards Paulo.

"Fuck yes. I can't wait to see you all decked out in a suit made for you in such a bold colour. I fucking love it, and I love you."

Cohen smiled, turning in Paulo's arms so he could kiss him quickly. "You should wear a matching kilt."

"Why?"

"Because you'd look fucking hot in a kilt." Cohen whispered, wishing they weren't being watched by a very curious tailor. "And you are famous so people won't comment about it at all. They'll see it as typically eccentric."

"You two are very cute together. I understand your vision now." Mac reminded them of his presence. Cohen expected Paulo to leap backwards, but he must've felt safe because he didn't move.

"Thank you." He wanted to bottle up this moment and keep it. Who knew that buying fashion could be so affirming? Not just of himself, but of his relationship with Paulo. It was a better gift than the suit itself.

"Okay, love birds. Let's get you measured up and you can go to this wedding and steal the show." Mac had set up an easel with a large piece of paper clipped to the top. Cohen kissed Paulo on the forehead.

"Let's do this."

CHAPTER 18

ENGLAND

Paulo paced in the hallway leading into the ballroom at Socrates' estate—Pewett Downs—as the announcers interviewed Lucien and this season's new Series E driver, Sri Anund, about their new car. Security for tonight's event was tight in response to the dramas last season when Socrates' World Championship trophies had been stolen.

Tonight Gamble Racing would be the first team to have a woman driver in one of the major teams with the announcement of Sri to drive beside Lucien in Series E. Like many women drivers, Sri had come through the rally ranks and had driven for Gamble Racing's off-road E-rally team last year. The team regulations for that division meant every team had a mixed pair—designed to give more opportunities to women drivers in a system biased against them— and Sri's performance had been so outstanding that she'd been given this opportunity.

Paulo paused and did some deep breathing exercises.

This would be his third pre-season car launch evening; he should be used to the attention and the media by now. Thankfully, Senior hadn't come this year, sending his brother Enzo to represent Sanchez Shipping. Okay, that wasn't much of a relief and anyway, he wasn't nervous about speaking on stage in front of the media and a bunch of wealthy sponsors. The real issue was that this was his first season launch since meeting Cohen and it felt so wrong to have spent the day being careful around him. This would be their first public outing, except not. In the off-season, Paulo had become so used to be in a relationship with Cohen, tucked away from the real world, away from his job. Cohen stood quietly beside the door to the stage, doing his job, and Paulo couldn't touch him. He wanted to rest his head on Cohen's shoulder and simply breathe in the reassuring scent of him before he stepped out into the limelight. He breathed in and out slowly; there was no need to be nervous, they'd already had a run through of tonight's event earlier today. He had done this before.

"Are you okay?" Cohen asked.

"Yes. Just a little nervous."

"I could tell."

"Is it obvious?"

Cohen nodded. "You've spent the last five minutes pacing up and down this hallway, muttering to yourself."

He gulped, feeling like this was his own fault. He just needed to embrace the idea that he had to pick between Cohen or his job ... well, he'd rehashed this a million times and he still had no clue as to what the right choice was. If he was deeper into his career and older, he'd probably just retire and choose Cohen today, but he'd barely started his S1 career. Most drivers spent a decade or more at this level unless they weren't fast enough. He sighed. Thinking like this wasn't helpful because he always hovered on that edge of being good enough to have his seat and knowing it'd been bought for him by his father. He was tired of trying to live up to Senior's conditions for his life. Oof—the sudden realisation of the core of his problem did nothing to ease the swirl in his gut.

"Tonight is—" He paused. Tonight had already burst the little bubble they'd created together away from the world during the winter break—a reminder that he was hurting Cohen by not choosing him openly. He tried to start again, but a hard thump on his shoulder interrupted.

"Come on. It's our turn." Ondrej paced past him towards the stage door. "Nice haircut, by the way."

Paulo had cut his hair short for the launch, and it wasn't until Cohen teased him about looking manly that he'd realised that it wasn't just habit to cut it for the start of the season. It was all part of the performance he had to do so he could keep Senior's money flowing towards Gamble Racing and allow him to have a chance at being the best he could be. He couldn't have long hair—not with Senior watching—and he rubbed the back of his neck, missing the way his hair curled against his skin. No, he missed the way Cohen threaded his fingers through Paulo's hair and gripped it, pulling and tugging, until Paulo moaned for him. He breathed out. Shit. He really shouldn't be thinking about sex right now. Getting an erection in his new racing suit would be awkward as fuck.

"You are late."

Ondrej grinned. "No, you are early. Relax. You've done this before."

"Yes, I'm not a rookie anymore." He swallowed as Ondrej winked at him. The door opened and one of the Gamble staff waved at them. Ondrej walked towards the door, so Paulo followed with Cohen slipping quietly through behind him. As soon as he rounded the curtain and stepped onto the stage, noise surrounded him. Cohen faded into the background, always there and never seen, which Paulo refused to see as a metaphor for their relationship. He cleared his throat quietly, so it wouldn't echo through the microphone clipped to his racing suit.

The huge ballroom at Socrates' mansion was filled with tables, each of them surrounded by diners—sponsors and fans—all waiting to hear what he had to say. Jaxxon, Socrates, and Mike sat at the table closest to the stage. They'd already spoken to the audience earlier; something Paulo knew from this morning's rehearsal. The car sat on the front of the stage, covered with a black sheet, and his stomach stopped churning. His car. He'd done this before. He knew how to handle himself in public. It was time to be Paulo Sanchez, S1 driver.

There was a spot on the stage where he was supposed to stand, so he walked there, and looked at the two presenters; Freddy and retired rally car driver Alicia Blasi. He focused on his breathing, just as he would before a race.

"Let's give a big welcome to this season's Gamble Racing S1 drivers; Ondrej D'Grieg and Paulo Sanchez."

The crowd cheered politely.

"It must be so exciting to be here, ready to reveal this year's car to the world."

"Thank you." Ondrej said. "Paulo and I are lucky to have worked with the excellent engineering and mechanics teams here at Gamble Racing. We've seen this season's car and driven it in the simulator. Now it's time to share it with everyone." The audience cheered. A shadow moved behind one of the cameras. Cohen. Paulo's heartrate slowed a little. It helped to know Cohen was close by, watching the crowd, and keeping Paulo protected.

"We are all so excited to see the new car, not just tonight, but also on the track. Paulo, is this year's car different to drive in the simulator compared to last year?" Freddy asked.

"Hopefully it's faster." Paulo replied easily. Having Cohen standing behind one of the cameras was the best, because he automatically glanced at him to see if he was going to roll his eyes at the semi-scripted comment. They'd run through tonight's program and outlined the gist of the questions asked, so they could plan answers, but they hadn't scripted it because these things were always more natural and fluid for the audience that way. Paulo really appreciated the forethought from Cohen in his choice to stand behind the camera. He obviously knew Paulo couldn't help search for him, even now with a live audience and who knows how many people watching online, and now everyone would think he was staring at the camera. Like he was supposed to.

"Speaking of faster, you ended last season with four top five finishes."

"Yes, it was a nice way to end a season that included a

win at Spa and a podium at my home track in Brazil." He threw that one in for Senior and Enzo. Senior had loved having his business name all over the local news; and Paulo wished that result could be enough to justify the continued sponsorship without the worry of Senior's bigotry.

"Was there something that you changed for those last few races, and are you going to bring the same energy into this season?"

"I hope so. I've been working hard on my mental game as much as my physical one, and the end of last season was the result of that work." Paulo had known this question was coming—it was an obvious thing to ask given how he'd ended the season with much greater consistency than the earlier part of the season—and his answer was essentially what Melati had recommended. She didn't know about Cohen yet. Should he disclose that? If anyone ought to know how to deal with any photos of them, it was Melati. He caught the end of a question from Alicia Blasi.

"I'm sorry. I missed that. Can you repeat it?"

"Sure. I was asking about your focus."

Paulo laughed. "Obviously it needs some work since I missed your question." The audience laughed too, and he breathed out gently, trying not to sigh into the tiny microphone pinned to his racing suit.

"As long as you focus when you are in the car. Let's not have a repeat of Shanghai from your rookie season." Ondrej shoved him on the shoulder playfully, as he referred to the race where Paulo had crashed into Ondrej. Paulo had been exiting the pitlane after boxing for tyres, and Ondrej had been flying past. Paulo's car took the brunt of the crash and he hadn't finished, while Ondrej had managed to get back to the pits for replacement parts, finishing out of the points.

Paulo covered his face deliberately then dropped his hands to show his big smile. "I'll never live that one down, will I?"

"I take it that the two of you are working better as teammates now?" Freddy asked.

"Apart from that race, I've always enjoyed having Paulo as a teammate. He works hard and listens to team orders."

Paulo made a big deal of rolling his eyes. "Says the driver who benefits from team orders the most often."

"How about we leave it there? Team orders is far too a contentious topic for tonight's launch." Alicia smiled. "Let's talk about the upcoming season. What preparations have you been doing over the winter break, Paulo? You mentioned mental health, which is such an important topic."

"To be honest, I spent the first month doing nothing much. It's a very long season and I felt it was important to get away from racing for a while and recharge everything." Paulo couldn't help looking at Cohen. The urge to tell the world he'd spent the winter break getting fucked by his incredible boyfriend flourished for half a second of raw panic before it faded, and he managed to aim for saying something bland. "I guess I just did normal things; hanging out with friends, binge watching a few tv shows, eating, that sort of thing."

"Did we see photos of Edinburgh on your social media?"

"Yes. I did have a fun couple of days in Scotland doing some shopping for a friend's wedding." He wanted to tell everyone about Cohen, so he quickly changed the subject to avoid the temptation. Enzo was here for fuck's sake. "I met a few fans while we were there, who wanted photos. It's always great to talk to people who are as excited for the upcoming season as I am."

"Fans make this possible for all of us," Freddy said.

"Very true. I appreciate every fan, even when they make memes that don't show me in the best light."

"Let's leave that one for now," Alicia laughed. "I'd rather hear about your shopping trip. Everyone loves a good wedding. I hope you bought them a present they'll love."

"Of course. I went all the way to Scotland specially to get it." Paulo grinned. "But I'm not going to say any more, because they might be watching tonight, and Scotland is enough of a hint."

Alicia nodded. "Nice. It sounds like your friend is very lucky. And you, Ondrej? How was your winter break?"

"It was excellent. We had a big family Christmas, and then my husband, Hudson, had a research job that took him to Australia, so we spent a few weeks there." The way Ondrej spoke about having a husband so easily would always be amazing to Paulo. "Like Paulo said, it's good to have that time away from racing. The season is long and intense and requires a high level of focus..."

"Huh?" Paulo interjected just for the laughs, and the audience loved it.

"Sanchez, how many times have I said..."

"Don't eff ... ing drive into me." Paulo grinned. He waited until the laughter died down. "Shall we take a look at the car now?"

"Great idea. This is the moment, we've all—"

A shout rang out. "Jesus hates gays."

Paulo's body instantly shifted to high alert—just like the beginning of a race—his heart beating in time with the lights going out one by one. His heart thumped. A blonde man jumped onto the raised platform near the car. Cohen burst from behind the camera. Paulo's heart thumped in time with Cohen's long strides. Just like driving into a corner at high speed, the world slowed down. His focus increased. He moved to protect the car, bumping shoulders with Ondrej, who'd done the same. Cohen leaped. He flew through the air and crash tackled the man. Thud. There was a split-second silence. Paulo held his breath until Cohen moved. More incoherent screams about Jesus filled the air. Louder than the thundering of Paulo's heart. His ears roared with noise.

"Holy shit." Freddy's voice rang out clear through his microphone. The man shouted again. Then nothing. Cohen rolled the man over, and stood above him, holding the man's hands clamped together at an awkward angle. More of Gamble's staff arrived on the stage. Together they dragged the intruder off the stage. The audience applauded. Paulo's chest puffed out. Look at his amazing boyfriend. He glanced at Ondrej who stood beside him, between the altercation and the front wing, protecting the car.

Alicia was the first to recover. "Please excuse the unscheduled interruption to our programming."

"And how about another round of applause for our security personnel?" Freddy's professionalism shone out too. Cohen bowed, then walked back to where he'd been standing. Paulo used that as his cue to walk back to his spot on the stage. The diners cheered and clapped.

"Shall we move on?" Ondrej asked once the general applause died down. "I'm rather keen to show everyone the car."

"Yes. The car." Paulo added, kind of uselessly, but he was still stunned at the whole drama. His ears still roared with the rush of blood in his veins. Cohen had put himself in danger to protect everyone; not just Paulo. What if the man had a knife? He swallowed, trying to shake off the image of Cohen lying on the stage injured and bleeding. It hadn't happened. Cohen had done his job. He'd removed the threat. Effectively. The blood rushing in his veins started to move to a new beat. Lust.

"Everyone. The moment we've all come here to see. The GR-S390." Freddy's announcement was followed by dramatic lighting, loud music, and the slow lifting of the cloth cover from the car. Earlier today Paulo had been dreading this moment because Victor had named the car the S390 as a joke. It meant that the engine had failed to get past 400kph during testing, something that irritated Victor. No S1 car had reached those sorts of speeds in racing conditions, and it was unlikely given the regulations. An impossible goal, and yet one that Victor wanted to reach. The highest ever straight-line speed during a race was 372.5kph, a record set a few years earlier. Victor's goal was a long way off reality. But none of that mattered now. Not after the intrusion, because all he wanted to do was kiss Cohen and tell him how fucking incredible he was. He wanted to reveal the car—get the job over with—and spend the rest of the night with Cohen. Ondrej nudged Paulo and he lifted his head with a start. Shit.

"Looks good, huh?"

"It looks fast." It was the obvious thing to say and required zero thought, which was good because his brain was actively trying to distract himself from wanting Cohen. Desire burned inside him.

"Almost as fast as our security staff dealt with the intruder." Ondrej's smile did nothing to help the fire inside him. He glanced over at Cohen who was doing that thing where he looked relaxed but was scanning everyone carefully. Paulo forced himself to focus on the event. He was being recorded; and his own reactions—his desire—would have to wait until later.

"Yes." He shook his head to try and clear the way lust was making everything foggy. "That's why we have security staff, although I doubt anyone could've predicted a religious bigot at a car racing launch party." His voice sounded weird; rumbling and rough. He covered the microphone clipped to his collar and coughed.

"Anything is possible. Gamble Racing is starting to get a reputation for drama at their car launches," Freddy said. "Last year, stolen trophies, this year..."

"Perhaps next year, we'll disappoint everyone and go back to boring car reveals where everyone applauds politely and says all the right things about the car looking fast." The crowd laughed at Ondrej's comment.

"It'd be nice to live a world where our security revolved around design. I'm grateful that we have security personnel, especially tonight, because as entertaining as it might be for Freddy, interruptions ... especially those with a bigoted message targeting some of the Gamble Racing team, well they take the attention away from the point of tonight." His heart was still thumping hard at Cohen's efforts to protect him and Ondrej. "Let's not give any more attention to hatred. Tonight we are here to celebrate the GR-S390, a car that I'm incredibly excited to drive at pre-season testing. Gamble Racing has an extraordinary talent in our Chief Engineering Victor Tsui and the design team he has assembled." He was rambling now. Damn it.

"Speaking of design, do we see some innovations on the bargeboards?" Alicia asked. Thank fuck for professionals. He forced himself to breathe a few times instead of answer and keep on talking and talking.

"Do you?" Ondrej walked around the side of the car and peered at it closely. "Paulo; can you remember what last year's bargeboards looked like?" Ondrej's exaggerated wink and his cagey answer created a wave of whispers through the crowd.

"Well, I can't wait until pre-season testing," Freddy said. Paulo couldn't wait until tonight's launch was over and he could lean against a wall—any wall—and be kissed by Cohen. He wanted to get on his knees for him and show him how hot it was to have him literally fly through the air to protect Paulo.

"Then we'll see how fast this car really is," Ondrej said.

"And on that positive note, that brings our launch presentation to a close. Everyone. The GR-S390," Alicia said. Loud applause filled the room and the lights changed, with one bright light focused on the car, and the rest of the stage dark. The four of them walked off the front of the stage towards the tables reserved for them. He sat beside Socrates and Ondrej joined their table too.

"Nice work by your bodyguard." Socrates picked up his

glass of sparkling water and Paulo grabbed his own water glass and tapped it against Socrates' one.

"Thank you." He couldn't wait until tonight was over and he could show Cohen exactly how he felt on seeing Cohen leap through the air to protect him and the car.

CHAPTER 19

Finally, the party was over. He'd gone through the motions of talking to his brother, Enzo, and the various clients of Sanchez Shipping who'd been invited to the Sanchez sponsorship tables for the dinner and launch. It was time to rush with Cohen back to their room in Socrates' massive house and beg to be fucked. Quietly so that no one could hear—although it was likely the rooms besides theirs were empty—and mostly because it was fucking hot when Cohen told him to be silent. The agony of it was exactly what Paulo adored. He wanted all the energy of Cohen's protective tackle aimed at him. He would be obedient and earn Cohen's affection.

After saying good night to Socrates and Mike, he signalled to Cohen, and they walked away from the ball-room together. The rabbit warren of hallways in Socrates' ancient mansion eventually led him to a staircase and the northern wing to the room he and Cohen wore in. The house had been built by a Duke hundreds of years ago and had centuries of additions had turned it into a massive space that could easily host a hotel, but without any room numbers or staff or even a map to help anyone navigate their way around the place.

"This place is incredible. It's like being in an old movie." Cohen walked beside him along the hallway. It was late at night with long shadows cast by the dim infrequent lights. At some point in the last century, they'd been upgraded to electric lights, yet it was still gloomy in the hallway. Imagine how dim it would've been when they were candles.

"It probably has been in a few movies. Socrates has a house manager who does all that sort of stuff." Paulo grew up in a similarly sized house, although the Sanchez mansion was much newer; custom built when Senior made his first billion. Senior's home had plenty of staff to run the whole place, and it wasn't until he left at fourteen to go to driving school, that he'd realised it wasn't normal. On the scale of rich kids at his school, he was at the top end. It had always fascinated him how it was the kids who were the least wealthy—barring the few on scholarships—who worked so hard to prove they belonged in the rich kid's club. Class differences still existed among the wealthy with billionaire's children at the top of the pile. He'd done nothing to earn that spot. It'd been granted to him courtesy of Senior's wealth and in hindsight, the whole thing was strange as people aspired to be him, when all he'd wanted was to drive and race. Back then, he'd hadn't realised what a privilege it'd been to not worry about money and could just focus on his goal.

"I mean, look at the detailing on each door." Cohen

stopped to trace one of the old oak doors that led to one of the bedrooms.

"I'd rather spend my time looking at you." Paulo's feet were itchy with the need to get Cohen into their room and undressed.

"Aren't you sweet?" Cohen sounded more snarky than usual.

"Are you alright?"

"Yeah." Cohen sighed. "Yeah, I'm okay. Just a little unsettled by tonight's thing."

Paulo pushed open the door to their room—the aptly named Screaming Cock room—with bright wallpaper covered in hand-painted roosters strutting across the walls. Trust Socrates to call the room something that was both rude, apt, and spectacularly over the top.

"Unsettled? I thought you were incredibly sexy."

"You did?"

"Yes. I'd watch you take out weird ... um, religious bigots every day."

Cohen blushed. "I'm sure someone has made a gif of it."

Paulo rolled his eyes. "Fuck. What a world we live in."

"Says the celebrity who has hundreds of gifs of him in existence." Cohen's shoulders slumped and Paulo reached out and hugged him.

"Hey. You were great. I'm really proud of you."

"For doing my job?"

"Yes. And being generally awesome."

Cohen sighed, a long deep sigh. "But I'm not awesome. I didn't see him until he was on the stage with you. I left it until it was almost too late."

Paulo cupped Cohen's cheeks. "Repeat after me. I'm good at my job."

"I'm good at my job. "Cohen's gaze darted away.

"Again. You are good at your job. I'm safe. Please don't bash yourself for some invented—"

"It's not invented. I was too busy looking at you to notice him."

"But you did notice, and you weren't too late. You saved the day. Heroically. In spectacular fashion."

Cohen frowned. "Thanks."

Paulo kissed him on the end of his nose. "Seriously. I was very impressed, and I'm the only person you need to impress."

"What does that mean?"

"I don't know. I just want to solve your problems and make you feel better. It's not like you to be so hard on yourself."

"I'm allowed to have high expectations for myself. Please don't dismiss my observations."

Paulo swallowed. "No. I ..." He paused. "Tell me why you think you weren't amazing tonight."

"I'm too invested in us. I was distracted by watching you do your job. You looked incredible and all I could think about was kissing you after the show. And then that man was on stage screaming obscenities at you. I should've seen him earlier. I didn't even notice that he had his poster and I should've. I'm only hard on myself because it's my job to make sure you don't have to listen to stuff like that when you are—"

"Working?"

215

"No. When you are still uncertain about who you are." Cohen's frown deepened.

"Cohen. I'm not uncertain about who I am."

"You aren't?"

"No. I'm the world's tenth best driver. I'm pansexual. And I'm in love with you."

Cohen's mouth gaped open, and Paulo reached out to brush his thumb over Cohen's bottom lip.

"I worry about telling people about us for external reasons; money, my career, my father. I definitely doubt whether I can be openly me. I don't doubt that I love you. If my life was simple, and there wasn't a team of six hundred people relying on my father's sponsorship, then I'd be open and out with you."

"So it's not ...?" Cohen's pause made Paulo's heart clench. He wished he could shout their love to the world. Having Enzo at tonight's dinner and the scowl on his face and the nasty little jibs afterwards reminded him why he couldn't.

"You. No, it's not you. I love you." He stepped closer to Cohen, holding his face gently. "I know that when we met, I wasn't out to anyone except a few random people I'd hooked up with once, and I had a lot of internalised homophobia to deal with. I'm still dealing with that, and will be for a while if I'm honest, but being with you has taught me something wonderful. That a life lived in the shadows isn't a life at all, and of course I'm going to be careful around my father. I'm not sure I can be careful forever. I just want to tell everyone how amazing you are and how I get to kiss you."

"Oh."

"What's the matter?" His speech had fallen flat.

"Your team pays me handsomely to protect you. Tonight, I almost didn't do that. What if next time I fail?"

Paulo kissed Cohen on the forehead. "You are a person, Cohen. People make mistakes."

"I should've been scanning the crowd, not watching you." The idea that he was so distracting for Cohen sent a shiver of delight up his spine. He knew he'd fallen hard for Cohen, but to hear it worked the same way for Cohen was incredible.

"Maybe, but in the end it doesn't matter because you fucking smashed that guy and it was awesome." Paulo kissed Cohen before he could protest again, pouring all the lust from tonight into the kiss. Cohen responded by gripping Paulo on the hips and kissing back. The kiss said everything Paulo had already told him; he adored Cohen, loved him, and wanted to spend all his days with him. Paulo kissed Cohen as if this was the last time he'd ever kiss him and he needed to retain his taste forever.

"I forgive you and I love you." He whispered in Cohen's ear, then dragged his lips over Cohen's cheek.

"Thank you. Next time I will focus on my job. A fuck up like that won't happen again." Cohen kissed him with that raw confidence that Paulo had adored from the moment they'd met; kissing him with long strokes of his tongue, the same, delicious, dominant way he always did. The moment that Cohen took charge filled Paulo with heat; he fucking loved it when Cohen did that with a subtle angle of his head and a simple push with his hands on Paulo's hipbones. Paulo's spine hit the back of the door with a thump and before he knew it, he was pushed up against the door, surrounded by Cohen. Trapped in heaven; if the pearly gates were on fire with heat licking at his skin. And when Cohen rubbed himself along the hard length of Paulo's cock, he shuddered, having to concentrate carefully so he didn't come in his racing suit. The suit was designed to keep fire out, away from his skin, not to boil him alive with lashing of desire.

"Please."

"Take off your clothes." Cohen's command sent a rush of blood to Paulo's cock and a hot shiver down his spine.

"I can't. You are in the way." Paulo protested, remembering how Cohen had enjoyed that last time they'd done this.

"Do it anyway."

"Fine." Paulo slid his hands down Cohen's face, deliberately trailing his fingertips along Cohen's jaw, through his beard, and down his throat, enjoying the way Cohen's breathing sped up. Paulo undid the neck piece of his suit with a simple pull, then unzipped the suit down his front as far as he could, which wasn't far as Cohen pressed his body hard against Paulo, making progress difficult.

"Can you give me a little space?"

"Because you need it or because it'll make it easier to do as you are told?"

"Cohen." Paulo wanted to be told what to do and he wanted to touch Cohen now.

"Well?"

"I want to be naked for you."

"So do it."

Paulo had to wriggle to get his suit undone and taking out his arms was even trickier with Cohen pushing against him. He managed to get it off his torso and pushed down to his thighs. A sheen of sweat broke out—hot and needy—as he wrestled with his racing suit in the enclosure of Cohen's arms. This was the best sort of delicious torture, from the way Cohen protected him and surrounded him, to the way his cock rubbed against Cohen's body, making every wriggle thrilling.

"I knew you could do it." The casual praise nearly had Paulo spilling prematurely. He almost swallowed his tongue as he tried to stop himself pleading for release.

"You saved my life tonight. Tell me what I can do to thank you."

Cohen scoffed. "That's overstating it a little."

"'Tis not." His protest disappeared and his eyes rolled back in his head as Cohen wrapped his fingers around Paulo's cock and stroked gently.

"I don't need to be rewarded for doing my job. I'm already paid well enough."

"Then let me help you come because I want to."

Cohen smiled for a second before kissing Paulo so thoroughly he could hardly breathe. He sucked in air through his nostrils under the onslaught of Cohen's attentions; from his mouth against Paulo's mouth to the way he stroked Paulo's cock. It was all ... a lot.

"Are you close?" Cohen licked Paulo's cheek before whispering in his ear. Cohen's neat goatee tickled Paulo's neck, adding more sensation to the raging fire inside him.

"So close." Paulo whined, needing more, but not wanting it before Cohen had found his pleasure.

"Good." Cohen took one of Paulo's hands—he had left them resting on Cohen's shoulders—and guided it down

Cohen's body until his hand was trapped between them. The backs of their hands rubbed against each other, squeezed by their bodies, and Paulo pressed his thumb hard against Cohen's public bone. Cohen still wore jeans, and the fabric was oddly rough under Paulo's hand. He pressed hard in the place where Cohen loved it the most and was rewarded by a growl from Cohen.

"More."

"Like this?" Paulo rubbed and pushed until Cohen shouted out, coming hard, and with each pulse, Cohen gripped Paulo's cock tighter. Cohen nuzzled against Paulo's neck, scraping his teeth over Paulo's skin. The sharp contact was all it took. Bright white heat exploded behind Paulo's eyes and his body filled with a rush of sensation as he came, hips bucking against Cohen. They stood there leaning against the door, breathing heavily for a long time.

"Yes. Just like that." Cohen's voice was all rough as he held Paulo. Paulo was glad for the door as he'd lost the ability to hold himself up.

"Come on, let's get cleaned up and go to bed." Cohen tugged Paulo's hands and he followed Cohen towards the plush bed.

"Need sleep." Paulo collapsed on the end of the bed, still woozy from coming so hard, and flopped backwards. He was only half aware of Cohen pulling off his suit, and then cleaning his skin with a warm cloth. "You are so fucking amazing, Cohen."

"Shh, go to sleep. You are due on the simulator early tomorrow."

Paulo groaned, but then rolled himself until he was in bed properly. If he wanted to be the best, then he'd better sleep and be ready to work tomorrow morning. Pre-season testing was in two weeks, then Cohen's sister's wedding, then the first race.

After a hectic breakfast with Socrates and the rest of the core team members, Paulo walked beside Cohen to the main engineering building on the estate. They walked past the horse racing stables, past the string of prancing Thoroughbreds being ridden towards the big gallops at the back of the estate, and past the outbuilding that housed Socrates' car collection. The engineering building was relatively new; purpose built in the 1990s with a testing track that wound its way through the forest to the left of the mansion. The horses—trained by Socrates' niece Xenia—lived and worked on the right side of the mansion, maintaining a separation between the two different types of racing.

"Do the horses get upset at all the car noises?" Cohen asked.

Paulo shrugged. "I don't know. I guess they must be used to it. We don't drive this season's car here anyway." The track was mostly used by Socrates and a few others to drive Socrates' car collection.

"Why is that?"

"S1 regulations only allow the cars to be driven on race weekends and in formal testing sessions."

"Doesn't that mean you don't spend much time in the actual car? That doesn't seem safe."

"It's fine. The main reason is to keep the racing as even as possible. Testing costs money, so if everyone was allowed to do private testing, the richest teams would do more testing and more improvements. Winning matters more than balancing the budget, especially for the top teams. This is a competition." Paulo started to get that competitive alertness inside his body, like an increase of blood in his brain, and all his nerves switching on, buzzing with readiness. The countdown to the season had begun and he was keen to get in the simulator and be ready. Today was a good day to push himself harder than he had yet. More neck strengthening exercises, more reflex testing, more of everything he needed to be faster and better. He didn't need the distraction of having Cohen hanging around, or maybe he did. Maybe he needed to practice his focus with Cohen standing beside him, because Cohen would be at all his races and Paulo couldn't afford to expend any energy on Cohen during a race. It wasn't harsh, just the reality. If he was going to push this car right to the edge, he needed everything intensely focused on winning.

"Work time." He pushed open the door to the engineering building, not waiting for Cohen. For the next four hours, the only thing that mattered was doing everything physically and mentally possible to get him ready to win at Bahrain in four weeks.

"Let's get you ready to win."

"Thanks." Paulo twisted around and smiled at Cohen. Having someone who supported his drive for success was brilliant, and he made a note to properly thank him later.

CHAPTER 20

Cohen stared at the Chateau du Colline. The sprawling thousand-year-old fort dominated the top of the hill as they drove up a winding road in country France. Trust Lilly-Anne to go all out with something so staggeringly ancient and monumental. The building certainly made a statement; it was solid and unflinching and looked over the surrounding land. A metaphor for a good relationship? It suited Lilly-Anne and Felix.

He wished he could have Lilly-Anne as his only family and screw the rest of them. His leg jiggled against the passenger seat of the car they'd hired from the small airport nearby in the Gascony region. He really shouldn't care that his parents would be there; he'd already decided that he didn't need them in his life, however it was one thing to enforce a boundary and stay clear of them and another to be thrown into the same room as them.

"Are you nervous?" Paulo asked.

"A little. I haven't seen either of my parents for a long time, and Lilly-Anne said they'd both be here."

"Lilly-Anne will also be there and so will I. We've all got your back."

"Thanks." Cohen needed to talk about something else. "Hey, remember when we first met, and you tried to kill me."

"What? I would never."

"In my car. Fuck, I never want to go that fast again."

Paulo chuckled. "You were never in danger. But I am sorry about destroying your car."

"I don't care about the car. I thought I was going to die as you drove around all the traffic, weaving in and out of traffic."

"You weren't going to die." Paulo's supreme confidence in his ability with a car was magnificent. Cohen just didn't want to experience it again. He was content with watching from a distant location. Content, no. He would never get used to the way his heart galloped whenever Paulo got into his race car. The more time he spent on the S1 circuit, the more he learned about the history of the sport. So many dead drivers. They'd spent last week at the pre-season testing and after watching Paulo drive over seventy laps each day, Cohen had been exhausted from the stress of it. The grin on Paulo's face after stepping out of the car after the first session had been amazing though. It was when he spun off the track in the next session that Cohen's heart had practically stopped beating until that radio call came through his headphones.

"Sorry, lost the back end." That was when he'd known Paulo was fine, because he simply talked about work, and his race engineer, Monica, hadn't even asked if he was okay, which seemed to be pretty standard for crashes. Not asking meant it wasn't necessary to ask because he was fine. He shook his head, this train of thought wasn't helpful, and he'd have to learn how to cope with watching Paulo do his job and risk his life. It helped that Paulo didn't worry about death.

"Is that why you didn't want a ride around Socrates' track in his 1960 Lotus Le Mans race car?"

Cohen nodded. "Yeah. I'm not going at those speeds again."

"I should take you around the Nurburgring sometime." Paulo's musing wasn't funny.

"The what?"

"It's an old racetrack built in Germany in the 1920s. The Nordschleife is thirteen miles long and a public road. It's legendary and anyone can drive it for the price of a small toll."

Cohen shook his head. "Fuck off. Nope."

"I could drive you around it in a slow car, like a little city electric car or something."

"Still no." The idea might be amusing if it wasn't Paulo and his innate ability to get a lot of speed out of any car, even Cohen's old piece of crap.

"What about in a rally car? They have all the proper safety equipment."

Cohen gulped. "No. You'd be a fucking demon in a car designed to keep you safe when you crash."

"Hmm, I suppose that would be too much like my work. It'd be fun though and don't you always tell me I need a hobby to escape the pressures of my job."

"Paulo. No. Drive the fucking thing yourself."

He chuckled. "Maybe I will. Oh, and by the way, we've arrived." Paulo parked the car and Cohen blinked.

"Did you just distract me on purpose with all this talk of trying to kill me in a fast car?"

"You started it."

True. He had, but Paulo had taken it further with his talk of rally cars and whatnot.

"I'd keep you safe. Speed is fun."

"Maybe for you."

"Are you nervous now?" Paulo asked with a little wink. Cohen slapped him lovingly on the thigh.

"No. Damn you. And thank you." He breathed in and out a few times. "Okay, let's do this."

Cohen walked beside Paulo, hating the way the shoe was on the other foot now. He was employed to protect Paulo and he knew how to do that, but he was walking towards a potentially fraught meeting with each of his parents. And thanks to their divorce years ago, he was going to have to do this fucking ugly drama twice. His heart trembled in his chest, and he hoped he wasn't going to vomit. He breathed in deep to try and centre himself, to find his usual confidence. Well, *fake it 'til you make* had gotten him through many situations when he'd been younger.

"Thank you." Paulo handed over the rental car keys to one of the staff and took a small key card. "Cohen, come on, let's find our room and freshen up. The staff will bring up our bags from the car and park it."

"You are in the main castle as a special guest of the bride, Mr Wright." The staff member wore an incredibly sharp suit with a blue jacket and red brocade on the shoulders that looked like it'd come out of a movie set, or a museum.

"What about the bride's parents?" Cohen asked.

"Ms Wright has placed them in the village. Only the groom's parents, the groom's sister, and yourselves are here in the castle itself."

Cohen almost choked at the evidence Lilly-Anne had put some sort of boundary in place for them both. "Well. That sends a message. Good for Lilly-Anne." The tumultuous storm in his gut started to ease.

"Please follow me."

"Oh my God. Cohen. You are here." Lilly-Anne rushed up to him and hugged him. She wore an elegant pants suit with a satin blouse and looked incredible; like a lawyer attempting to be casual, a look that suited her perfectly.

"Settle down. We saw each other at Christmas."

"Hey, I'm allowed to hug my baby brother." She hadn't let go yet. "I'm so glad you are here. Why the fuck did I ever entertain the idea of doing this in Texas? Jesus, it would've been so fucking stressful."

Cohen nodded.

"Hi Lilly-Anne." Paulo said.

"Paulo. Bring it in." Lilly-Anne waved one of her arms, and Paulo stood awkwardly to receive a hug from her. "Relax, man. I won't bite."

"Are you sure?"

"Yeah, I'm so happy you two could make it. You are the sweetest couple."

"Thanks."

"Come with me. Felix and his sister, Tasha, are out in the courtyard having some champagne." Lilly-Anne

RENÉE DAHLIA

released them from her fervent hug and marched off through the castle. Cohen started to follow her because he had a bunch of questions about this weekend.

"You okay?" Paulo asked.

"Yeah. It's good to see Lilly-Anne so excited." Cohen just needed to keep his focus on that because that's why they were here.

The introductions went smoothly. They hadn't met Tasha at Christmas because she'd been with her partner's family for the week.

"And this is Essie, my wedding planner."

"Hi. It's nice to finally put a face to the name."

"You could've just looked Paulo up on the internet." Lilly-Anne laughed.

"I meant your brother. Now, did Lilly-Anne talk to you about the ceremony?"

Cohen shook his head. "No. We just got told to turn up and that everything was under control."

Essie smiled. "I'm pleased she has the confidence in me. Given the short time frame that I was given to plan this, we've decided to go with a simple ceremony with no best man or bridesmaids."

"Simple is what I wanted. No fuss. I just want to marry Felix because he wants to marry me." Lilly-Anne's pragmatism earned her a kiss on the cheek from Felix.

"Darling. Do you blame me for wanting to put a ring on your finger and holding on tight to you?"

"I'm not going anywhere, piece of paper or not."

"Aren't they just gorgeous?" Essie grinned. "It's easy to love my job when I get to work with couples like you two. Now, I understand there are some potentially problematic relationships that I need to ensure the staff are aware of."

"Our parents are divorced, and our Dad is bringing his latest trophy wife. Mom's biggest issue is that she's determined to dead-name Cohen, and we need all the staff to tell her no one of that name is on the invite list." Lilly-Anne's practical response reminded Cohen that people cared about him. He didn't have to do this alone.

Essie nodded. "Yes, I've been over that issue with everyone. I've worked with this castle before and they have a very inclusive well-trained group of staff, so I'm confident the staff will support you on this matter. Do you need us to run interference and keep her away from you?"

Cohen frowned. "No. I can handle her myself." He ought to be happy that Lilly-Anne had gone out of her way to ensure he felt safe and welcomed. If only she hadn't invited Mom at all, but he would never suggest that to Lilly-Anne whose complex relationship with Mom was very different to his lack of connection with her. Lilly-Anne was nine years older than him, an overachieving older sister with all the baggage that went with that, and Cohen understood Lilly-Anne had her own journey to take with Mom.

"If our mother causes any problems I'll stab her with Paulo's sgian-dubh." Cohen paused deliberately, and after everyone had gasped, he grinned. "I'm kidding. I've never stabbed anyone who didn't attack me first."

"What's a sgian-dubh?"

"A little Scottish dagger."

Paulo winked. "You'll see."

"What will we see?"

"We might have gone a little overboard and made

matching outfits for the wedding tomorrow. Cohen is going to look awesome." Paulo blushed. Fuck, he adored the way Paulo just blurted out stuff and then dealt with the emotions after he'd realised what he'd said. It was so different to how he behaved around the press.

"No. It's Paulo who will be incredible." When they'd gone back to Scotland for a final fitting, Cohen had been thrilled with how his suit looked. A perfect fit that made him look so masculine, and to see Paulo in a kilt made of the matching fabric with all the extra pieces that made up the whole Scottish outfit was adorable.

"Did you say matching outfits?" Tasha asked and he blushed, ducking his head so everyone wouldn't see his heated cheeks. "That is adorable."

"It's almost a shame that you have a no social media policy." Cohen nudged Paulo, just to let him know that he was joking. He understood how much Paulo feared being outed to his father.

Paulo paled for a second, and Cohen squeezed his thigh, pleased to see Paulo recover quickly. "Maybe I'll pose for a photo with the groom and get Melati to post it."

"It's such a shame that your sponsorship deal requires you to be single." Lilly-Anne told the lie that Cohen had concocted to protect Paulo from his father's nonsense. A flash of confidence puffed out his chest; yeah, he could handle anything at this wedding. Together him and Lilly-Anne could deal with their parents. He had her back as much as she had his, and the ease with which she told Paulo's manufactured reasoning only proved Cohen's point.

"Yeah. People like to think of their drivers as young and

available, I guess. It's good for the sponsors at this stage of my career. I try not to listen to all of that. I just want to win."

"I'll make sure that we strictly enforce the photo ban and remind people that the several famous sports stars at this wedding value their privacy for commercial reasons as well as personal ones."

"It should be enough that people value their privacy for personal reasons, but if money makes people toe the line, then we will use everything we have to make them do as they ought." Felix's sister Tasha proved she wasn't someone Cohen wanted to come up against in an argument. "No one wants to be sued because someone lost a multi-million-dollar sponsorship deal." Tasha worked for the same legal firm as Lilly-Anne, so her quick summary of the situation wasn't at all surprising.

"Shall I get everyone something to drink?" Essie jumped up and waved at one of the staff who walked over. The woman in the tailored uniform took their orders efficiently.

"This place is incredible. I can't believe you got it at such short notice." Tasha smiled at Essie and Lilly-Anne.

Lilly-Anne shrugged. "Well, money talks and I didn't really have any preferences which also helped. I just wanted somewhere private with enough accommodation for everyone, and if it had a bit of a cool atmosphere, that was a bonus."

"You've nailed the atmosphere. This place is amazing."

Felix leaned towards Paulo. "Just a heads up, most of my teammates are coming along, and they've seen your Austin video."

Paulo tensed, and Cohen slung his arm around Paulo's shoulders. "Don't tell me. They want Paulo to take them for a drive."

"Abso-fucking-lutely. But take me first!" Felix laughed. "I can't believe I know a real S1 driver. Please drive me somewhere."

Cohen didn't want to encourage Paulo to be reckless, but he was so happy when going fast that Cohen stopped himself before he said something that would annoy Paulo.

Paulo shook his head. "Sorry, next weekend is the first race of a new season and I'm not keen to take any unnecessary risks before then."

Cohen breathed out slowly. Good. Except... "Hey, you told me I wasn't at risk."

"Unnecessary risks." Paulo tilted his head a little. "All of life is a risk, it's just the degree of risk. And I'm not willing to take people for a joyride a week before the season opens. Driving to get to an important meeting on time is different. And you were the perfect passenger."

"What? Scared shitless?" Everyone laughed at Cohen's response and he grinned along with them.

"No. Quiet, focused, only talking when I needed directions. You allowed me to concentrate on getting us there safely. Taking people for a joy ride comes with a certain level of ... distraction and that increases the risks beyond what I'm willing to do."

Lilly-Anne's irritated expression should've been captured on camera. "So you'll speed with my brother on board, but you won't take our friends for a ride?"

"Not this weekend. If they want to come to Gamble's headquarters, I can take them out in one of Socrates' cars on the test track, or…" Paulo grinned and Cohen wanted to say no, he better not. "Or we could meet at the Nürburgring during the summer break." There it was. He tried to hide his discomfort at the idea of Paulo taking Felix and his friends for a race around some trumped-up old racetrack. It was one thing to watch Paulo drive at ridiculous speeds for work, knowing all the safety equipment he had as well as knowing the track had rapid response teams everywhere, and quite another for him to take any old car around a track that didn't have all of that.

"Let's do that," Felix said with a grin.

"What is the obsession with men and speed?" Lilly-Anne asked.

"Compensation?" Tasha smirked. Cohen wanted to press his hands to his cheeks to hide the flash of heat that surely everyone could see. He knew Paulo wasn't compensating for a lack of size, that's for sure.

"Can't be that. You've made my brother all embarrassed."

"Fuck, Lilly-Anne. Some things should stay private." Cohen wasn't keen to listen to people joke about Paulo's dick size in public.

Paulo rolled his eyes and grinned. "It's cool."

"I bet, since Cohen has just implied that you don't need to compensate." Tasha raised one eyebrow and Felix shoved her on the shoulder.

"Don't you have a boyfriend?"

"So does he. I'm allowed to joke, Felix."

Paulo cleared his throat. "Whatever. You didn't ask the right question about speed anyway. An obsession with speed is not gendered. My race engineer, Monica Gastrell, was a champion rally car driver in her twenties, and the S1 journalist Alicia Blasi holds a category speed record at Monza. Car racing doesn't have a great gender balance among drivers, but it's one of the few sports where people compete against each other without gender divisions."

The wait staff arrived with their drinks, and Cohen sipped his beer as the sun started to set over the edge of the castle courtyard, listening to the ebb and flow of the conversation. Tomorrow he'd have to deal with his parents. Tonight, he could enjoy being with Paulo, Felix and Lilly-Anne; his real family.

CHAPTER 21

The words of the marriage celebrant washed over Cohen as he sat beside Paulo in the front row of the small chapel at the castle. The chateau had its own chapel, complete with very religious stained-glass windows, although the angels had rather masculine arms. Paulo looked incredible in his kilt, sitting with his bare leg curled around Cohen's ankle in a wildly intimate gesture. There was something special about the way Paulo slowly allowed the world to see more and more of himself, although it was still very contextual. During the public practice session last week, Paulo had been distant and focused. Yesterday, among friends, he'd smiled and made a joke about them wearing matching outfits.

The wedding would be amazing if it wasn't for Cohen's parents, who were seated a few rows behind them. Cohen tried not to imagine the cold prickles on the back of his neck as their judgemental stares. The wedding itself was gorgeous. Lilly-Anne looked stunning in a designer lace gown that flowed over her, and Felix was magnificent in his tuxedo. His family, in traditional Cote d'Ivoire dress, filled the church with colour.

Paulo had taken his time getting ready, fussing over his outfit, until they were late, and it wasn't until they were seated that Cohen realised that he'd likely done it on purpose so they wouldn't have to talk to Cohen's parents before the ceremony.

"And now you may kiss each other." The celebrant's deliberately chosen words sounded exactly like something Lilly-Anne would pick—ungendered and lacking in the traditional heteronormative marriage power balance—that Cohen had to pinch his lips together to stop himself laughing in delight. The newly married couple kissed enthusiastically, and Cohen joined in the cheers of celebration coming from Felix's side of the church. Soon enough, papers were signed, the couple walked down the aisle, and everyone stood up to follow.

"Shall we?" Paulo asked.

"Yes."

"Just a second." Paulo shifted on the pew. "Okay now stand."

"What?" Cohen wasn't used to Paulo giving him orders.

"I just wanted a better view. I hope that's okay."

Cohen grinned at his goofy boyfriend and the pleading expression on his face. "Sure." He stood with a flourish, then waited until Paulo stood up before he leaned in close and whispered. "You just wanted to see my ass better." The bug-eyed gaze and the flare of lust in the way Paulo's bottom lip sagged were priceless.

"Yes. I do adore the way the fabric stretches over your ass."

"Says the guy who isn't wearing any fabric on his ass!" He loved that Paulo had decided to wear the kilt in traditional style, meaning he wore nothing under his kilt.

"Just for you."

Cohen leaned in closer and whispered in Paulo's ear. "Tonight, I'm going to bend you over one of the stone walls here and fuck you with your kilt flipped up around your ears."

"You promise?" Paulo's voice was rough and needy.

"Come with me." Cohen strutted out of the church, loving the idea that Paulo would follow him anywhere. When they were like this together, Cohen felt like he could conquer the world, more than his usual dose of natural hard-won confidence. The best part of all was that Paulo wanted this, he loved it when Cohen commanded him. Cohen was so fucking lucky to have had Paulo stumble into Horny's and his life. Fuck. All this wedding stuff and talk of love was making him sappy.

"Excuse me." Hearing his dad's voice before he saw him didn't give Cohen much time to prepare himself. All the good vibes fled, and his heart thumped unsteadily. He tried not to curse.

"Yes?"

"Not you." Cohen's dad dismissed him and turned to Paulo. It must be the beard; the last time his dad had seen him, he'd only been on T for a few months. Since then, his shoulders had broadened, and he'd muscled out nicely as his body developed to match how he felt inside. A hysterical giggle threatened to burst out and he shoved his hands in his suit pants pockets.

"Are you Paulo Sanchez?"

"Yes."

"Interesting choice to wear a kilt to a wedding in France."

"It's a very deliberate choice for reasons I don't need to disclose to anyone but the person I'm wearing it for."

Cohen's dad shook his head slightly as if he was trying to make sense of Paulo's comment, and Cohen was too busy enjoying the thrill of Paulo hinting that he was fond of Cohen to think too much about the fact that his own father hadn't recognised him. This was so much better than he'd been worried about.

"Do you know the groom?"

"I'm here with the bride's brother."

Cohen's dad frowned. "The bride doesn't have a brother."

"She does. Dad, I am Lilly-Anne's brother." Cohen didn't want to have this conversation.

"Meet Cohen Wright, my personal bodyguard and very close friend," Paulo said. "I'm honoured to have been invited to his sister's wedding today."

"Cohen Wright?" Cohen's dad blinked slowly. The speed of realisation was farcically glacially slow. "I thought that was just a phase?"

"No. I've always been your son, Dad. The only difference is that now I live freely as myself."

Cohen's dad stared for a while and Cohen couldn't stop the tension building across his shoulders. If this continued, his shoulders were going to touch his ears soon.

"If Paulo Sanchez says it's okay, then I suppose I have a son now."

Cohen wanted to argue with his dad about how pathetic it was to only accept him on the condition that some random famous guy said so. "Okay."

Cohen's dad stuck out his hand to Paulo. "Hi, I'm Mr Wright. Pleased to meet you." The gesture was weirdly awkward, and Paulo shook Cohen's dad's hand with an unfriendly glare. Cohen loved it when Paulo was in his corner, mad at the world on Cohen's behalf.

"Have you seen your mother? She's going to find this very confronting."

"As if you care." The words were out before Cohen could stop them.

Cohen's dad pursed his lips. "You are right. I don't care for her, or her opinions. But she's likely going to make a fuss."

"I'm aware of that." As if the fuss was the biggest fucking problem here. She could make all the noise in the world, and it wasn't going to change reality, but God forbid if someone wasn't polite.

"Cohen is more than capable of dealing with this without your help." Paulo's voice lowered in tone, a warning, and one that Cohen didn't hear often from Paulo.

"I'm not offering. It's just very confusing."

"It's not confusing at all. Cohen is a man. An incredible man who I consider my friend." Paulo said back off without saying it. "And not that it matters at all, but you seem like the type of man who values performance, so you should know that Cohen is outstanding at his job. To work in S1 is to be among the most skilled people in the world, and

Cohen excels in a competitive environment. You ought to be proud to call him your son, and the fact that you express any doubt is a nasty reflection on your own character." The tendons in Paulo's strong neck stood out and that vein in his temple pulsed.

"Let's go." Cohen turned and walked away with Paulo pacing beside him.

"I'm sorry."

"Why?"

"For that unhinged spray at your father."

Cohen shrugged one shoulder. "He deserved it. Besides, it's just a warmup for my mom."

"Fuck. Can we avoid her and head back to our room instead?"

Cohen grinned.

"How can you laugh?"

"I'm choosing not to be angry at her. She's a toxic cow who has already sucked up enough of my energy."

"A joy vampire."

"Yes. Fucking yes. That's exactly it. Feeding on the joy of others until everyone around her is depleted and worn out."

"Excuse me." Essie called out as she paced towards them. "Can you two please come with me?"

"Why?" Cohen wasn't in the mood for more fuckery.

"Lilly-Anne wants to have some photos with you."

All of Cohen's tension rushed out on a smiling sigh. "Brilliant. Let's not waste the artistry of Paulo's suit for a moment longer."

"My suit? You are the one wearing it."

"And you are the one who gave me the gift of picking

anything in the world and supporting my choice to wear a suit made from trans flag inspired tartan. It's your suit as much as mine."

"Does that mean I get to decide when to take it off you?" The cockiness in Paulo's voice—in public—was a bigger thrill than Cohen had ever experienced. He loved the way Paulo was starting to reveal himself and feel comfortable to flirt with him in public. He leaned in close and whispered in Paulo's ear.

"No. Only I decide that."

The way Paulo blinked, and the delicious rush of colour across his cheeks, had Cohen forgetting where they were.

Essie coughed. "This way." She rushed off and Cohen chuckled. Oops, flirting with Paulo while others could hear what he was saying wasn't a habit he should get into, but it was such fun. He grabbed Paulo's hand and they followed Essie, walking hand-in-hand, around the corner of the chapel building and along an uneven stone pathway until they reached a turret jutting out at the edge of the cliff. Lilly-Anne stood there with the wind rustling her dress, with the low stone wall behind her as the only thing that stopped her blowing off the edge of the cliff into the valley below.

"Wow."

"She looks stunning."

He cleared his throat. "I was thinking you'd look amazing standing there; like a warrior in your kilt with your dagger drawn, and the enemy vanquished to the valley below."

"I'm not going to take over Lilly-Anne's wedding photo shoot."

He shrugged, trying to look careless when his insides were melting at the thought of the wind catching Paulo's kilt and flicking it around his legs. "I'm sure the photographer can find time for a few shots of you."

"Only if I can get a few of you. I love your suit."

"I can send them to my father."

"Cohen. Please don't. Conditional acceptance is not real acceptance."

"I know that." He closed his eyes, and slowly unclenched his fists. He shouldn't have made that joke because now Paulo was being so soft and understanding and somehow that irritated the fuck out of him. With a deep breath, he realised he was annoyed at himself for caring about his father's reaction to him. It shouldn't matter. He'd decided long ago that he didn't care about his parent's shitty opinions about him.

"I don't want to fight about this. I understand what it's like to have a crappy father." Paulo's nose was all wrinkled up in distaste.

"But he accepts you as you are." Oh, right. His mouth knew what his brain took a while to catch up and understand; that was why Paulo's comment about conditional acceptance pissed him off.

"Senior doesn't know who I am, and he only accepts the parts that are useful to him. Your dad did the same thing to you just now."

"So you aren't mad because he hurt me, you are mad at your own father by proxy."

"What?" Paulo leaned back against the stone, almost slumped. "No. Yes. It's both. I'm angry that your father hurt you and I'm resigned to my own father hurting me."

His hurt whisper did nothing to ease the churn inside Cohen. "Did I fuck up?"

"No." Cohen growled under his breath. "I don't think it's as simple as me or you fucking up. Let's not argue now and just smile for Lilly-Anne."

"Okay. I care for you, Cohen."

He knew that and he knew Paulo was doing his best to unlearn his upbringing. He breathed out, ignoring the nasty little burn in his lungs. Lilly-Anne turned to wave at Felix, who joined her for a few poses. Cohen's heart ached for them, the simplicity of their love for each other, as if no one else in the world mattered. Oh. He had that and he couldn't throw that away thoughtlessly.

"I'm not mad at you. I'm angry at your father." Cohen reached out and held Paulo's hand, rubbing his thumb across the calloses on his palm.

"You are?"

"Yes. He's actively forcing you to make an impossible choice. I want the freedom that Lilly-Anne and Felix have; to be exactly who they are and happy to show the world."

"I want that too."

"But you can't. I understand. It's okay."

"Is it?"

Cohen grimaced. "Well, it's not a hundred percent okay and that's why I'm mad at your father."

"If it helps, I'm mad at him too. And I'm mad at your father. Ergh. Fathers." Paulo closed his eyes and breathed out. "Actually, no. It's not fair to say that. Ondrej's father is accepting and supportive; many drivers have supportive families. Socrates and Mike have been incredible fathers to Xenia. We are the ones who lucked out."

"Yes." They had more in common with their family backgrounds than he'd realised. Paulo's family money made it tricky for Cohen to see that they both had toxic parents who didn't accept who they each were. Money made many problems disappear. Not this problem, though. "We can make our own family. Family isn't about a DNA connection, it's deeper than that."

"I agree. And I have a plan to deal with Senior so that I am not reliant on his money as much for my work, and then we can be a family, not just at home, but everywhere."

"You do?" It was a lot to take in. Lilly-Anne stood fiercely in Cohen's corner, except for the complicated way Lilly-Anne saw their mom. And now Paulo had a plan to do the same.

"Yes. This season, I'm going to prove that I'm among the best. I'll be consistent and that will allow the team to get different sponsors. Then I'll be free to be with you, out and open, just like the rest of my team. I want to show the world what you mean to me..." Paulo opened his eyes. "I just have to earn it first."

Cohen couldn't breathe. As far as declarations of love went, it was perfectly Paulo and just fucking everything. He wanted to fuck Paulo right now, just bend him over the stone wall and shower him with kisses and love. Paulo pulled him closer and leaned forward to kiss him. The kiss tasted like home. A flash went off.

"Oh my god, you guys are so cute." Lilly-Anne's voice broke through their kiss and Cohen pulled back.

"Your timing sucks." Cohen turned around to growl at his sister.

"It's my wedding. I can say and do whatever I want. Isn't that what you told me?"

"Fine. Yes."

"Then kiss again. I want more photos of you two."

Paulo leaned closer and whispered. "Please. I enjoy kissing you, and we know the photos will be just for us. One day, once I've earned a new sponsor, we can share them with the world."

"I'd like that." Cohen loved looking at the gold flecks in Paulo's big brown eyes. "Besides, we really need photos of you in this kilt." He placed his hands on Paulo's chest, gripping the lapels of his shirt, and pulled him closer for a proper kiss.

CHAPTER 22

Paulo always wanted to be kissed by Cohen. He'd never tire of it. Cohen was so damned good at kissing. Paulo melted in Cohen's arms, loving the way Cohen's beard brushed against his skin. Every kiss was a conversation with Paulo wanting to earn Cohen's affection and Cohen telling him that he'd already done enough, and he deserved all the attention being poured into him. He'd believe that when he was completely out to the world. Each stroke of Cohen's tongue sent flashes of heat through Paulo, as if he could absorb all of Cohen's confidence with this connection. He wished he could tell everyone about his amazing boyfriend. One day. One day, he'd be able to do it, when he'd earned it and removed the obstacle in his path. Slowly, with each brush of Cohen's lips, Paulo was starting to believe that he could have everything; Cohen, a career in S1, and team sponsors who accepted him completely.

"Lilly-Anne. I do not approve of your friends. Two men kissing in public is obscene and one is wearing a dress!" A judgemental voice sang out clearly across the open space.

"It's a kilt and Paulo looks fucking sexy in it." Cohen's shoulders shook as he spoke softly.

"I take it that voice belongs to your mother?" Paulo asked. He held Cohen tighter, then forced himself to relax so he didn't hurt him by clinging too much. He wasn't sure that the woman had heard Cohen.

"Yeah."

"Are you ... laughing?" He didn't understand what was going on.

Cohen's eyes sparkled and his smile shone brightly. "My mother just gendered me correctly for the first time in my life. I'm pretty sure she didn't recognise me."

"So that was just stock standard homophobia?" Paulo frowned. "Isn't that still bad?"

"It's not great." Cohen's nostrils flared as he breathed in deeply. "She shouldn't say that to you."

"And you."

"Mom, if you aren't going to be polite, you are welcome to leave." Lilly-Anne's voice had a careful neutral note.

"I am not going to leave. My daughter is the bride. I think I should have had some say in the guest list." The woman had dyed blonde hair, carefully cut into a fashionable bob cut, and she wore a beautiful pastel pink evening gown. She had that look of someone who'd been beautiful in her youth and was desperately clinging to it. The attempt failed because her face was marred by a sneering expression with her mouth turned down at the corners.

"Essie. Please escort this person from the grounds. She isn't welcome." Lilly-Anne cut off any issues before they began. Essie spoke into a radio and staff members appeared from all over, surrounding Cohen's mom. They escorted her away from everyone, marching quickly. The woman's protests faded away with every step. Lilly-Anne leaned against Felix, and Paulo hoped she wasn't going to faint. She looked very pale and wobbly. Essie rushed over with a little handkerchief and blotted at Lilly-Anne's face.

"I'm not going to cry."

"Later. We can analyse this later. You can cry then, and I'll hold you close." Felix rubbed his hand in circles on Lilly-Anne's back. Paulo stepped backwards. This felt all too intimate, like he was a bystander to something private, and he didn't know what to do. The idea of vaguely flinging himself over the stone wall appealed for a second, just so he wouldn't be in the way. It was the need to hide and get away that drove the urge. Instead, he stayed put, awkward, tense, and uncomfortable, unsure of what to do.

"Aren't they lovely together?" Cohen leaned against Paulo's shoulder.

"Huh?"

"Lilly-Anne and Felix."

"Yes." Paulo paused for a moment, enjoying the way Cohen's body fit against his. "When Felix said we'll analyse this later, is that something you want too?"

Cohen rose on his tiptoes and brushed his lips against Paulo's ear, sending a shiver down his spine. Every single time that Cohen touched his mouth to Paulo's skin, Cohen managed to take all of Paulo's uncertainty and switch it into something wonderful.

"No. I don't need to analyse it. I'm good. Honestly. I'm pleased that Lilly-Anne made the decision quickly. I don't need to be annoyed that she chose to invite her. I'm going to choose to see the upside in having her removed so rapidly after one awful comment."

"If you are sure, then that's enough for me."

"I am. Let's forget it and focus on celebrating Lilly-Anne and Felix."

"I have always found your confidence inspiring." Paulo blurted, then clamped his hand over his mouth. God, this environment with all the heightened emotions made him want to place everything he had—his heart most of all—at Cohen's feet.

"Thank you." Cohen bit him gently on his earlobe.

"Fuck, that's good." Paulo's breath rushed out of him as heat scattered across his skin. "Cohen."

"Yes?"

"I wish we were alone."

Cohen stepped back a half-pace and winked. "I'd bet you'd let me fuck you in public if I asked."

Paulo shivered. The image of himself being tipped against the stone wall, with his chest resting on the top as he stared down at the valley with all the early spring growth making the land green and lush, with his kilt flicked up over his back, and Cohen standing behind him with his suit pants around his knees as he fucked him. Fuck yes. He swallowed.

"You are seriously considering it, aren't you? Despite all the reasons why you shouldn't."

"Yes." Paulo hissed under his breath. He wouldn't want to do that if people were watching—he would never be an exhibitionist—but the idea of risking it in a public place where someone might see by accident ... Fuck. That made him tremble with need. His cock was uncomfortably hard against the wool of the kilt and the weight of the sporran.

"Good boy." Cohen traced his thumb along Paulo's bottom lip. "I'm tempted, but one of us has to have good sense and if the photos were made public... well, it's not worth the risk to either of our jobs."

Paulo couldn't get rid of the image from his head. Good sense? He had none of that. Desire pushed away anything that might constitute a logical thought process. "I don't care."

"Yes. You do." Cohen grinned. "But I love that I can make you ignore reality with just a few words."

"Fuck. Cohen." Paulo pleaded. He needed him. Now.

"You'll have to wait. This is just the release of adrenalin."

Paulo swallowed again, trying to breathe. He nodded, unable to talk.

"This feeling is the same thing as at the end of a race when you've had a good result." Cohen's explanation made complete sense. He'd only been to four of Paulo's races at the end of last season, and yet he already knew this. It was just another way Cohen was the perfect person for him. After every good result, there was a rush of adrenalin and satisfaction, and when it wore off, Paulo was left with an emptiness that could only be fixed by chasing another victory. Competitiveness was so intertwined with his sense of self. It wasn't bad. It just was, and right now, he wanted to show the world his amazing boyfriend.

"How do you know?"

"You aren't usually this reckless."

"Reckless?" He gulped. "You accused me of that when

we arrived." The whine in his voice echoed the frustration at being cock-blocked by Cohen's sensible decision not to fuck in public at his sister's wedding. He stepped backwards and ran his hands through his hair.

"Fuck. I'm sorry. I don't know what got into me."

Cohen grinned. "Emotions make us do interesting things. And you weren't reckless with me that day in Austin. I just misunderstood. I thought people drove fast because they didn't care about themselves, or something."

"It's not that."

"Wait. Maybe that's true for most people. For you, I've noticed that it isn't about the speed exactly, but about being competitive. You understand the risks you are taking and you adjust to the situation." Cohen chuckled. "That's why this is so fascinating to me."

"Why?" He wasn't sure he followed what Cohen was talking about.

"You are so careful about your identity and who knows about you and us because you understand the potential cost to you and your team. And yet, you were willing to ignore that calculation now..."

"To show you that you matter more to me than anything. Hearing those words dismiss our kiss so horribly makes me want to tell the whole world and screw the consequences." He puffed out his chest. "I'll tattoo your name on me and put it on my socials."

"Please don't do that. If you are going to get a tattoo, please make it something special."

"Your name is special to me. You are important to me." Perhaps even more important than the single goal he'd spent his entire life aiming at. The shocking admission felt good. One day, if it came to it, and he had to pick between S1 and Cohen, he'd pick Cohen.

"Paulo." Cohen's soft exhalation around his name sank deep inside Paulo. He'd earned that one, all by himself, and he would cherish it forever. He stared deep into Cohen's eyes and tried to communicate everything that he felt; like he'd torn his heart out and given it to Cohen to care for.

"Excuse me," Essie arrived back, an abrupt interruption that jarred, tearing him away from what felt like a pivotal moment. "The offender has been removed from the property and the staff all understand not to let her back on the grounds. Shall we keep going with the photos? We are a little behind schedule."

"Heaven forbid that we upset the schedule." Felix laughed. "Come on darling. Let's pose with Cohen for a proper family photo."

"And Paulo."

Paulo nodded. "Okay." He almost told Lilly-Anne to take some without him just in case he could never be open about his relationship with Cohen, but he stopped himself. He'd made his choice. He could be in these photos—as part of Cohen's family—because he chose Cohen over everything else. As for the rest, he could still earn that with persistence and a reminder that driving S1 was his passion and his lifelong goal. He could have everything. Later. Most importantly, right now, was that this would be Cohen's family from now onwards and these photos would shine with the love and care they had for each other. He followed Cohen and stood where the photographer showed him.

"I'm so sorry, Cohen. I shouldn't have invited her."

"Can I say I told you so to the bride on her wedding

day?" Cohen's smirk was fucking perfect and the way Lilly-Anne whacked him on the shoulder, then laughed, broke all the built-up tension.

"No, but I'll allow it once."

"If everyone could look this way, please, and smile." The photographer waved their arm, and the process began. After countless photos, Paulo's face hurt from holding a smile. He must've taken photos with everyone, including an entire soccer team and various combinations of Felix's family. He'd made more promises to drive people around the Nurburgring than he could potentially keep and had taken selfies for people to upload to their social media. Yes, there was a social media ban at the wedding, except for one booth set up in a spare room at the castle that Lilly-Anne had sanctioned for selfies only. One of the hotel staff looked after all the phones to make sure they weren't used elsewhere to take sneaky photos of the more famous guests without their permission.

"Paulo, I've been looking for you." Cohen sounded exasperated.

"I'm here."

"Taking selfies?"

"With fans. It's fine because it's just me and them, and I'm cool with my image being on fan pages if it's just me and a fan or two. It's part of the job."

"That kilt is going to get the internet buzzing."

Paulo nodded. "I've already had a couple of texts from Melati about it." He'd told her about the wedding and to expect a few fans tagging him, but he'd forgotten to tell her what he was wearing. Opinions were apparently divided on whether it was appropriation or art. No one had made the connection to the trans flag yet and he was curious to see how long it would take for a clever fan to notice. With the way some fans were obsessed with any image of a driver doing something away from the track, it was bound to happen.

"Any problems?"

"No. I should probably text her the name of the designer of the kilt and the fabric."

Cohen's smile beamed with delight. "Yes please. It'd be a huge boost for Isabella."

"Are you first name friends now?" He teased Cohen who bit his bottom lip.

"I might have reached out on socials to thank her. It turns out we have a few mutual online friends, so she's joined our discord group now."

"That's super cool. Hang on, I'll grab my phone and text Melati now."

"And then we need head inside for dinner and dancing."

Paulo smiled. "I can't wait to dance with you." He spun around and the kilt flared out a little. Not enough to show his naked ass but just enough of a hint that Cohen's eyes flashed wider and darkened with lust. The rest of the night promised to be incredible.

CHAPTER 23

BAHRAIN

"The rise and rise of Gamble Racing." The headline on the front page after Ondrej won the first race of the season and Paulo finished just off the podium in fourth was incredibly satisfying. It was Monday morning after the race, and he lay in his hotel room bed with Cohen reading the S1 news on his phone. They had a flight to Saudi Arabia this afternoon for the next race and were both taking advantage of the sleep in.

"Um, Paulo. Have you heard from Melati?"

"No, I'm sure she's doing the usual post-race stuff."

"There is a photo of you online."

Paulo shrugged. "There are lots of photos of me online."

"Not like this." Cohen held his phone in front of Paulo's face. A blurry photo of Paulo in his kilt at the wedding, being swung around on the dance floor by Cohen, filled the screen. The photo was clear enough that anyone could tell it was him dancing with a man who wore a suit made of the same fabric as his kilt.

"Oh." He wasn't sure what to say. There was only one interpretation of that photo.

"SanchezKilt is trending."

"Again." It had on the day of the wedding last weekend too as people at the wedding shared their selfies with him. Paulo's phone dinged with a message.

> Melati: Have you seen the photo?

Paulo sent her a thumbs up emoji.

> Melati: I assume it was taken at the wedding. So much for a social media ban.

> Melati: What do you want to do?

"Melati wants to know what I want to do."

"What are the options?" Cohen asked. Paulo stared at the ceiling for a bit, unsure how he felt about the photo. They looked good together; which probably wasn't the point right now, but damn!

> Paulo: What options do I have?

> Melati: It's just dancing. You could ignore it.

> Paulo: Plenty of people dance at weddings.

> Melati: With other men too.

Paulo showed the text train to Cohen. "What do you think?

"I think people are going to notice that the suit and the kilt are the same fabric."

He stretched his neck muscles. "Fans of my sport are very good at details like that. I'm surprised Melati hasn't said anything."

"She probably doesn't want you to freak out."

Before the wedding, she would've been correct. "No. I'm not going to do that." He breathed in carefully, then rolled on top of Cohen, so he could gaze into his eyes. "I choose you."

Cohen blinked. "Are you saying you want to put out a statement that says 'this is my boyfriend'? Because you know what will happen if you do."

He'd upset Senior and lose his sponsorship. Except he'd just finished fourth behind his teammate who'd won, and he was still buzzing from the result. "What do you think I should do?"

"Only you can answer that." Cohen's face flickered with an emotion that Paulo couldn't name, and he gasped, suddenly realising something very important.

"Am I being selfish by wanting to announce us?"

"What on earth do you mean?"

His breath was stuck in his throat. "If we do this—announce you to my fans—the media are going to want to know everything about you. It's selfish of me to only think about what will happen to me if I make this announcement. If we do, there will be interviews and comments and the whole internet will have an opinion. Sometimes those opinions aren't great." He felt like such a shit. He'd wanted to be guided by Cohen, to talk about what to do for his own sake, and he hadn't even thought about how this might affect Cohen. Cohen was so confident, but that didn't mean Paulo could just blurt his whole relationship online without consulting Cohen's feelings.

"I take it you don't want to talk about us just yet."

"It's not that. I know that's been my focus for ... well ... since we met." He swallowed. "Um, fuck. I told myself at the wedding that if I drove more consistently then the sponsorship stuff with Senior would matter less because Gamble could get other sponsors, and then I'd be able to tell people how much I adore you. But it's not just about me. You should also get to choose if you are ready to deal with the type of ugly comments that this will bring your way."

"Stop overthinking. I've been on the internet for most of my life. I'm more worried about you than me." Cohen was—once again—protecting Paulo from the worst of life, or at least in this situation, the worst of the internet. Paulo really wanted to deserve the protection and care from this kind-hearted wonderful man who he loved very much.

> Melati: Who is the man in the suit?

Paulo stared at his phone. "Melati didn't recognise you."

"I guess that gives you options." Cohen rolled them both so he lay on top of Paulo, then bent his head and kissed him. The world and all his worries disappeared as Cohen's tongue slipped between Paulo's lips.

"At least there isn't a photo of us outside after dark." Cohen's whisper against Paulo's mouth was decadent.

"Of you bending me over the stone wall and fucking me?" It had been as good as Paulo had hoped, and just the memory was making him hard.

"Yes. Good times. A little bit of dancing is nothing compared to that."

"Could've been worse, so it's all good?" Paulo grinned, and then a second later, he sighed. "Fuck me. When I met you, the idea of a photo like that would've been my worst nightmare."

"And now?"

"Now I want the world to see how amazing you are."

Cohen kissed him again. "The world will have to wait. You have a good plan to sort out the sponsorship issue, and you are on target for that goal."

"I am." Paulo squirmed under Cohen. "I need to respond to Melati."

Cohen rolled off. "Fine. I'm sure that needs to be done right now."

"As soon as I do it, I'll be free for you."

Cohen wrinkled his nose. "I like the sound of that. The new dick I ordered arrived yesterday."

Paulo flushed, amazed that Cohen had bought it online and had it sent directly to their hotel in Bahrain. Even in plain packaging, it seemed quite ballsy to do that. "Is it the one..."

"With the ribs that I showed you? Yes. It's that one." So very like Cohen at his finest; confident that he was in control of life. It was Paulo's favourite thing about Cohen.

Paulo closed his eyes. "Why do you make it so hard to get anything done?"

"I'm not the one who is hard." Cohen shifted so he lay

beside Paulo, then Cohen placed his hand on Paulo's stomach, spreading his fingers wide across his abs, but not touching Paulo's cock. Damn it.

"Cohen." Paulo wasn't above whining. His fingers gripped his phone tight and he made himself relax them.

> Paulo: That's Cohen, my bodyguard and boyfriend.

Paulo sent her a thumbs up.

> Melati: I heard from Skye that you guys are an item.

> Paulo: You can't tell people. My father will pull his sponsorship

> Melati: I heard that. It's shit

> Melati: How about we ignore it and just see what happens? I'll keep an eye on the comments and then we can make a decision later.

Paulo sent her a thumbs up.

"What's happening?"

He showed his phone to Cohen who nodded. "It's a good idea. There's no reason to say something right away, and people dance with people at weddings. It's not a big deal."

"If I wasn't in the queerest team on the grid, then I'm sure no one would care." He couldn't stop that little worry, that he'd soon be getting a call from Senior.

"Stop thinking. Let Melati follow the comments and make a decision when you—"

"Have more data. Yes. I can understand that as a strategy.

Cohen took his phone off him and placed it on the bedside table. "My turn now."

While Paulo had been on his phone, Cohen had strapped on his new dick, a ribbed thick navy-blue beauty. Cohen licked Paulo's throat, a long decadent stroke that had Paulo whimpering, then he rolled so he lay on top of Paulo, using his weight to press Paulo into the mattress. Suddenly he didn't care about the photo or any of the implications. He was here with his man, this wonderful man, who took all of Paulo's dirtiest, darkest desires, the ones he used to be ashamed of, and created something beautiful and loving from them. Paulo writhed under Cohen's touch, gripping Cohen's spine with his fingertips, as Cohen played with him, moving on top of him. He bit Paulo's nipples, sending shards of heat through his body. He traced each muscle and every part of his skin, slowly making his way down Paulo's body. Paulo was overwhelmed by sensation, a ragged mess of desire, able to do nothing under the onslaught but cling on tight to Cohen's body. The guilt that he should be giving back to Cohen was whisked away when Cohen wrapped one hand around Paulo's cock.

"I love how you leak for me. I love how one touch can make you do anything I command."

"Anything." Paulo could barely whisper out his desire. The luxurious high thread-count sheets were scratchy under his heated skin, a riot of sensation as Cohen teased and taunted him by trailing his fingers and tongue all over Paulo's chest. There was nothing better in the world than the touch of Cohen's skin against his own.

"If I said stand on your head naked, you would?"

Paulo planned how he would do it. "Gladly. Anything for you."

"I wouldn't ask you to do something that might get you hurt. You have another race in a few days."

"I'd risk it for you." Paulo was beyond rational thought. All his blood, all his energy was focused on the way Cohen casually stroked his cock with one hand, and the rest of his torso with the other. Building tension with a few swift strokes, then a few lazy ones.

"Ouch." Paulo huffed out a breath as Cohen bit his nipple harder than usual.

"Too much."

"You know it's not." He squirmed a little. "Please." He wasn't sure what he was asking for, but he trusted Cohen to use his brilliant imagination to inspire him.

"Not yet. You have to be a good boy and earn it."

Oh fuck. He was going to die from pleasure before he'd even given Cohen anything. He reached out for Cohen's face and stroked his beard, and Cohen groaned deep in the back of his throat. Yes, that's what he wanted to do; to give pleasure to his lover. So he kept playing with Cohen's beard, loving the texture of his hair under his fingers, and especially loving the noises Cohen made and the flush spreading across his skin.

"I like that but it's not enough. You need to earn your reward."

"How?" He asked knowing full well that Cohen loved

this type of role play; where Cohen was in charge of the world and made the decisions. He loved it too, that's why they belonged together.

"Kiss me, then lick me there, behind my dick. Just like the fourth best driver in the world might do. A championship worthy licking."

Paulo shivered. Holy shit, he was woozy with the idea of it. He pulled Cohen closer, kissing him with everything he had. Pouring his love and his very soul into the kiss until Cohen melted in his arms. He loved it when that happened. He took his time, savouring the taste of Cohen's skin as he explored with his mouth and hands, all the way down Cohen's body. He focused on the parts of Cohen's body that Cohen was proud of; his biceps, his shoulders, the thin wisp of hair down the middle of his abs. God, those abs, so strong and defined; worth every day in the gym.

"Working for you has been great for my fitness." Cohen laughed as Paulo licked down the v muscle leading to Cohen's choice of dick for the day.

"You look great. You'll still look great to me when you are old and wrinkled and a bit pudgy." Paulo mentioned being together as old people on purpose because this was the long term for him. He wasn't messing about when he'd said he wanted forever with Cohen, walking together through life as equal partners.

"I want to grow old." Cohen's voice rumbled.

"And I want to be old with you. I'll become one of those annoying retired drivers who relives the glory days." It was much easier to talk while he was the one doing the taunting. He held Cohen by the hipbones and squeezed, then kissed him on the belly button.

"Let's go there one day." Paulo murmured against Cohen's stomach, revelling in the taste of his skin, slightly salty with a remnant hint of the hotel's soap from last night's shower. A bit of apple or something a little sweet.

"Where?" Cohen sat up, his dick sliding against Paulo's cock, and then Cohen leaned over to the bedside table and squirted some lube into his hands. He held both his dick and Paulo's cock together and ... fucking hell ... Paulo's eyes rolled back in his head and he lost all train of thought. He was on fire for Cohen, and yet he wanted to do more for him before he completely lost it.

"Gah." He couldn't think as heat and electricity made his skin alive with lust.

"Where should we go?"

"Ahh... Oldness?" Paulo's head was filled with a lusty fog.

"Paulo. I think time for talking is over."

Paulo nodded. He rolled them both to the side, so he could explore Cohen more freely. Having Cohen's weight on Paulo was one of his favourite things, but he hadn't forgotten that he'd promised to shower Cohen in kisses. Everywhere. The idea that Cohen wanted to be licked down there was unusual and surprisingly vulnerable for him. What a gift.

"I think you should sit on my face." He breathed out the words with his heart racing.

"Okay?"

"It'll give you more control over your body. Plus I love the idea of being under you."

Cohen nodded, a light blush on his cheeks. "I think that will work best for me."

Paulo kissed Cohen again, threading his fingers through his neat beard. They kissed for ages and Paulo loved it, loved the simplicity of demonstrating the depth of his feelings through this connection. Then Cohen pushed off up, moving in that lithe easy way of his, until he knelt astride Paulo's chest.

"Like this?"

"Or maybe facing away, so I have easier access?"

Cohen grinned and dragged his dick across Paulo's chin. The cherry scented lube was a little sickly sweet, but then Cohen winked and moved, twisting around so he sat facing away from Paulo's face. Paulo's overwrought senses leaped again, and he reached out to hold Cohen's hips. Cohen bent forward, giving Paulo a perfect view of Cohen's glistening body. He was wet, soaking wet with desire, and Paulo eased his face upwards while pulling Cohen slowly towards him until Paulo's lips met Cohen's ass. Paulo groaned at the sight of Cohen. Holy hell. He very carefully licked along Cohen's lean ass muscle towards his hole, loving the way everything clenched and how Cohen moaned. Paulo kept his grip on Cohen's hips tight and gave all his attention to Cohen's hole, careful to ignore touching anything that might give Cohen dysphoria. Paulo was rewarded by Cohen's knees tightening against Paulo's chest.

"Fuck, your cock is leaking so much." Cohen bent forward and kissed the tip of Paulo's cock. Paulo jerked at the simple touch, then focused on rimming Cohen. He'd been stressed because he'd never done this before for anyone; he was inexperienced but enthusiastic, and yet, it was simple and easy. All he had to do was listen carefully to Cohen's ragged breathing and the way he groaned to know he was doing what Cohen liked. With every moan, every groan, Paulo repeated the action that had caused that.

"Hold my dick and pull it close to me." Cohen's dick would press against his clit, stimulating him, so to comply was giving him a gift of pleasure in a way that he wanted. Paulo grabbed Cohen's dick, not capable of waiting anymore, and did as he was asked.

"Fuck. Yes." Cohen begged. So Paulo did it again, and he tried to time his strokes on Cohen's dick with the strokes of his tongue as he lapped at Cohen's ass. Cohen was so wet, dripping down towards Paulo's mouth and he wanted it all without being greedy and overstepping Cohen's boundaries. He waited until Cohen's musk reached his tongue and then he licked and sucked and tasted until soon enough Cohen cried out and slumped forward with his chest on Paulo's cock. Having Cohen's weight on his cock, and his taste in his mouth was all it took. Paulo came with his tongue in Cohen's ass, then collapsed back onto the pillow.

A good amount of time passed with them both lying there until Cohen shifted, first sitting up, then swinging his leg over until he slid down and lay beside Paulo.

"Was that okay?" Paulo checked in.

Cohen kissed him. "It was perfect. I'm all painted with your cum."

"Gross... But also kind of nice?" Paulo wasn't sure if he should cringe or yell his success to the world.

"Definitely nice. Better than nice."

Celebrations were in order. Paulo's chest puffed out and a wave of satisfied warmth surrounded him.

"Good." He was about to suggest a rest, then another round, when his stomach grumbled.

"I guess we should eat?"

"Yes. And then we can do this again."

Cohen laughed. "You sound like a keen puppy. Yes, I will throw your ball for you again and let you treat me like a god."

"You are my hero. I enjoy lavishing attention on you." Paulo didn't care if he sounded sappy. It was all true.

CHAPTER 24

"That was a disaster." Paulo hung his head in shame as he stood in the shower after finishing out of the points in the third race of the season. In every race this season, he'd been beaten by his teammate. He turned the water up slightly too hot, letting it scald his skin and wash away the disappointment of today's race. So much for his plans for consistency. Disaster.

"Why is that?" Cohen leaned in the doorway of the hotel's bathroom. He looked so good, but Paulo didn't deserve him, or the delicious way he leaned with one hand hooked in his jeans.

"Are you kidding me? Third in quali, second row on the grid, and then I fucking spun on the second lap." The car was good—faster than last year and less twitchy—and he'd fucked it up.

"I'm pretty sure you were tapped out."

"Maybe." Paulo conceded the possibility. "Whatever. It was a squandered chance. I should've been on the podium, not trailing the whole field in last place." He'd tried to hold out Letherbarrow at turn three, they'd made contact, and both had spun. Letherbarrow had retired, while he'd managed to rejoin the race, but had to pit for a puncture leaving him in last.

"Monica said it was a good drive to make your way from the back of the pack to eleventh."

Paulo growled. "No points though."

"Yeah." Cohen paused and Paulo scrubbed his hair with whatever brand shampoo this hotel used. It had an interesting smell and he read the bottle. Lemon myrtle and macadamia. Sounded like something to eat, not fucking hair product. Whatever. He breathed out, a long slow breath to release all the day's frustrations. It didn't help much.

"Shall I join you?"

He shook his head. "Not today." His plan to earn this relationship had turned to shit thanks to Letherbarrow's aggression and his own decision to get his elbows out to try and keep his track position. He ignored the annoying fucking voice in his head reminding him that one race didn't matter on the scheme of things. It sounded too much like Monica; winning one race didn't make for a consistent season and missing out on points in one race also didn't mean disaster. One good result or one bad result wasn't an indicator of the whole season. The first two races were top five finishes; solid points for the season.

"Take all the time you need." Cohen left and closed the door. Paulo scrubbed his hair digging his fingers into his scalp. Damn it, he wanted Cohen to stay, and he also wanted some space, and his whole head was a fucking mess. And one thing threatened to overwhelm everything; the niggling worry that he was abusing his power by making the decisions on whether Cohen stayed or went. He bowed his head and let the water rinse off all the suds. The hot water slowly helped centre him again. It was one bad result; being tapped out happened in racing and he'd driven well from last into eleventh. It was time to apologise to Cohen for pushing him away, so he quickly finished his shower. Once he was dry, he wrapped the towel around his waist and walked out of the ensuite.

"Look at this." Cohen held up his phone, showing him a photo of him at the wedding standing alone, leaning on the stone wall of the chateau.

"Where did you get that?"

"From the photographer, of course. It's my favourite. I love the glow in your eyes."

"That's because I'm staring at you."

Cohen grinned. "If the world knew how sappy you can be, they'd ... well, I don't know actually. I don't think people expect their race car drivers to be uber masculine anymore."

Paulo laughed. "None of us are uber masculine. We're all lean with quick reflexes, not muscle bound and angry."

"Are you sure? I've heard you guys on the radio."

"What?"

"He fucking cut me off." Cohen repeated the exact phrase Paulo had used when Letherbarrow had tapped him in today's race.

"Well, it was true."

"Read this." Cohen flicked his thumb across his phone to the S1 app. The top headline was the Letherbarrow had been given a two-place grid penalty for the next race for arguing with the stewards over his initial penalty for causing a collision. Good. Having it validated as not his fault helped settle the unease inside him.

"I told you he tapped you out." Cohen grinned.

"Look at you, learning all the rules and slang of my sport." It was easier to joke than ... "Hey, I'm sorry. I overreacted just now. One race isn't a disaster. It's a small hiccup in my plans to earn our future."

Cohen gripped Paulo's bicep. "Stop."

"What?"

"Stop putting pressure on yourself with this earning nonsense. You don't have to earn me. I'm already here."

"But you aren't completely with me. I want to tell everyone."

Cohen squeezed gently. "We've talked about this, over and over, and I'm happy for you to take your time. There is a whole season ahead of you. Please stop stressing about ... this. It's time to eat, then sleep, and tomorrow we have the whole morning to explore Melbourne before our flight home in the evening."

They would head to Monaco this week and he'd focus on training before Imola in a fortnight. "Okay." He let Cohen pull him towards the bed, loving the way Cohen's fingertips dug into his muscles, and the heat of his palm against his bare skin. "I'm so pleased I walked into that bar and met you. I love you."

Cohen chuckled. "I fucking adore the way you blurt out your feelings."

His cheeks heated. "Only for you, Cohen." He spent so much of his life tightly held, focused and controlled. Cohen's gift to him, every day, was that he could relax and be himself around Cohen. He treasured those moments more than anyone—not even himself—truly understood.

"I'm glad you walked into Horny's too. I'll be forever grateful that Stanley begged me to take your absurd job offer."

"Absurd?"

Cohen stretched up on tip toes and kissed Paulo on the forehead. "You didn't know me. We'd just met and you offered me a signing bonus for a job with great pay, awesome benefits, and the chance to travel the world. It was absurd, so out of context. I was so sure I was going to get scammed."

"Never. From the moment you leaped over the bar and kicked that guy in the face, I knew I wanted you to work for me. I wanted you." He breathed shakily. "I might need time before I tell the world about us, this, but I love you. And I trust you to protect me."

"I know you do, and it stuns me every day that I'm so lucky. Not just to have a stable job that lets me save for a rainy day, but also that I get to have a future, and of course, the icing on the cake, I've fallen in love with someone who wants me exactly as I am."

"Bossy in bed, and protective everywhere else?"

Cohen bit his bottom lip, as if holding back a smile.

"Cohen, you are the love of my life, and one day I'll tell the world."

The smile broke through, making Cohen's face glow with joy. "I know you will. I can wait."

"You deserve better."

"I have everything I need already. This push to tell the world is your thing."

"But that day in Monaco when you ran away?" He'd been so ashamed of his own shame that day, wishing he could be braver and tell everyone how he felt about Cohen. Hiding was so problematic, especially when he was the rich and famous one. After that, he'd told his team and no one had cared, except to tease him in an accepting way. If only his father, and the rest of the world, could be the same.

"I just needed a moment to remind myself of all the good things. I'd become so used to being with you and being loved by you in our little bubble in Monaco for the off-season that your reticence to be with me shocked me right back into my worst fear. That I was only here on your benevolence."

Paulo cringed; he was the one with the fear, putting his job first, protecting himself from Senior at the cost of Cohen's happiness. It was a good reminder that he held so much power in this situation. "What can I do?"

"Keep listening and learning." Cohen waved his hand in the air. "Look at society and how the world sees me. Think carefully. Ask before doing anything."

"I worry about the power I hold because you work for me."

Cohen shook his head. "I don't work for you. I'm employed by your team."

"A good distinction." He loved Cohen and the way he didn't mince his words, and how he only told Paulo reassuring words when he meant them, not to ease Paulo's often confused feelings. Internalised homophobia, learned from his family, was a bitch to unlearn and he appreciated the way Cohen helped him.

"Every extra day that I work means I can build up my savings and my CV. You've given me options."

"Okay."

"I don't need this job anymore. In less than half a year, I've saved enough that I can go anywhere and take any job I want."

"Do you want to leave?" He stopped breathing.

"No. I'm trying to tell you that we both bring things to this relationship. I have enough money now that I don't have to stay. I'm here because I choose to be."

Paulo picked Cohen up and twirled him around, then kissed him with everything he had. He was so fucking lucky to have met Cohen; this incredible man who loved him and all his desires.

"Get in bed." How did Cohen do that? The lowered tone in his voice was fucking everything Paulo had always desired. He dropped his towel and leaped into bed. Cohen threw back the covers, and trailed his fingers lightly over his skin, tracing every muscle. His fucking incredible boyfriend took his time, slowly igniting him until every touch was a flame flickering inside him. Cohen pressed his fingertips into the muscles at the top of his thighs, right in that spot that always got tight after a race, and he let out a groan.

"You like that?"

"You know I do."

Cohen massaged it deeply. Not in the same way that Paulo's physio would tomorrow in his post-race session, but in a way that demonstrated how well Cohen knew his body. He closed his eyes and tried to let his body sag into the bed. A sharp pain shocked him awake. Cohen had flicked the end of his now-rigid cock. It was the very best of pain.

Exactly what he desired most of all, and what he'd never been able to admit to himself until he'd met Cohen.

"Put your hands wide."

"Cohen." He whined a little, wanting to kiss his boyfriend.

"Do it or I'll stop now and go to sleep."

He fucked loved being told what to do by Cohen. He obeyed, stretching his arms wide across the bed.

"You look so good. All the work you put into this body, all the training... The results are stunning." Cohen flicked his nipples, then traced all the way down his abdomen, over his trembling muscles, past his cock, and down his thighs. The way he stood beside the bed, looming over him, fully clothed, added to the erotic experience. Paulo was completely and utterly at Cohen's mercy. The best. He'd driven a whole race today, his body was tired, yet he was alert to Cohen's every touch, loving the way he dragged his gaze, as if planning what he was going to do with Paulo next. He wanted all of it. Every dirty thought in Cohen's head.

"Roll onto your side, facing away from me."

"Do you want my arms still spread wide, or..."

"Yes. Twist." Cohen waved his hand in a hurry up gesture and Paulo rolled onto his side, first with both arms to get his body placed how he hoped Cohen wanted it, then he moved his arm back behind him, stretching so his hands were as far apart as possible.

"Like that?"

"Perfect. Are you ready?"

He closed his eyes and listened carefully to the way Cohen moved. There was no other noise in their hotel room, not a breath of wind, or a quiet radio, only the ragged sound of his own breath as he waited impatiently for Cohen. He didn't have to wait long, only a couple of breaths, when Cohen kissed his palm. The soft wetness of his lips against his skin and the gentle brush of his beard were a sensation overload. He wanted to grab his cock and stroke it, knowing he wouldn't be far away, but he never would. It wasn't about him; he wanted to obey Cohen, to submit to the pleasure Cohen was about to gift him. This dance was familiar now and yet, he still felt that flicker of shame deep in his gut that he was wrong to want this, wrong to enjoy being at Cohen's mercy. He needed to unlearn that shame. It helped to focus on the way Cohen's tongue licked his wrist, first with light little touches, then long succulent licks, all the way along Paulo's arm to his twisted shoulder. Cohen's fingers followed his mouth. The first slap on his ass shocked him into a yelp.

"You like that?"

"Please. Again."

Cohen used his hand to paddle his ass over and over until it stung. The noise, the impact, the perfect touch of flesh against flesh. It was everything Paulo desired. He wanted to kneel at Cohen's feet and worship him.

"You are enough. You don't need to earn me."

"I do."

"No." Cohen slapped him again and he groaned as pleasure spiked. "You already have me. I can't be earned. I choose to be with you."

Paulo curled his spine, arching into Cohen's touch. One more slap. Fucking hell. "I'm going to come."

"Not yet." Cohen kissed his ass, soft on the tender flesh. "I could do more. You don't have to drive for a fortnight."

"Yes. I want it all."

One lick from Cohen across the same area he'd been slapping, and Paulo squirming with joy.

"Not yet. You can't come yet." Cohen kissed and licked his ass until Paulo grabbed the sheets and his eyes rolled back in his head. He fought the urge to come, needing to obey Cohen because it was his favourite thing to be told to wait, to be sent to the edge of desire and have to wait for permission.

"I need..."

"This?" Cohen dipped his tongue into Paulo's ass.

"God yes."

Cohen kissed and rimmed, and Paulo's whole body shook with the need to do as he was told and not come. He was so close, so very close. Cohen shifted, kissing all the way up Paulo's spine, and he couldn't help but protest. Not in words, he was beyond words.

"Shh, it's going to be fine." Cohen took his hand and carefully placed it on his cock. "Now, Paulo, now you can come."

He roared, arching his spine, and his eyes filled with stars as he came. And when he finished, sated and soft, Cohen rolled him gently on his back and knelt across his thighs, grinding his groin against Paulo's slackened cock. Cohen leaned forward and kissed him, a long luxurious kiss that had Paulo clinging to Cohen's hair. He put all the love he could into the kiss, all the thanks, until Cohen moaned deeply and grabbed Paulo's hand, shifting it onto Cohen's ass. Paulo caressed Cohen's body, sliding his hand under

Cohen's shirt onto the skin of his lower spine. And it wasn't long until Cohen came with a soft groan into Paulo's mouth.

"What a gift you are, Paulo. Now sleep." Cohen kissed him on the forehead, climbed off the bed, and tucked Paulo under the sheets. As he drifted off, he thought he heard Cohen murmur softly, thanking him. He hoped it was true and not just a good dream.

CHAPTER 25

Cohen walked beside Paulo after the post-race team meeting in the hotel. Paulo moved a little stiffly, as if his ass was still sore from being spanked last night. Nice. It'd been so hot, how Paulo had been desperate to come and had waited and waited until Cohen gave him the command. Now, it was back to business as they headed back to their room to pack and get ready for a flight back to Monaco tonight.

"Let's do something fun. I've never been in Australia before."

Paulo twisted around with an odd expression. "Like what? Cuddle a koala or something?"

"Yeah, sure. Or just walk around Melbourne together and look at the sights."

"We only have a few hours spare."

"Aren't you rich?" Cohen teased his boyfriend who nodded and pulled his phone out of his jeans pocket and leaned against the wall of the hotel hallway as he typed into it.

"I'll change our flights home. How long do you want to stay?"

"It's up to you. You have Imola in less than a fortnight, and it's a long flight and the jet lag could be an issue for you too."

Paulo nodded. "Most of the team is going home today."

"All those happy couples. We can be the same."

"In public, for a day?"

"Yes. Relax. No one is going to care about an S1 driver and his bodyguard."

Paulo tensed for a moment. "Do you really want to cuddle a koala?"

"I want to spend a day with you, somewhere new. You promised me travel and adventures."

Paulo shook his head. "I guess I did." He relaxed then typed something into his phone. "Okay, I've changed our flight for the same one tomorrow. That'll get us back to Monaco by Wednesday."

Cohen opened the door to their hotel room with his swipe card, and waved Paulo inside. "Get that uniform off. I'll get us a ride share."

"To?"

"Wherever koalas live. The zoo, I guess." He stripped off his black Gamble Racing shirt and grabbed a dark grey t-shirt from his suitcase. Just as he straightened up, Paulo kissed his spine.

"You are so handsome."

He glanced over his shoulder to see Paulo kneeling behind him, his arms folded across his chest.

"You can touch me."

Paulo placed his hands on Cohen's ankles, slowly

tracing his legs all the way up. He kissed and sucked at the same spot on Cohen's spine, and damn if it wasn't hotter than last night. This fabulous man, on his knees for Cohen, showing him how much he wanted him. The gift of him was enough to push him closer to coming. Cohen undid his jeans with trembling fingers, and guided Paulo's fingers to where he needed them.

"Suck harder. Leave a mark."

Paulo obeyed and the heat of his mouth on Cohen's back was delicious. Cohen used Paulo's fingers to rub himself just how he needed, building pressure with every stroke until he came in a rush of hot and cold, with everything unfurling inside in a shockwave of sensation. Fuck, he loved this man and the way he happily worshipped Cohen. After a moment to recover from the lightheaded softness left after his orgasm, he carefully turned around, stepping clear of Paulo's knees to kiss him on the forehead.

"You are precious." His voice was raspy in the aftermath. He tugged on Paulo's hair and his boyfriend stood up in an athletic movement.

"Thank you." Paulo stood with his head bowed, and Cohen held his chin and tilted his face upwards.

"No, thank you." He kissed him softly on the lips, then stepped away to grab his discarded shirt. "Let's go and cuddle a koala."

Paulo nodded. The outline of his hard cock in his jeans gave Cohen a little thrill. Perhaps it was mean of him, but he wanted Paulo to wait, to stretch out the pleasure for as long as he could.

. . .

They chatted about inconsequential things during the long ride share journey to the animal sanctuary that had koalas for cuddling. Cohen spent the drive planning how he was going to tease Paulo into coming, somewhere almost in public, because he loved pushing Paulo's boundaries. Not for the sake of it. Just because Paulo loved it too; he loved anything where he had all his usual power and fame stripped away, consensually, where he had to submit to Cohen's care.

Paulo had used his fame to get them a last-minute booking at a wildlife sanctuary, promising to put it on his social media to give the place a boost. Cohen wasn't sure he'd ever get used to this lifestyle, and just how easy being rich and famous made everything, but he wasn't complaining. He was going to take every opportunity gifted to him and enjoy it, because he knew how fragile life was. It might be cynical of him to realise that love wasn't always enough. Things happened, and he needed to be prepared. Besides, he'd much rather be in a relationship where they stood beside each other, looking out at the world together, than one of co-dependence where they only saw each other and none of the external threats.

"We are here." Paulo stated the obvious with a little shake in his voice.

"Don't worry about the world. You have me to keep you safe." Cohen jumped out of the car, checking their surroundings before Paulo stepped out. From there, he did his job as Paulo walked up to the entrance and gave the name of the person they were to meet. As he watched Paulo pay with a wave of his phone, he noted the decent donation Paulo added to their entry fee and his chest puffed out with pride for his lovely boyfriend. The quiet way he used his money to help people and animals without the need for people to pay attention to him was so beautifully Paulo. Understated and focused.

After introductions, they followed Dr Sarah Amdst to the koala enclosure. "Koalas sleep a lot, so I can't promise that you'll have the opportunity to hold one."

"It's fine. Cohen isn't the type of brash American to demand you wake the animals."

"And yourself?"

"I'm just here because my bodyguard wants to do this."

Dr Amdst's eyes widened slightly. "Do you often take your staff on adventures?"

"I'm rich, young, and famous." As if that were any type of answer, and yet it was the only explanation Paulo needed to give because people accepted that he didn't need to explain himself.

"I see." Dr Amdst's voice conveyed disapproval, but she lifted her chin with a shallow breath outward. "We would love to have a photo of you for our website." Money talked.

Paulo nodded. "I did promise that. With or without a cuddly little bear."

"Koalas are not bears. They are marsupials."

"Okay." Paulo frowned a little at the veterinarian.

"This way." Dr Amdst opened a door and they both walked through. Dr Amdst collected a large camera from a shelf in the small corridor, before leading them through a door that opened into an enclosure filled with a large group of sprawling tree branches. "Oh, look Kylie is awake. Come this way." They dutifully followed the veterinarian under some of the branches towards a lump of grey fur sitting in the nook where two branches met. Cohen hadn't spotted the animal until Dr Amdst reached up towards it. The koala gave her a bored stare, before allowing itself to be collected off the branch it was sitting on. The koala snuggled into her shoulder, and she cooed at it. It always amused Cohen how some people were so soft with animals and so abrupt with people, he low-key loved to see it, because people could be tricky.

"Okay, stand here. It's the best light for photos."

"You first." Paulo gave Cohen a little push and he grinned.

"I suppose it was my idea."

"The ultimate tourist thing to do in Australia!" Paulo pulled his phone out of his pocket and stood over to the side, ready to take some pictures. Dr Amdst moved Cohen's body and gently placed Kylie the koala in his arms with gentle instructions about how best to hold the animal.

"She is heavy."

"Yes. People often say that." Dr Amdst stood to the side, just out of shot. "You can take as many photos as you want now." She grabbed some leaves and held them up for Kylie who munched on them casually.

"This is amazing. Thank you." He stroked the soft fur, paying attention to the long claws, just as Dr Amdst had indicated. Eventually, the veterinarian took the animal off him, and indicated that Paulo should come over. The whole process was repeated, with the only difference being that Dr Amdst took a whole lot of photos of Paulo with instructions on his hand placement and smiling and whatnot. She was obviously well versed in how to best present her koalas for the camera and her social media. Cohen took a few photos on Paulo's phone.

"Shall I send some to Melati?"

"Yes. I forgot to tell her we were doing this. She'll love it. I'll send her a bunch of photos and stuff and she can upload them when she wakes up. It's close to midnight in England."

"Excuse me?" Dr Amdst asked. "What are you planning to do with the photos?"

"Melati, my social media manager, lives in England. She will upload photos to my socials for me with all the right tags and stuff. If you email me, I'll forward it all to her with the information you want shared."

"I thought you'd do it yourself."

"No. I don't like to read the comments, and with over a million fans and followers, it's too distracting and time consuming. Melati manages all my social media, and for several other people in our racing team. She's amazing at it and it allows me to focus on my job, on driving well, not on everyone in the world's opinion of me." Paulo allowed Dr Amdst to take Kylie from his arms, and the koala was gently placed back on the branch. It grabbed some leaves and ate, apparently unconcerned at the interruption to its day.

"I'd be happy to email everything to you." Dr Amdst smiled, for the first time that day. "I'm sorry if I was a little gruff. It's hard for the koalas to do this outside their routine and I worry so much about them, but I also understand the need for promotion and getting a big audience to help get us donations to keep going. We have a valuable collection of koalas here who are disease free, and they are part of a wider study being shared between several sanctuaries like this one."

"That's awesome. I hope my photo helps a bit."

"It will. A million followers?"

Paulo shrugged. "Something like that. S1 is a very popular sport, especially in Europe."

"You have a British accent?"

Paulo nodded. "I was born in Brazil, but did all my schooling in England, so yeah, that's where the accent comes from."

"Would you like to see any of our other animals?" Dr Amdst asked. She'd relaxed a lot since Paulo had mentioned his social media following, and the realisation for what Paulo offered—more than just being an influencer or whatever—seemed to have helped Dr Amdst relax around them both. She indicated that they should leave the enclosure, and they walked back through the door into the corridor, then out into the main part of the zoo.

"I'd love to." He glanced at Paulo who shrugged one shoulder. A few people were looking their way, mostly groups of parents with toddlers which made sense since it was midday on a Monday.

"Sure."

"Most people like to see the kangaroos and wallabies. What do you think?"

Cohen didn't really care, he wanted to hang out with Paulo and see him enjoy life. "Why don't you show us some of your favourites? I'm American. I'm pretty sure all of your wildlife is going to kill me, so..."

Dr Amdst laughed. "And yet you happily cuddled a drop bear."

"A what?" Paulo asked.

"It's a mythical creature based on the koala. Drops out of trees in the middle of the night and lands on unsuspecting people. Some people draw them with fangs or whatever. It's hilarious."

"As if Australia didn't already have enough dangerous creatures, you have to make up some as well?" Paulo was grinning. "I like Cohen's idea. Why don't you show us your favourite?"

"They are all my favourites."

"Really? Because I definitely have a favourite car."

Cohen frowned. "You do?"

"It's this year's one, the GR-S390."

He scoffed. "I should've known it would be the fastest car you've driven."

"I'm sorry, but I was told by the front desk that you were famous. I'm confused."

Paulo stuck out his hand. "Paulo Sanchez. I drive Series One cars for Gamble Racing."

"Neat. I assume you were here for the Grand Prix this weekend, then?"

"Yes." Paulo shook his head.

He winked. "Don't ask him about the race."

"Oh, why not?"

"Paulo was tapped out by the rookie Letherbarrow and it was a tough day at work. We are here to relax before heading to the next race."

"And you are?"

"Cohen Wright. Paulo's personal security." The crowd of people had slowly grown into a decent sized group.

Dr Amdst frowned. "I don't think that's necessary around here."

"Are you sure?" He indicated subtly to the group of people gathering.

"Oh. I didn't notice. Shall we head to the platypus? It's nice and quiet in there, and we can go into the staff only section, if you'd like."

He nodded. "Good plan. Paulo, did you want to sign a few things first?"

"Sure. It's always like this after a race weekend." Paulo walked towards the group of people and Cohen stalked beside him, scanning each person. It took half an hour to chat to everyone who was interested, and take selfies, and sign things, before they'd run out of people and were able to carry on with the tour.

"Sorry about that."

"No, it's fine. Hopefully it'll be good publicity for the sanctuary and we can raise some much needed funds."

"Do you need much?" Paulo asked.

"Always and ongoing. Feeding animals is expensive, and that's without the cost of their health needs, and everything else. We only break even most years."

"I'll make a donation on the way out."

"You don't have to do that. You are already doing enough by being here. We don't get many famous visitors."

Paulo glanced at Cohen and he knew, from that one glance, that Paulo was only donating to Dr Amdst's sanctuary because holding the koala had made him smile. He almost missed the toddler who launched himself at Paulo's legs, but quickly picked up the child before Paulo was touched.

"I'm so sorry." A blonde white woman rushed over and grabbed the child.

"It's fine." It wasn't, but the situation diffused quickly when the woman rushed away holding her child's hand and Cohen let out an uneasy breath. Stopping a toddler from grabbing Paulo was easy on the scale of things.

"Who knew being a famous person's security guard meant fighting off rambunctious toddlers?" Dr Amdst laughed.

"We have had a couple of instances where people have tried to use their children as an excuse to get close to Paulo. It's usually easy resolved."

"Cohen's job allows me to focus on mine. And I appreciate his presence." Paulo's simple words hinted at much deeper feelings; in public with a random stranger. It meant more to him than agreeing to change their flights so they could be tourists for the day.

CHAPTER 26

Paulo leaned back in another ride share as they left the koala sanctuary and headed into the city to grab lunch. Dr Amdst had recommended a place down a laneway that was quintessentially Melbourne; whatever that meant. His phone buzzed with an alert from the S1 app. "Sanchez Shipping, sponsors of Gamble Racing and owned by the father of driver Paulo Sanchez, has signed a three-year contract with S1 for all the logistical transportation for every team."

"Typical."

"What's that?" Cohen leaned over and Paulo showed him the headline.

"I can't believe I'm the last one to know. I should ring Senior and congratulate him."

Cohen pulled out his phone and tapped something. "It's midnight in Brazil, so maybe not now."

"How do you know?"

"I have a time zone app. It helps me work out when to call Lilly-Anne, wherever I am in the world."

The simple pragmatism once again reinforced why employing Cohen had been a good idea. Paulo was so often caught up in how much he loved Cohen that he took for granted how competent he was at all the different facets of his job. He really needed to pay more attention.

"That's really cool. Could you please remind me to call him when he's going to be awake."

"Why not send him a text?" Cohen's suggestion made sense, so he quickly typed out a congratulations message and hit send before he could second guess himself.

"Done. Now for some lunch."

The car drove down a tight laneway and stopped outside a grey concrete building. Ten people stood in a line outside the building.

"Thanks, driver." Cohen jumped out and Paulo followed. He kept his head low and his new koala sanctuary branded cap pulled down over his forehead. They joined the line of people waiting. They stood beside each other like equals, rather than like a famous guy and his security detail, not just because it was strategic and less likely that people would recognise Paulo, but simply because he believed Cohen was his partner and his equal. He needed to get better at showing it.

"Are you sure this is the right place?" Cohen's expression mirrored the uncertainty inside Paulo.

"It's the one Dr Amdst put into the ride share app." He tried not to stare forlornly at the commercial rubbish bins across from the small doorway where the line ended. A couple of plants in pots were a futile attempt to make it look welcoming. Almost. If they weren't standing outside an industrial building with no indication that it contained cleanliness, let alone quote the best coffee in Melbourne unquote, or whatever Dr Amdst had said.

"The food better be as good as promised." Cohen shrugged. "But I guess the people waiting to go in is some sort of indication?"

"If you've come here for food, you've been misled." The white man in the line in front of Cohen turned around. He had a long beard and thick rimmed glasses, paired with a brightly coloured shirt and loose jeans. He had a dark grey jacket slung over his arm.

"Excuse me?"

"It's coffee only. There's no seating inside. That's why the line moves so quickly, just order your ... you look like an almond milk latte type actually; but order whatever you like ... and then move through to the other door. A few people stick around and sit on the milk crates outside if the weather is nice like today, but it's Melbourne, so."

"So, what?" Cohen asked.

"Classic Melbourne, you know, four seasons in one day. I hope you brought a jacket." The man indicated his own coat.

"Thank you for the advice."

"You American or something?"

"Yes." Cohen answered sharply, and Paulo was glad he didn't have to say anything. His mostly British accent was bound to result in far too many questions from this overly friendly person who dished out advice without being prompted.

"You are in for a treat then, mate. I heard Americans have dreadful coffee. You'll get the best coffee in Melbourne here, so it'll be better than anything you've ever had before."

"Okay."

Paulo touched Cohen on the elbow. He really didn't want to take food recommendations from this rather enthusiastic person with a very interesting taste in fashion. "Shall we get coffee, then walk until we find something for lunch?" He kept his voice pitched low, but the man responded on Cohen's behalf, so it was a wasted effort.

"Oh, mate. Yeah. At the end of the laneway, and down to your right is a little Vietnamese place that does the best pho. If you want burgers or something more like familiar to an American palate, go left instead and there's a burger joint that's pretty good. It's next to the pie place. Now that place is awesome. They do a different flavour every week."

Paulo listened to the man babble on about different food options. He would hate to stereotype this guy as not being into sports, but there didn't seem to be a big risk that he'd be recognised by him. He didn't have to guess as the man kept talking.

"You know what I love about this place. It's so carbon friendly. They use paper straws and recyclable cups." The man was about to get dangerously close to having a negative opinion on his sport. People still thought car racing was a climate disaster, with ignorant opinions about it, instead of understanding that S1 engineers had created the most efficient engines in the world, and this flowed into the everyday car with improvements in efficiency too.

"Thanks." Cohen was typically understated in his response. He had a patient expression on his face, like he was waiting for the man to stop talking.

"What's an American doing in Melbourne anyway? You here for long?"

"Only a few days."

"That's a shame. There's so much to see around here. Where are you going next?"

"Italy."

"Seriously. I thought you were going to say Sydney. Like they are all a bunch of financial wankers up there, just care about money and stuff, but Italy. That's cool, man."

Paulo bit the inside of his cheek to prevent a laugh, and thankfully the man stepped inside the grey metal door, leaving them outside. More people had lined up behind them, so Paulo didn't risk saying anything in case the rest of the locals were so opinionated.

"I'd heard that Australians are friendly, but wow, that was a lot," Cohen said.

"I'm just happy he didn't—" He wanted to say recognise him, but there were other people in the line behind him now and he really didn't want to mention that he was someone who might be recognisable.

"Yeah. At least we have some food options now."

Paulo chuckled. "Is American coffee really as bad as the reputation?"

"Well, it's not a monolith. Some places are good, others ordinary, like anywhere, really. I'm so not getting an almond latte though!"

"I think it's our turn, then we can go for a walk and check out those different food options." He opened the door for Cohen, who raised one eyebrow at him. "Yes, I know that's your job, but we are tourists today, not working."

"I'm always working when you are in public." Cohen whispered, his breath a gentle breeze against Paulo's ear. Cohen's suggestion that they hang out today had been a good one, and he couldn't wait until they were back in their hotel room so he could kiss him thoroughly.

Several hours later, Paulo collapsed on the couch in their hotel room. They'd spent the afternoon walking, occasionally hiding in small shops during rain showers—the weather was as erratic as promised by the man at the coffee shop—and had enjoyed dinner together in the city, before heading back here. He closed his eyes, happy to just rest for a bit.

"Wake up. You are trending."

"Sanchez? It's probably the new logistics contract."

Cohen shook his head, his lips pinched. "No. There's a photo of us holding hands and a bunch of different tags."

"Good or bad?"

"You aren't freaking out?"

He needed a drink of water. "I think I might be?"

"Why don't you call Melati and see what she advises?" Cohen spoke good sense, an excellent reminder of his pragmatic qualities that had always drawn Paulo to him. "I'll grab your phone." Cohen jumped up and grabbed Paulo's phone from his jacket. He'd tucked it in there earlier in the day and had been ignoring it.

"There are a lot of notifications."

Paulo held up his hand and Cohen tossed him the phone. He plucked it out of the air; thanks reflex training; and sure enough, the home screen was filled with notifications.

Enzo: That better be a publicity stunt.
You were supposed to be the real man in
the gay team.

Paulo's hands shook and he dropped his phone.

"What's the matter?"

"My brother is being ... well, he's just proved that I was right to not say anything."

"Show me."

Paulo swallowed and picked up his phone to hand it to Cohen.

"You, Paulo, are definitely a real man. As am I. We are human and exist in reality, which makes you real. What a toxic jerk your brother is."

He sighed. "Part of me wants to come out in public, own the photo, and post an even louder, queerer one, just to be petty."

"I'm loving that energy, but I sense a but."

"Just the usual. If Enzo thinks like that, he's only mimicking Senior, and Senior holds the financial power. If I'd finished in the points today..."

"No. You aren't the problem here. They are." Cohen wrapped his hands around Paulo's face, pulling him close and kissing him on the forehead. He held him for a long time, just their foreheads pressed together, breathing quietly until Paulo's heart slowed back to a normal rate. "You are absolutely a real person whose desires are no one's business but yours. You are loved by me, adored by your fans, and one of the best drivers in the world."

"Thank you." Paulo wasn't going to be afraid anymore. He was worth it, and Cohen was worth it. "It's time to face the truth." He grabbed his phone and called Senior before he talked himself out of it.

"Paulo." Senior's voice almost made him hang up, but no, he could be brave now.

"Congratulations on the logistics contract."

"Yes, I saw your text. It's a good opportunity for us."

He breathed in deep. "I have a little bit of news too."

"I assume this is to do with the photo Enzo showed me."

"Yes."

"Was that real?"

Paulo swallowed. "Absolutely, yes, sir. I was holding hands with Cohen, my bodyguard. We are in a relationship."

"You are fucking your bodyguard?"

"Yes sir."

There was an impossibly long pause. Paulo pulled his phone away from his ear, but it was still connected. He opened his mouth to ask Senior if he was still there when Senior spoke.

"I don't like it, but I respect your honesty."

"You are not..." Going to pull the sponsorship money? He didn't have the chance to finish as Senior barrelled on, interrupting him.

"Boy, I've always suspected that you might not be completely the son I wanted." Senior's comment hit him hard in the solar plexus and he gasped.

"I'm pansexual." He glanced at Cohen and just blurted it out, because the sting of hearing Senior say that he wasn't straight enough for him cut deep into the old hurt he'd carried for years.

"Is that a fancy word for it?"

"It being queer? I'm not sure you want a whole history of queer identities."

"Indulge me."

Paulo gulped. There had to be a hidden backhander here. "Pan is Latin for all, so pansexual means that I'm attracted to all forms of sexual and gender identity. It's more about personality for me, than what someone looks like."

"Basically you'll fuck anything and anyone." Senior was typically crude.

Technically, although it was a little more complex for him than that. "All humans who are of legal age and consent to be with me, yes."

"Pansexual, huh. It's the greedy one; wants to fuck everyone." Senior laughed and Paulo winced. Yeah, there was the backhander.

"I don't want to fuck everyone in the world." Just Cohen. He paused, unsure if he should bother explaining this to his bigoted father.

"You could, though. You are a super star. Famous, young, rich."

"I could." He made the concession out of habit, and then was annoyed at himself for agreeing with Senior. People didn't disagree with billionaires, not even their children.

Senior made an odd noise. "I won't pretend to understand any of that modern stuff, but I understand greed."

"Okay?" His father had managed to miss the point completely, but if this was some sort of imperfect acceptance, he'd take it. Conditional acceptance was as shitty as he'd imagined when the same thing had happened to Cohen at Lilly-Anne's wedding.

"Keep driving fast, son." Senior hung up, leaving Paulo stunned.

Cohen didn't ask any questions, he simply held Paulo and waited while Paulo ran the conversation around and around in his brain, trying to let it all sink in.

"I think he's okay with us?" Eventually he managed to communicate his conclusion, although he wasn't overly certain.

"You think?"

"Yeah. I mean, he wasn't kind, but he also didn't cut the sponsorship and he told me to keep driving fast."

Cohen kissed him hard on the mouth. "My brave Paulo. Look at you; facing your biggest fear and coming out on top."

"Take me to bed, Cohen. Let's celebrate." His worst nightmare had just happened, and it hadn't been terrible, not even bad. Just annoying, with an unsurprising bigoted overtone.

Cohen shook his head. "No. You need to sleep first. And when you rested and this has all settled in, then we will celebrate."

"I'm so fucking glad I have you in my life."

CHAPTER 27

MIAMI

ohen stood at the side of the podium in Miami, out of sight of the huge cheering crowd, as Paulo stood on the top step. His chest was so puffed up with pride for his boyfriend—the race winner and with the fastest lap for maximum points—that he thought his team shirt would rip down the seams.

The anthems played, the trophies were handed out, and then the three drivers celebrated with champagne spraying all over each other. Paulo's smile and the triumph of his expression was everything. His boyfriend had taken on the world's fastest drivers and won. Cohen's pride in Paulo's success was only beaten by how proud he'd been of him after he'd told Senior he was pansexual. He was still buzzing about that, and how Paulo had told Melati to confirm via his socials that he was pansexual and in a relationship, but that he wanted to keep things private for now. Of course, people had spent too much time on the internet trying to figure it out, and Paulo hadn't bothered to correct anyone who'd guessed. Let them enjoy the search, he'd said.

Most people had been supportive, a few had been awkward, and even less had been bigoted. It said a lot for Jaxxon and the way he ran Gamble Racing that people could be safely themselves there.

"How good is this!" Jaxxon slapped Cohen on the shoulder and handed him the constructor's trophy for the race.

"You can't give me that." He cradled the trophy awkwardly.

"I just did. You earned this as much as him. He's improved so much since you've been in his life."

"He did that himself."

Jaxxon smiled. "Don't underestimate a team effort."

A very sticky Paulo leaned on Jaxxon's shoulder. "How good is this!" Cameras flashed all around them, so it would be obvious to anyone looking that Cohen held the trophy for some reason, and then Paulo kissed Cohen on the cheek. Cohen didn't think his chest could get any bigger, as he puffed with pride for his incredible boyfriend.

"It's what you've worked for your whole life. Now, let's go and do some more interviews."

"I already said enough before the podium celebration." Paulo wrinkled his nose but didn't stop smiling the whole time.

"Come on. Let's do what the boss says, then we can get you into the shower and cleaned up." Cohen didn't mean for it to sound so dirty, and when Jaxxon cackled, his cheeks flashed with nuclear heat.

"There's some motivation." Paulo winked. "I suppose Freddy wants to chat."

"It is his job. Here, give me the trophy and I'll get it

cleaned up for you." Jaxxon took the winner's trophy from Paulo, and they stood awkwardly for a second, before heading down the stairs to the waiting press.

"Time for interviews."

Freddy was the first one to shove his microphone in Paulo's face as they stepped off the staircase. "Your second ever S1 win. Congratulations."

"Thank you." Paulo slipped back into media mode, and Cohen did the same, standing protectively to one side. He was still holding the constructor's trophy, so he handed it to Jaxxon who hovered nearby.

"It's been a big improvement in points for you this season compared to last."

"Victor's car is the biggest reason for Gamble Racing's excellent results so far this year."

"And your newly announced relationship."

Paulo glanced sideways with a grin. "I am aware of the speculation online about my relationship and how that has apparently affected my driving."

"Love makes you faster?"

"No. Being loved gives me confidence and most importantly, I have the freedom to be exactly myself. I'm very fortunate that my family supports my career, and they also support my relationship, which is a huge privilege that many queer people don't get."

"You are queer?"

"Yes. Should I be clearer? I am pansexual and I'm in love with Cohen." Paulo glanced over at him, but he shook his head and stayed out of the public light.

"That is clear. Could we meet this Cohen one day?" Freddy was being a little disingenuous, given that they'd met privately hundreds of times. Freddy was in a relationship with Team Principal Jaxxon, and they were always hanging together at Socrates' mansion and in the workshop whenever they could.

"The internet has already seen him. In a tartan suit at a wedding, holding hands in Melbourne, and I believe there are photos of us kissing from Imola last weekend?"

"Yes I have seen those. You two are very cute."

"Thank you."

"Go and celebrate your second podium, Paulo. Congratulations." Freddy moved away and Cohen took the chance to hustle Paulo away before someone else corralled him. They walked quickly back through the paddock to the Gamble Racing section, and as soon as they were inside, away from all the cameras, Cohen hugged Paulo tight.

"I can't believe you said that out loud for the world to hear."

"Believe it."

"I do. You were awesome today."

"Now I just have to do it again for the rest of the season."

He raised his eyebrows. "How about you enjoy today first? Then you can take this energy into the next race and the one after that and the one after that."

"You are the best thing that has ever happened to me, Cohen. Without you, I would never have been brave enough to come out, and I would never have found this confidence in me to thrive. It truly is the difference between mid-field and winning."

"I thought that was just the car."

Paulo kissed the end of Cohen's nose. "The car is a huge help."

He didn't want to kill the mood, but he had to ask. "Will you love me this much when you are losing?"

"When I met you, I was losing. I lost in Australia, and I still love you. I have more than enough evidence of loving you while losing. Today ... like you just said ... I'm going to enjoy winning while loving you."

"Thank you."

"To team work and the best man in the world." Paulo kissed him again, and Cohen adored the way Paulo always wanted more. "That's you, by the way."

"Oh, I thought you were talking about yourself. Isn't that the sports thing to do? Talk in third person about yourself. Sanchez drove a great race today."

Paulo rolled his eyes. "If I ever get that pretentious, please make me stop."

"I promise." Cohen grinned. "But only because I love you."

———

Want to know what happens at the end of the season? The Gamble Racing series epilogue is available as an exclusive bonus when you sign up for my newsletter. http://www.reneedahlia.com/books/gamble-racing/news/

———

Go back to where it all began with DRIVEN TO DISTRACTION, the first book in the Gamble Racing series.

A race to the finish line, and a family secret ...

Car racing driver Ondrej D'Grieg has one goal in life. Be a champion. To achieve that he needs to focus. That's why Ondrej has no time for his father's insistence on him being involved with some old family drama about a missing rare car. He can ignore the mystery, if only Hudson, the historian investigating it, wasn't so distracting.

Hudson Lockley has a research job to do, and falling for the son of his employer is a no-no. But only one thing is more fascinating than this puzzle; Mr D'Grieg's famous racing car driver son, Ondrej.

When their interest turns to kisses, then more, the race to figure out this attraction between them starts. But a small mistake could cause a crash that breaks both their hearts.

ACKNOWLEDGMENTS

I pay my respects to the Wangal people of the Eora Nation, who are the traditional owners of the land on which this book was written.

My kids, who are huge S1 fans, for working out the fake race season results for my drivers in this series and helping with other technical details. If you want to see the full spreadsheet, it's an extra on my Patreon.

Thank you to Lina, the Word Makers, Rachel Reid and the Carina discord. You've all championed this series and your support has kept me writing during a difficult year in personal life.

A huge thanks goes to Penny Aimes for the description of Austin with a lot more detail than I used in this novella. And a special thanks to May Peterson for this article, which is a must read: http://www.maypetersonbooks.com/2022/03/08/breaking-the-trans-bubble-and-how-you-can-help-do-it/

AUTHOR NOTES

The Marsha P Johnson Institute (marshap.org) protects and defends the human rights of Black trans people.

ALL BOOKS BY RENÉE DAHLIA

Thanks for reading DRIVEN TO PROTECT. I hope you enjoyed it. Reviews can help readers find books, and I am grateful for all honest reviews. Thank you for taking the time to let others know what you've read, and what you thought. If you write a review for Driven To Protect and email me (renee at reneedahlia dot com) with the link, I will send you a free copy of one of my other books of your choice.

If you'd like to know more about me, my books, or to connect with me online, you can visit my webpage www. reneedahlia.com and if you sign up to my newsletter, you can grab a free book.

Twitter https://twitter.com/dekabat

Facebook https://www.facebook.com/reneedahliawriter/

Instagram https://www.instagram.com/reneedahlia_author/

Patreon https://www.patreon.com/reneedahlia

BookBub https://www.bookbub.com/authors/renee-dahlia

You've just read a book in my Gamble Racing Series.

Contemporary: GAMBLE RACING

Driven to Distraction (#1) - mm: A race to the finish line, and a family secret ...

Driven by Passion (#2) - mm: Engine fires, sabotage, and two friends falling in love....

Driven by Ambition (#3) - mm: Two men in the spotlight with too much chemistry...

Driven to Protect (#4) - mm: Paid to protect him ... But at what cost?

Contemporary: SERAPH'S BURLESQUE CLUB

Show Up (#1) - wlw: A fake date ... a real secret.

Show Off (#2) - wlw: From casual hook up ... to something more?

Show Queen (#3) - wlw: Online friends, real life enemies ...

Show Time (#4) - mm: When a fake date becomes real thanks to a romantic island setting.

Show Dance (#5) - mm: Best friends to lovers and a wonderful costume.

Contemporary: CRICKET SLAM

Captain's Knock (#1) - wlw: Secret hook-ups between teammates turn into an HEA.

Sweet Spot (#2) - wlw: Available in the Mistletoe and Markets anthology

Contemporary: BISEXUAL SING TEAM

Count Me In (#1) - wlw: A fallen rock star meets a scrapbooking queen.

Strum Me Hard (#2) - wlw: A down on her luck popstar meets a polite socialite entrepreneur with a scandalous secret life.

Tune Me Up (#3) - wlw: A marriage in trouble. A meddling daughter. A reminder that love is worth it.

Contemporary: KAPOW! ADVERTISING AGENCY

Out of Her League (#1) - wm: She is his greatest fan. He wants more than adoration...

His Buxom Beauty (#2) - wm: Image is everything, or is it?

Craving His Spotlight (#3) - mm: Can a second chance at fame avoid repeating old mistakes?

Her Pregnant Rival (#4) - wlw: Society expects them to be rivals, but what if the best revenge is love?

Contemporary: RAINBOW COVE

His Christmas Pearl (#1) - fm: One gourmet party. The taste of love?

His Christmas Pride (#1) - mm: One gourmet party. The taste of love?

Contemporary: MERINDAH PARK

Merindah Park (#1) - wm: 'Money lost, nothing lost. Courage lost, everything lost.' Can two people take the ultimate gamble and fall in love?

Making Her Mark (#2) - wm: Her best friend's brother

and a betting scam. Can the rules be broken to help a friend, or will it only be hearts that are broken?

Two Hearts Healing (#3) - wm: It should be the perfect country romance between next door neighbours, but an accident threatens to stop it before it begins. Can they overcome the guilt and find love?

Racetrack Royalty (#4) - wm: One fast horse, and a whirlwind romance set among the glamour of Royal Ascot. But what happens when everyone goes home?

Contemporary: FARRELLTON FOSTER FAMILY

Betrayed (#1) - wm: What happens when your best friend betrays you? Can you forgive a teenage mistake?

Forbidden (#2) - wm: Love between foster siblings should be forbidden... unless you've never met until now.

Liability (#3) - wlw: When Maiden Heaven crashed into Jessica's organised life, nothing would be the same again...

Contemporary: Margaret River TV Boxed Set

Featuring two novellas; Homage (wm) and Uplift (wlw), and a bonus short story (wlw).

Historical (Regency): DESIRING THE DEXINGTONS

Love Wasn't Built In A Day (#1) - mm: A friends to lovers gay Regency romance with a delicious slow burn.

The Secret Life of Spinsters (#2) - wlw: An expected alliance between spinsters...

The Highwayman's Surprise Bride (#3)- wm: Coming to KU in The Regency Abduction Club

The Summer of Second Chances (#4)- wlw: Coming to KU in Summer Secrets at the Soho Club

The Widow's Modiste (#5) - wlw: A bored widow, an incredible dress, and a modiste with a secret.

Historical (WWI): GREAT WAR

Her Lady's Melody (#1) - wlw: An aristocrat hiding from her past, a doctor hiding from her grief, a journey that will be a danger to themselves... and their hearts!

Her Lady's Fortune (#2) - wlw: An assertive bank manager, a wary heiress. . . A one night stand they can't forget.

Her Lady's Honor (#3) - wlw: The war might be over, but the battle for love has just begun.

His Lord's Soldier (#4) - mm: Two best friends torn apart by war. Could the re-enactment of four Christmas dinners create a love worth fighting for?

Historical (Victorian): BLUESTOCKINGS

The Shipwrecked Earl's Bride (Prequel) - wm: A Spanish fisherman's daughter might be the best wife for a banished Earl.

To Charm a Bluestocking (#1) - wm: She wants to be one of the world's first female doctors; romance is not in her plans.

In Pursuit of a Bluestocking (#2) - wm: When he goes hunting a thief, he never expects to catch a bluestocking...

The Heart of a Bluestocking (#3) - wm: When an uncommon lawyer meets an unusual doctor, their story must be extraordinary...